TITLES BY HARPER ST. GEORGE

The Gilded Age Heiresses

THE HEIRESS GETS A DUKE
THE DEVIL AND THE HEIRESS

PRAISE FOR *THE HEIRESS GETS A DUKE*

"A delightfully entertaining read, rich with romance, glamour, and lush Victorian detail. Harper St. George truly captures the spirt of the era."
—*USA Today* bestselling author Mimi Matthews

"*The Heiress Gets a Duke* is a charming, compulsively readable delight and I can't wait for the next book from Harper St. George's magical pen!"
—*USA Today* bestselling author Evie Dunmore

"A sexy, emotional, romantic tale . . . Harper St. George is a must-buy for me!"
—*USA Today* bestselling author Terri Brisbin

"Wit, seduction and passion blend seamlessly to create this deeply emotional romance. St. George weaves an intriguing plot with complex characters to provide the perfect sensual escape. There's nothing I didn't love about *The Heiress Gets a Duke*, especially its lush, captivating glimpse into history."
—*USA Today* bestselling author Anabelle Bryant

"Rich with period detail, *The Heiress Gets a Duke* brings to life the Gilded Age's dollar princesses in this smart, sexy, and oh so satisfying story."
—Laurie Benson, award-winning author of The Sommersby Brides series

"You'll sigh, you'll cry, and you'll grin yourself silly as this independent and cynical heiress finally gets her duke." —Virginia Heath, author of *Beguiled at the Wedding*

The
DEVIL
AND THE HEIRESS

HARPER ST. GEORGE

JOVE
New York

A JOVE BOOK
Published by Berkley
An imprint of Penguin Random House LLC
penguinrandomhouse.com

ISBN: 9780593197226

First Edition: June 2021

Printed in the United States of America
1   3   5   7   9   10   8   6   4   2

Book design by George Towne

To my parents for encouraging my love of reading and writing all my life.

I love you.

Chapter 1

A proclivity for wickedness in his private life combined with his distaste for those he judged inferior rendered Lord Lucifer completely unsuited to her. That did not save the heiress, however, from her fascination of him.

V. LENNOX, *AN AMERICAN AND THE LONDON SEASON*

LONDON
MAY 1875

Humor me, my lord, and tell me why you wish to marry my daughter." Griswold Crenshaw, American industrialist, sat behind his large mahogany desk, hands arrogantly folded over his stomach, cigar clenched between his gleaming teeth, eyes mere slits of condescension. He was a man secure in the knowledge that he held all the power in this negotiation.

It chafed that the bloody fool was right.

Christian Halston, Earl of Leigh, was accustomed to privilege. It meant that he was never required to answer questions or to even ask them very often. Information was gifted to him like tributes wrapped in golden paper. However, a wise man of privilege knew the benefit of a little humbling now and then, or so he had been told. Actively forcing his jaw to relax, he said, "I should think that is self-evident. Miss Crenshaw is—"

Crenshaw leaned forward and tugged the cigar from his mouth. "Beautiful. Cultured. Educated. Pardon me, my lord, but I have met my daughter, and I am aware of her many attributes. I am asking why you are interested in obtaining her hand."

It appeared the humbling was not over yet. Reasonable when dealing with a wealthy American and his daughter, Christian supposed. To be fair, he found the London Season to be one of the more inane rituals imposed upon modern man. It was all pointless chatter and insincere flattery that ended with men carrying home their brides. The whole thing could be condensed into a week if everyone were honest about the matter. It was a welcome revelation that Crenshaw wanted the truth rather than adulation.

Christian could deliver the truth. "I am rather interested in her fortune."

Crenshaw grinned, and the oxblood leather creaked as he leaned back in his chair, straining the springs. "Now we're making progress." Amber liquid swirled in his tumbler as he picked it up, indicating that Christian should do the same with the identical one he had been provided upon arrival a few minutes earlier. Christian complied and let the drink roll across his tongue.

"What has you in need of funds? Debts, my lord?"

The tone the older man used made it seem very much as if the *my lord* bit was optional. Did Christian even want this man for a father-in-law? No, he bloody well did not. He closed his eyes and imagined Violet. Beautiful Violet with her dark hair, creamy skin, chocolate eyes, and the piles of money that came with her. He could do this. There would eventually be an ocean between him and Crenshaw, after all.

"No debts." Those had been dealt with when Christian had inherited the earldom at age twelve. After finding out that his father had left his small savings to his mistress and his children by her, Christian had happily sold almost everything not bolted down or entailed and had never once looked back. That had taken care of his father's debts. Montague Club, the club he had opened with his half brother Jacob Thorne and a friend, the Duke of Rothschild, kept him comfortable.

Crenshaw's eyebrows shot up into his hairline. "Astonishing. I was led to believe that most of you aristocrats were . . . insolvent."

Christian stifled a cringe at this uncouth talk of funds. The man had every right to believe that, and there was a bit of truth to it. Almost every eligible noble in London had been clamoring for one of his daughters. Rothschild—not Sterling any longer since he had come to accept his position as duke—had ensnared the elder daughter already, though their engagement had not yet been announced.

"I consolidated some years back when I inherited. The family seat in Sussex and my home in Belgravia are in working order." Though they were in desperate need of repairs since the rents at Amberley Park barely covered the minimum needed to keep the place running.

"Well then, that's commendable." Crenshaw took another sip of his drink. "Might I ask why you require funds?"

"I own a small estate in Scotland. Blythkirk. I inherited it on my mother's side, and it holds sentimental value. There was a fire recently, so it requires extensive refurbishment." Years of practice made his tone sound benign. There was no hint of the fact that the home had been his refuge from a father intent on making his life hell. That its near loss had opened a well of pain that he would rather not face.

The older man grinned as if he did not quite believe a mere estate could be worth a wife. "Her settlement will provide for more than that, my lord."

Christian inclined his head in acknowledgment of that fact. "Indeed, it will. I am certain to make good use of it.

While I am not insolvent, my ancestral estate, Amberley Park, drains my income. There are improvements I would make there. Furthermore, there are several investments I am interested in procuring. For one, I have a stake in—"

Before he could elaborate, Crenshaw said, "I am going to stop you there, my lord. As you are aware, I am a man of industry. As such, it is not enough that I find my daughter a suitable match, but that I look out for the interests of Crenshaw Iron Works in the process. To be very honest, there are more men who can fulfill the former than the latter."

Christian stared at the man. The rules of matrimonial negotiations were a bit outside his purview given that he had never considered obtaining a wife before Blythkirk's devastation, having been content to allow the earldom to pass to a distant relative, but he was almost certain that the bride's best interest should at least slightly outweigh those of a business. "Are you saying that you need a candidate who can bring business ventures to Crenshaw Iron Works?"

"That's it precisely. The ideal would be someone who meets with our Violet's approval, of course, but can present opportunities for Crenshaw Iron's expansion. Now that we are in the beginnings of setting up operations here, well, the world is open to us." His hands skated through the air in a smooth glide, mimicking the opening of a presumed gateway to the world. His eyes fairly glittered with greed.

"Like Rothschild." Christian knew that the main reason Crenshaw had encouraged and even pursued Rothschild's interest had been because of his title and the doors that title could open in Parliament. Being related to a duke willing to speak on Crenshaw's behalf would give the company nearly unfettered access to the railways being constructed in India.

Crenshaw's gaze narrowed. No one outside of the family was supposed to know that Rothschild had followed their elder daughter, August, to America. Christian, however, had been with Rothschild when he had made his mad dash to the Crenshaws' rented townhome off Grosvenor's Square to propose only to find his beloved ready to set sail. He had followed her to Liverpool and boarded her ship just in time. The ship was still en route, meaning no one knew how that had turned out, though Christian would guess the couple would wed very soon.

"Yes, like the duke."

"I have influence with my seat in the House of Lords," said Christian even as a hollow was opening up in his belly. He did not like the direction of this conversation. Crenshaw was a shrewd man. Access to Parliament granted, he would be looking for another advantage.

"Of course, my lord, and that is not inconsequential." A note of consolation had crept into Crenshaw's voice. The hair at the back of Christian's neck bristled. He was about to be refused. "We are very flattered by your interest."

"But you have another offer." A better offer. Christian clenched his jaw so hard that his molars ached. He did not intend to lose Violet to another man. She had fascinated him from their first meeting. If he was forced to consider a wife, then it would be her.

Crenshaw would have grimaced had he not been so accustomed to tense negotiations. Christian could see the urge lingering there in his expression. The corners of his mouth turned downward a small degree, and his eyes sobered. "Nothing has been finalized, but there is a tempting proposal on the table, yes."

"Who is it?"

"Well, now, I wouldn't want to give anything away until things are further along."

Christian searched his memory, trying to remember every man who had ever paid attention to Violet at the various balls he had seen her attend. The list was nearly endless, because she was an heiress and beautiful. Even though her older sister, August, should have been the talk of the season, and she had gained her share of admirers, it was Violet who had commanded the greater share of attention. Part of that was because Mrs. Crenshaw had been very active in taking Violet to every social event imaginable. Part of it was because everyone knew that August was a blue-stocking and more concerned with working in the family business than getting married. In fact, she had publicly claimed to not be interested in marrying soon. Until Roth-schild had changed that.

Violet, on the other hand, was more refined, more of what was expected in an aristocratic wife. There was a fire lurking beneath her cool exterior that she hid well. It made most believe she would be biddable. Christian knew that she would not, but he wanted her anyway. Perhaps because of that. He liked the way she met his gaze instead of demurring to him. She would challenge him, and if he had to face a wife daily, then why not rise to that challenge?

"What has he promised you?"

Crenshaw sighed dramatically as if he did not want to reveal more but had been given no choice. He smiled again, a practiced one meant to placate. "Mineral rights."

One of the many things Christian did not have to offer. "And you will give your daughter away for mineral rights?"

The smile did not fade, but it cooled so fast that it hardened. "You would have me give her away for less."

Touché. "I would have you present all viable options to her and allow her to choose."

"You believe yourself to be a better option, my lord?"

"Naturally. I understand that I've gained a reputation of sorts. You must have heard the rumors." Women. Deviance in the bedroom. Violent brawls and general debauchery. Christian watched Crenshaw's face closely for any reaction to his boldness in bringing up that subject. There was none. Crenshaw was good at what he did. "The women," Christian elaborated.

Crenshaw gave a brisk nod. "Women can be dramatic creatures. I do not put much stock into their reactions."

"Nevertheless, I would assure you that the rumors exaggerate." For example, the gossips claimed his leg had been broken by an irate husband. That he had been set upon by the husband in a dark alley. As if he would be so careless. "Rest assured, I would never put your daughter at risk."

"I am not concerned with your fidelity. Violet will learn that the state of a husband's personal life is his own affair."

"Then it is purely material gain you are after?" The words were strangely bitter on his tongue.

Crenshaw laughed and rose, placing his cigar on the edge of a crystal dish. "I will be certain to keep your proposal in mind." Which meant that he wouldn't.

Dammit. Christian had no way to counter a bloody business proposal when he had only come armed with a title, charm, and an admiration for the man's daughter. He had wrongly assumed that the business need that accompanied marriage would be resolved now that the elder daughter's union was all but assured.

Christian got to his feet and waited for the predictable throb of pain that shot through his ankle to pass before gripping his cane and following Crenshaw to the door. "Then at least tell me whom I should congratulate for winning her hand."

Crenshaw tipped his head. "I cannot say."

Christian's grip on the silver hawk's head of his cane became a fist, but he forced a lazy tone. "You cannot say?"

"All right." Crenshaw grinned like a boy who had glutted himself on a treat. "I will merely say that you may visit and admire my beloved daughter later this summer in Devon."

Ware. Pallid and weak. It had to be him, because his family seat was in Devon and he seemed to always be at hand when the Crenshaw sisters were about. The man-child could not hold his own against a mildly strong gust of wind much less an angry suitor bent on having Violet. Unfortunately, the issue would not be decided in a bare-knuckle boxing match. More's the pity.

And to add insult to injury, Ware was a mere viscount.

"I shall look forward to it." Christian bid good day to the infuriating man and made his way to the front stairs as if he had not been rebuffed by a man whose recent ancestors had been scoundrels and thieves. There was no doubt in his mind that he would be the better match for Violet Crenshaw. The fact that his lack of resources was the only thing keeping her from being his grated.

Ware was a slug. The man wouldn't know what to do with a woman like her. He'd keep her hidden away on his estate, justifiably afraid that a better man would take her from him. Christian, however, would keep her in the light. He would allow her to host as many parties as her heart desired and enjoy as many theater outings as she wanted. She would dance and flirt and everything else that was socially acceptable to a newly married bride, but she would be his, and no man would be foolish enough to overstep. The reputation his fists had gained him would work in his favor there.

His old leg injury flared up on cold, rainy days but otherwise was a mere annoyance that caused a barely noticeable limp. He carried a cane for the occasions when standing excessively was necessary, or for the random uneven pavement or gravel walkway. Stairs were another problem. No matter how he tried, navigating them was slower than he would like and required the use of a well-mounted handrail. Today, however, he was grateful for the delay as he made his way down. It gave him time to notice the most beautiful and haunting voice he had ever heard. Hearing it instantly helped to dissipate his anger.

He knew immediately that it was Violet singing. The soft rasp of her voice coming through the closed door was unmistakable. A pleasant chill tingled over his skin and down his spine. By the time he neared the foot of the stairs, it was over, to be replaced by light applause. Violet said something, but her voice was too muffled to distinguish the words. Laughter followed. The music room door clicked open, and a maid hurried out, leaving the door ajar behind her.

A decent man would have kept walking and not lingered as he passed the partially open door. He would have smiled at the giggles spilling out of the room and hurried on his way to his next appointment. Everyone knew that Christian was not a decent man. He owned a reputation notorious for indecent things.

He stopped at the gap, arrested by a swirl of pale yellow and an upswept chestnut coiffure that hurried past the open door. The woman's face was not visible to him, but like the voice, he knew she was Violet. She clapped her hands once, rounding up her charges—all debutantes her own age—to have them give their attention to the next performer. He could not see the poor girl who started the next song, but her voice was atrociously high. Pity that she had to perform after Violet might have stirred within him had Violet not come to stand on the far side of the room directly in his line of sight. She stopped everything for him.

In profile, it was obvious that her nose was possibly too strong for her small features and that her mouth was likely too wide, but taken together they were perfect. Her foot tapped along to the music, making him smile because it was not the least bit proper. The hem of her gown fluttered as the toe of her shoe worked in a steady rhythm. He followed the vibrations of the fabric up to her small waist and the hug of pale yellow over her bosom where it ended in a ruffled collar at her neck. Hungry for another look at her profile, his gaze continued upward, and his heart nearly stopped in his chest when a pair of irate dark eyes settled on his.

Her mouth quirked in displeasure.

He had met Violet twice. The first time they had been introduced at a ball and briefly exchanged pleasantries. He had found her both charming and alluring. The second time had been when he had come to this very house several days ago with Rothschild in his quest to win back her older sister. They had exchanged words then. Unpleasant words.

You, she had said to him here in this exact entryway. *Why are you here?*

Because I like fireworks, he had answered.

It appeared she was prepared to repeat their exchange as she made her way to him. Taking hold of the door, she glanced into the entryway, noting the footman at the door before allowing her gaze to fall on Christian. "Lord Leigh," she said, her voice low, giving it a smooth huskiness that rasped pleasantly across his ears. An elegant brow rose in question, and she stepped out of the room, drawing the door closed behind her. "What a surprise to see you here again."

"Miss Crenshaw." He inclined his head. "It would appear I cannot stay away for very long." He teased her simply to see her flush with displeasure.

Her eyes flared in annoyance. "How lucky we are, my lord." Her tone implied the opposite.

She was not above having her feelings known, even if she was refined enough to couch them in polite words. It had been years since he'd felt this spark of interest when talking with a woman. Despite his best intentions to keep it contained, a laugh escaped him.

Violet openly glared at him. "You find humor in that?"

"I was just thinking that I very much enjoy our encounters."

She had the grace to blush as she undoubtedly recalled how angry she had been during their conversation here in this entryway. She had mistakenly believed Rothschild to be unfaithful to her sister and hadn't held back her disappointment. Instead of being a good friend and pleading Rothschild's case, Christian had baited her.

Swallowing, she asked, "Is there something you wanted, my lord?"

You. All of you.

"I am just leaving from a meeting with your father," he said instead.

"Ah, then please do not allow me to keep you."

Swirls of amber flame glittered at him from the depths of her brown eyes. No, he decided then and there, Ware would not have her. She was too good for the likes of him.

Inclining his head, he said, "Good day, Miss Crenshaw."

"Good day, my lord." She opened the door and stepped back into the room.

He crossed the entryway, aware of the weight of her gaze on his back when he had expected her to close the door between them immediately. The footman opened the front door for him, but instead of stepping out, Christian glanced back at her. She was staring at his shoulders, her gaze slowly moving down his back. The glaze of attraction in her eyes was unmistakable.

She flushed when she realized he had caught her and closed the door firmly between them.

He stared at the lacquered wood grain for the space of a few heartbeats. He knew because he felt each of them as his blood rushed through his body. Talking with her always had the effect of making him more aware of himself and less aware of everything around him, except for her. He was glad for the lengths he'd already gone to attain her hand, lengths that weren't quite aboveboard but would be worth it in the end.

Finally, the footman made a nervous sound in the back of his throat. As Christian walked out to his carriage, he decided that he would bypass her parents in his bid to win her. They were set against him, so it made much more sense to approach the woman herself. It would not be easy given the unfavorable impression of him she had thanks to Rothschild, or perhaps she had heard murmurs of his past, but he could overcome that. It would be a simple matter of finding her heart's desire and giving it to her. Then she would be his.

Chapter 2

❧

Rose Hamilton was in London for one reason—to enjoy the Season. The number of potential husbands her parents threw her way would not change that. Perhaps it was this misunderstanding of her own nature that caused her to lower her guard.

V. LENNOX, *AN AMERICAN AND THE LONDON SEASON*

Violet sat at the table in the small parlor off the garden the next morning having breakfast alone. Mother was still in her room, and Papa kept up his Manhattan work routine even though most of London was still in bed, which meant he had already been ensconced in his office for hours. Violet didn't mind. She enjoyed her mornings alone. Lately, mornings like this were the only time she had to herself to write.

The gorgeous little room had a row of windows that looked out over the cheery walled garden in the back of their rented Mayfair townhome. A short break in the rain allowed watery sunlight to filter in through the windows, casting a golden glow over the table and the papers spread out before her, her second manuscript and one she hoped to publish under the name V. Lennox, Lennox being her mother's maiden name. A name was scrawled at the top of each sheet with a list of attributes below. Each name was a character that she had created to represent a person she had met in London. So far she had six characters, which was fine because she was only on chapter four of her manuscript, but she needed two more gentlemen for a ball scene she had planned. The problem was that she was having a terrible time creating characters that were . . . well . . . not the same. While the gentlemen she met were almost certainly individuals with their own needs and wants, she only knew them superficially and hadn't yet been able to dig deeper to find out who they really were. It was the problem with only meeting men at balls and dinner parties where everyone was on their best behavior.

Sorting through the short stack, she took out the two based on her dear friend Camille, Duchess of Hereford, and Hereford himself. In her book they were the Duke and Duchess of Helford. She, a tragic figure who had been sold into marriage by her parents to a much older man; he, a fortune-hunting aristocrat who treated his bride more like a wayward stepchild than a treasured wife. The characters were so close to the truth of the situation that it made her ache to write them. She definitely needed to change the name to something far different. Marking through Helford, she made a note to herself.

The next characters were an older couple. Snooty and full of their own influence in their small corner of the world, the Ashcrofts were everything Violet had come to expect from the older nobles, but they had been kind and welcoming to her family. Because they were friends with her parents, she had changed their names considerably to Lord and Lady Garfield.

Placing those aside, she picked up the last two: her American heiress and her English suitor. Lord Lucifer, the name she had chosen to represent Lord Leigh. She could not help the smile that tugged at the corner of her lips as she read the attributes beneath his name. Arrogant and entitled, he exuded wickedness. The whispers she had heard told the story of a man who overindulged himself in sensory pleasure—women, cards, and drink (possibly more). He owned a club with the Duke of Rothschild where all manner of illicit things happened. But it wasn't only hedonism that she discerned in him. No, there was a danger about him that she couldn't quite understand. As someone who believed herself capable of assessing the character of a person within a matter of minutes, that alone made him very intriguing. It didn't hurt that he was also devilishly handsome. With thick dark hair, pale gray eyes, and cheekbones that could cut glass, she imagined that Lucifer himself would take his form should he deign to set foot upon the earth.

And the way he had gazed at her yesterday. A tiny thrill of pleasure worked its way down her spine as she remembered the look in his eyes from across the music room. He found her desirable. She would never encourage his pursuit because she was already engaged and that danger coupled with his debauched tendencies made him entirely unsuitable regardless, but she was flattered nonetheless. He was . . . something.

A polite knock sounded at the door a moment before a footman stepped inside. "Pardon me, miss."

"Yes?" She hurried to arrange the papers so that he couldn't read them. If this novel was ever published, it would have to be anonymously if she wanted to continue a peaceful relationship with her parents.

"This came for you special delivery." He stepped forward and placed an envelope on the table next to her scone with strawberry jam and clotted cream, a delicious indulgence she didn't believe needed to be relegated to teatime only.

She recognized the tight loops and practiced penmanship, even before she saw the sender's name—Theodore Sutherland. Teddy had finally answered her pleas. Too late, but it was nice to see his name.

"Thank you," she said to the footman. He gave a short bow and left her alone.

She and her family had arrived in London for the season only a month earlier. Violet and her sister, August, had naively believed that they were there to visit their friend from New York, Camille, the newly minted Duchess of Hereford, and partake in the city's amusements. Little had they known that their parents were secretly plotting to wed one of them off to a nobleman.

The Crenshaws were considered new money among the Old New York crowd, hence they were often shunned in the established ballrooms on Fifth Avenue. A duke in the family would change everything. Violet had been their parents' initial offering to the Duke of Rothschild, but he had decided to pursue August. No one had been more surprised than Violet when her older sister with her business-minded ambitions had fallen in love with him.

In a panic after Mother had proposed the marriage idea to her, Violet had both telegrammed and written to Teddy. He was the man she intended to marry. Yes, his family was from St. Louis and had earned their fortune in breweries—neither would gain him entrance into New York Society—but she didn't care a whit about that. He was kind and thoughtful and supportive of her writing. After spending two summers together in Newport, he had asked her to marry him and she had said yes. She was not giving him up because her family wanted her to marry an aristocrat.

But all was settled now. She would have to write Teddy back and tell him so. She probably should have already written to him. Strange that she hadn't felt the urgency to do so before now. Perhaps because she had been so relieved that August was happy.

Setting the letter aside, she took a sip of her tea and allowed herself to revel again in the character of Lord Lucifer. Perhaps she should have him indulge in an attempted seduction of the young American heiress in her book who was in town for the Season. Perhaps that young American heiress wouldn't be nearly as virtuous as she should be.

Heat suffused Violet's cheeks as she imagined him stealing a kiss in a secluded corner at a ball.

"There you are, Violet, darling," said Mother as she hurried into the room.

Violet startled to attention, nearly spilling her tea all over her papers in her bid to put them away. "Good morning, Mother."

"What do you have there?" Mother's artfully plucked brow rose as she sat down across from Violet at the round table.

Violet knew her mother meant the stack of facedown papers, but she picked up the letter to intentionally redirect her attention. "This? A letter from a friend."

"Which one?" Mother asked, pouring herself a cup of tea. "I wasn't aware the post had already come."

Violet's mouth went dry. Her parents didn't quite approve of Teddy, and she wasn't a very astute liar. That point had been driven home the one time she had wandered away from a summer party to walk with Teddy along the beach. They had done a fair bit more than walking. Mother had discovered her coming home with sand on her shoes and skirts, and one lie had led to another until the whole party had left to search for a missing bejeweled hairpin and a bedeviled seagull.

But Violet could hardly admit that she had written to Teddy in a pique of desperation.

"Amelia," she said. More words threatened to spill from her lips like marbles scattering across the floor, so she bit her tongue to stop them.

After giving the letter another questioning glance, Mother seemed to accept the explanation. She couldn't read a thing without her reading glasses anyway. "When you reply, please send my regards to her mother."

"Of course." Violet stifled her sigh of relief and tucked the letter into the papers, gathering the whole stack against her chest. "I'm sorry, but I was leaving."

"Already? But I just sat down."

"Papa has asked that I help him transcribe some letters. You know how illegible his own handwriting is."

Mother nodded. "It is quite awful. I suppose with August running off, someone has to." Neither she nor Papa had been very happy when August had accompanied their brother, Maxwell, on his return to New York, though knowing that the duke had joined her on the crossing had soothed them. August had been Papa's right hand here in London, and with her gone, drafting correspondence had fallen to Violet. Not that she minded the extra task. It allowed her to spend time alone with him, and she appreciated the glimpse into the world he inhabited with her brother and sister. Working at Crenshaw Iron wasn't in her blood, not like it was for them, but Violet enjoyed being useful.

"All right, then. I shall see you a little later. Don't work too hard. Remember, we have the ball tonight. Lord Ware has agreed to play escort."

"Lord Ware?" Pallid, dull, and with a tendency to stare at her breasts, Violet didn't particularly care for him.

"Mmm." Humming through her first swallow of tea, Mother said, "Do humor him, dear. The young man is all alone in London with no parents or relatives at all from what I can tell."

"Fine." Violet sighed. More stodgy people, but she shouldn't complain because it was all fodder for her novels. Her other finished novel had featured the characters of High Society New York, so it was nice to have this change.

Violet clutched the papers to her chest all the way to her bedroom where she hurried to her small desk and dropped them. The envelope fell out of the stack to lie on the polished wood surface. Funny how two weeks ago that letter would have meant everything to her. Now, it was a pleasant way to spend the next few minutes. Taking a seat, she turned toward the window and opened the letter.

Dear Violet,

Your words have caused me so much distress that I believed it best to answer your plea in a handwritten letter. When I last touched my lips to yours, my darling, I never dreamed that it might be for the last time. You are the sun, moon, and stars of my sky. Without you, my world has turned gray.

My love for you shall go on into eternity, ceaseless in its quiet ferocity, but even I know my limitations. I haven't the capability to compete with a British noble. My God, a duke of the realm and you, a duchess! Violet, my fair and clever girl, though it causes me great pain, I will release you from our childhood vow of matrimony. It was foolish of me to believe that I could dare hold your hand for more than a moment.

Go to your brighter destiny with my blessing but know that I weep for myself. I have thought of nothing but holding you in my arms again since you left, and it seems that longing will never be assuaged. However, it is a burden that I gladly bear for your happiness.

Please give my highest regards to your parents and give your father my thanks. He will understand the reason.

Forever yours,
Teddy

Childhood vow? Childhood vow! It was only last summer when he had proposed to her. She was hardly a child, and he would be graduating from university soon followed by law school. He made it sound as if they had made a foolish agreement as a pair of adolescents.

She read the letter over again, convinced that somehow she had misunderstood. But no. He was turning down her pleas for help and even encouraging her to accept another suitor. A stranger! What a toad! Did he even miss her? Had he already moved on to some other woman?

His declaration of love and subsequent proposal had seemed so sincere. It hadn't been a formal proposal. There had been no ring, and he had not asked her father's permission, but to Violet it had been no less real for the lack of those things. They had been sitting on the beach on a piece of driftwood, and he had quietly spoken his heart to her.

I love you, Violet. When I imagine my future, I only see you. Will you promise to marry me?

She read the letter yet again, unable to believe this was written by the same man. Each florid stroke of his pen seemed more like insincere babble with every pass. How had she not noticed his terrible writing voice before? This time she fixated on his closing. *And give your father my thanks.*

Thanks for what, she would like to know. Had Papa gotten to him? Had Teddy's affections been so easily bought? He couldn't possibly need money, so what favor had Papa performed for him? Her parents had been so set on her marrying Rothschild that perhaps their desperation had pushed them to it. She didn't want to believe that, but the idea had been planted.

She wouldn't accept Teddy now if he pleaded on his knees for her, but she had to know if her parents had interfered. Stifling the urge to throw the letter into the nearest fireplace, she folded it and placed it in her desk drawer. She was too angry to be sad.

Was she even sad? Shouldn't she feel devastated? To be honest, she hadn't spent very much of her time in London missing Teddy. She had told herself that it was because she didn't see him much during the year anyway, but could there be more to it? Could it be that she had only felt mild affection for Teddy and had seen him as a safe way to thwart her parents while continuing her writing?

She didn't like what that said about her, but she also couldn't deny there was some truth to that.

Pasting a smile on her face, Violet knocked on her father's study door several minutes later.

"Come in," he called.

"Good morning." She closed the door behind her and made her way to the carved rosewood side chair at the end of his desk where August usually sat.

He glanced up, spectacles perched on the end of his nose. "Yes, thank you, darling. I have a few letters that need to be sent out. You know I don't have the patience for letter writing."

Or the penmanship, she silently added. "Of course, Papa," she said, reaching for the parchment and pen he had set out for her. "Oh, I received a letter from Teddy today."

"Teddy?" He muttered, distracted by the papers scattered in front of him.

She stared at the gray wave of hair artfully arranged above his ear, idly wondering if her anger would be enough to ignite it. Keeping her voice light, she said, "Theodore Sutherland of the St. Louis Sutherlands. We know him from Newport."

"Sutherland . . . Sutherland." He repeated the name as if he didn't know it. "Aha." Picking out the piece of paper he had been searching for in the assortment before him, he placed it before her. "This letter is the one I dashed out this morning." It was a combination of chicken scratch meshed with dangerous ink slashes. August had taught her the secret of deciphering his nearly illegible writing. "I'll need it to go out in tomorrow's post along with the ones you will write now."

Accepting it, she said, "About Teddy. He sends you his thanks."

Papa finally looked up at her, confusion still clouding his expression. Dear Lord, could he have truly forgotten that he had paid a man to call off his proposal so easily, or was he simply a good actor?

She smiled. "He sends his highest regards to you and Mother, and then specifically writes to give you his thanks."

The fog cleared the very moment he realized who Teddy was. "Ah yes, Sutherland." A satisfying flush rose to the apples of his cheeks. At least he had the grace to be a little ashamed of himself.

"Why was he thanking you, Papa?" She glanced down at the paper as if his answer was not the least bit important to her.

"Oh . . . uh . . . nothing really."

"It didn't sound like nothing. Don't be so modest."

"I wrote a recommendation for him so that he could pursue his legal studies."

A heaviness settled over her. Is that all she had cost? Surely there was more to it than that. "Is that all? He made it seem as if there was more."

Papa shrugged a shoulder but glanced down, clearly uncomfortable. "Also a small contribution to him."

"How small?"

He shrugged again.

"Papa?" All pretense at nicety gone, her voice filled with warning.

"His parents had discontinued his allowance because of his poor grades. The boy was nearly a pauper. Don't worry, darling, it was hardly any amount we'd miss. You'll finish your Season in style."

Perhaps it was the last bit that sent her over the edge. Her parents always insisted that their ideas were her own. She wasn't the one who wanted to accept every single invitation. That was Mother. She wasn't the one who insisted on a new gown for every dinner and event. That was also Mother. "I do not care about finishing the Season in style.

I care about what you demanded from Teddy in exchange
for those funds."

His eyes widened in apparent shock at her forcefulness.
She was supposed to be the mild-mannered one. "That is
hardly any of your concern."

"Hardly my concern? You had him withdraw his proposal!"

"It was not a serious proposal." He sighed, not even
bothering to deny it. "He is too young to marry."

"He was twenty-one on his birthday, barely a year older
than I am."

"And he would not have gone through with it anyway,
not without my blessing."

"But why would you refuse your blessing?"

Sighing again, he took off his reading glasses and pinched
the bridge of his nose. Finally, he said, "Violet, answer me
truthfully. Would you like to marry a man who could so easily be bought away from you?"

The chair was suddenly uncomfortably hard at her back.
She shifted like a nervous child. "No, but that isn't the issue
at hand. Why are you so against him?"

"Because he isn't good enough for you. Frankly, I have
received multiple offers for your hand, and Teddy is by far
the lowest contender on the list."

She gasped. "Multiple offers? You have offers aside
from the initial one from Rothschild?"

"Of course. His Grace was one of our top choices, but
there have been others since and even before Rothschild. All
of them titled gentlemen. Not one of them a ne'er-do-well
who cannot make the marks needed to keep his university
career on track."

"Are you saying that you are considering these offers?"

"What sort of father would I be if I didn't?"

"A father who listens to his daughter. Have you considered that perhaps I do not intend to wed yet?"

"No." He laughed. "Because you decided to betroth

yourself to Sutherland, I assumed the state of marriage was something to which you aspired. Was I misguided?"

Anger brought her to her feet. "You might have considered that I loved Teddy."

He stared at her solemnly. "Do you love him?"

She pressed her lips together so hard that they started to go numb. Teddy had confessed his love to her, but she had never said the words back to him. It wasn't that she held no affection for him, but the words had never seemed right. "That is hardly any of your concern now, Papa. You are still insistent upon me marrying a nobleman, aren't you? No matter that I would prefer to return to New York."

"I did you a favor. Any man who would walk away from you for such a paltry sum does not deserve you."

He said it with such vigor that she was momentarily stumped. She couldn't refute him, because she would not have Teddy now under any circumstances.

"I simply want what is best for you, darling," he continued. "A secure marriage with a secure future. A home with a respectable social position for you and your children. Is that so very terrible?"

"Yes, it is if it means that my wishes do not count for anything." She was disappointed that she had allowed her emotions to get the better of her, but even more disappointed that her parents were not satisfied now that they would most certainly be getting a duke for a son-in-law.

They wanted more. That more meant that she would be bait on a hook.

"Will you at least grant me the opportunity to present a suitor for your consideration? Believe me, Violet, no one wants to force you to do anything."

Violet took in a steadying breath. She had learned from their ordeal with the Duke of Rothschild that outwardly thwarting their parents had gotten them nowhere. She would have to be smart about this, which meant she needed to get a handle on her emotions. In that spirit, she said, "Fine. As

long as we both understand that I won't be forced into anything, then I will cooperate."

"Thank you in advance for your cooperation." He smiled
and indicated the rosewood chair. "Now, could we please
continue?"

She sat, but as she worked, her mind was consumed with
the issue. Her parents had their duke with Rothschild. They
should be satisfied. But if it turned out they weren't and
insisted on her marrying, then escape would be necessary.
Was she truly prepared to go to such an extreme? The glimmer of a plan began to form.

Chapter 3

His lordship regarded her with the same curiosity with which she observed him, cautious but bewitched, nonetheless. She was not his usual quarry, but this was not his usual hunt.

V. LENNOX, *AN AMERICAN AND THE LONDON SEASON*

Not only had Lord Ware been eyeing Violet's cleavage all evening, but he was scowling at every man who dared to dance with her. The look did not suit him, making him appear a petulant adolescent with a hairline in imminent danger of receding. When the waltz she danced with Lord Atherton ended, she requested he escort her to the opposite end of the ballroom from Ware. And that was exactly how she had phrased the request. Much to Lord Atherton's delight, if the curious tug at the corners of his mouth was any indication.

When he gave a stiff bow and left her, Violet smiled at everyone she passed, slowly making her way toward the terrace. Every one of these stately townhomes seemed to have a terrace. This one ought to, but between the bodies ahead of her she could only see a row of tall windows with no doors. Damn.

She turned on her heel and changed course toward a corridor that would lead her to the ladies' dressing room.

Anywhere for a few minutes of peace without Ware making eyes at her bosom. His head was already bobbing between the crowd on the other side of the dance floor in search of her. Spurred on by her girlish delight in thwarting him, she nearly ran from the room. A laugh broke from her throat when she left the room and loped down the deserted corridor, mindful of the way her shoes pinched her toes.

Wouldn't it be lovely to meet Lord Leigh roaming these halls? He always seemed to be skulking about at these events. Never dancing. This would be the perfect scene to write with her heroine escaping to an assignation with Lord Lucifer. Her face burned hot at the mere thought, and she giggled again at her own foolishness. Aside from his physical attributes, she didn't care for the man. All that wickedness couldn't be healthy for a person.

Turning into the first open door she came to, she found herself in a salon surrounded by priceless artwork on either side. It was a room that called for graveness, so she stifled her laugh as she hurried through it. The next room was similar, but with one very important difference. There were already two people inside, and the very angry man said, "I cannot believe I allowed you to come tonight. You are an embarrassment."

Violet pulled up short in the open doorway and meant to back out of the room before they could see her, but she realized the golden-haired woman was Camille, who was with her much older husband. He faced partially away from Violet, but his distinctive muttonchops made him hard to mistake for anyone else.

"I have nothing to do with your embarrassment, Hereford. You're overreacting." Camille crossed her arms over her chest and raised her chin, but her expression seemed stricken. Twin spots of color rose high on her cheeks.

"Do not tell me I am overreacting. My wife strives to be a strumpet. Not only do you traipse about London at all hours without a care for your reputation or mine, but the moment I allow you out of the house, you are throwing yourself at every man who dances with you. We are at a ball, Camille, not a brothel."

Camille's gasp was audible from across the room. "How dare you? I only danced, and there was absolutely nothing improper about our conversation."

Hereford's voice hardened. "I will decide what is proper and what isn't. And this is not a conversation I will have with you here. You are going home for the evening."

"Hereford, you're being unreasonable." She rolled her eyes. When he moved toward her, Camille took a step back. "I've done nothing wrong, and I'm staying here. I was having a lovely time until now."

"You are going home. I will simply tell everyone you developed a headache." He followed her retreat and took her arm in what appeared to be a viselike grip.

Violet flinched at the contact, wondering if it was a sign of further unseen violence. Uncertain what to do, but knowing she had to intervene, Violet stepped farther into the salon and said, "Camille?" Both heads whipped toward her. Camille's expression was horrified, and Hereford's merely a reflection of his anger, but at least he dropped his hold Camille's arm. "Is everything all right?" Violet asked.

The very air stood still, simmering with tension as it waited for someone to act. Finally, Hereford turned back to his wife. "I shall go have the carriage summoned. Do not force me to come and retrieve you." Ignoring Violet, he left through the far door, letting it slam behind him.

Camille's face crumpled the moment he disappeared, her hands coming up to muffle her low sob. Violet hurried over and pulled her friend into her arms. "That was awful. Are you injured?"

Camille sagged against her friend for a moment, accepting the comfort before she pulled back. Giving her head a shake, she wiped at a tear that threatened to fall. "No, he didn't hurt me." Though the pale skin above her elbow-length gloves was pink from his grip, it didn't appear as if it would be bruised.

"Does he hurt you, Camille? Are you safe with him?"

"He doesn't harm me, not in the way you mean."

"In what way, then?"

Camille only shook her head, clearly struggling to find her composure. Violet felt helpless to do anything to help her, and she hated the way that set heavy on her chest. Camille was nearly the same age as her and should be enjoying herself back home in New York by going to parties with friends. She was far too young to have been married to a stranger nearly three times her age and shipped across the ocean with no family or friends.

Anger spurring her words, Violet said, "It's obvious he cares very little for your well-being. Come home with me."

Camille gave a short bark of laughter and shook her head. "You are right on that count. He was merely greedy for the money my father settled on me. I am an inconvenience he doesn't need or want."

"Then do it. Come home with me. He likely won't even care," Violet urged.

Camille put her hand on Violet's shoulder and shook her head sadly. "You're very sweet, Violet, but I can't possibly do that. Everyone will know, and as much as I am unhappy, I cannot bring that disgrace upon my family. It's not fair to them."

"But it's not fair to you, either."

"No, but I did marry him. If I leave, he will see it as a personal affront. I simply have to figure out a way to make do." The misery in her eyes when she glanced toward the door Hereford had exited through tugged at Violet's heart. "Besides, your parents wouldn't allow me to stay."

"Then we can go away somewhere." If Violet had to escape, it would be no hardship to include her friend.

"But where?" asked Camille.

Home to New York? No, they would be found easily,

perhaps even before the ship left Liverpool. Even if they made it to New York, the scandal and gossip would give them no relief. Besides, Teddy wasn't there waiting for her. They needed to go somewhere where they wouldn't be found for a bit. Somewhere they could find relaxation and comfort.

"Windermere. I read an advertisement in the paper a few weeks ago about an estate there accepting boarders. It's something of an artists' house. Women only. We can go there together, and no one will know where we are." Saying the idea out loud gave it some weight, as if it were actually a viable alternative. Violet had kept the advertisement because it had seemed like a very romantic place to dream about. But all of this marriage business made it seem much more of a possibility. She refused to end up like Camille.

Her friend gave her first genuine smile. "An artists' house? How lovely." Then she seemed to shake herself from her wistfulness as she asked, "Oh, dear, have you heard back from the publisher about your manuscript? I'm sorry I haven't asked you before now. We haven't seen very much of each other since you've been in London."

Violet had sent in her finished manuscript weeks before they had left New York along with her forwarding address in London. Every day she waited felt an eternity. "I haven't heard yet, but I hope to soon. And please don't worry. We've both been busy." Though to be truthful, Hereford had been angry that Camille had gone with August to a bare-knuckle fight in Whitechapel a few weeks ago and had essentially kept her prisoner in their home since then with very few approved outings or visitors. The little they had seen each other, Violet's mother had been present, so they hadn't been able to properly chat.

"I hope you hear soon. I'm certain it'll be good news. And, Violet, I so appreciate your concern, but you don't want to run away. You have the rest of the Season to look forward to."

"I suppose, but it wouldn't be a hardship." Violet was almost surprised at how easy it would be to leave. She was enjoying herself, but she would enjoy spending time with her friend even more. "I'm afraid that my parents still have marriage to a nobleman in mind, so it might actually be a welcome escape."

Camille stiffened. "What do you mean? Did something happen with Rothschild and August? In your letter you said that he followed her to America."

"No, nothing's happened. I assume they have reconciled and Max is having a devil of time keeping Rothschild off her on the crossing." Violet teased in an attempt at levity.

Camille relaxed somewhat, but she still held an air of alarm. "That's good, then. A duke in the family will get your mother onto Mrs. Astor's guest list."

Violet nodded. "That's true, but Papa asked me to consider a few suitors."

"Violet, no!" The blood drained from Camille's face, leaving it as white as chalk. "You cannot let them force you into marriage. Not under any circumstances. Do you understand me?" She held Violet's hand in a grip that was almost painful.

"It's not my intention to marry."

Camille faced her fully, getting closer and lowering her voice. "Violet, listen to me. There are things that happen between a husband and wife that you don't understand yet." A rosy blush bloomed across her cheeks as she spoke. Under normal circumstances it would have made her appear quite lovely, but coupled with her wide, fearful eyes, it was alarming. "The marriage bed for one. It is an indignity in the best of circumstances, but imagine being forced to bare every part of yourself to a man you despise, or worse, to a man who despises and resents you. To give your entire being over to him."

An image of Viscount Ware came to mind. His eyes were nearly as cold as his touch. Thanks to an anatomy book she and August had stumbled upon years ago, and snatches of overheard conversations, she knew the basics of what went on between a husband and wife. She had never considered what it would be like to lie with Lord Ware in that way, but the very idea of it shook her to her core. Papa hadn't said, but surely if he had been allowed to escort her tonight, then he was a contender for her hand. "And for two?" she asked, quite certain that she didn't really want to know more.

"He controls your entire life. Who you visit, who your friends are, where you live, what you eat, the clothing you wear. Now imagine giving that power to a person who believes you to be beneath him. He marries you for your money, but deep down he remembers that you come from common stock and he resents being brought so low. Please promise me that you will only marry someone of your choosing? Someone for whom you feel affection?"

Violet couldn't speak past the lump in her throat, and her chest ached with sadness for Camille and her obvious misery.

"Please, Violet? I need to know you understand."

Violet nodded, forcing herself to say, "Of course. I promise."

Camille pulled her in for a quick hug and then wiped at the corner of her eye once more. "Good. Let me know if you need any help, but I'm afraid it will likely have to be in the form of a letter. I have a feeling I won't be allowed visitors for some time."

She started to walk away, but Violet took her hand, fearful that she might not see her friend for a while. It was within Hereford's power to withhold her from everyone for as long as he wished. "Please promise me that you'll let me know if *you* need help. We can go away. Anywhere."

Camille smiled. "Don't worry for me. It's not that terrible. I am being a touch melodramatic, but I wouldn't wish it for you."

"Nevertheless, I'll have your promise," Violet insisted.

"Fine, I promise. Now I have to go before he comes back." Giving Violet another smile over her shoulder, she hurried out of the room.

Christian had never found much use for Ware and other men of his ilk. Haughty and with an inflated sense of superiority, they did nothing and accomplished even less. Their whole purpose of existing seemed to be to enjoy themselves to the detriment of everyone else. Not that Christian frowned overly much on that sort of existence—his own hovered somewhere around that level minus the damage to the undeserving—he simply despised their dishonesty about it all.

Their initial dislike had formed at Eton where the viscount had been a year behind Christian, but the depths of Christian's loathing had hit a new low when Ware had walked into the ballroom with Violet on his arm earlier that evening. Their courtship was proceeding faster than Christian had anticipated. His only consolation was that Violet appeared to not favor the man at all. She had mostly ignored him, leaving Ware to glare at whomever had her attention. It was a sign of an insecure man, which meant Ware wasn't at all certain of his intended and Christian needed to act fast.

Violet had left the ballroom only moments earlier, but Ware was already on her trail, having caught sight of her as she hurried out. Christian rushed through the crowded room but lagged behind Ware's faster progress. When Christian finally broke into the corridor, Ware had paused at the far end as if determining whether to turn left or right.

"Ah, she got away from you, did she?" Christian called, lessening the distance between them with each word. When he reached the other man, he said, "You will have to be more vigilant to catch an heiress."

Ware's eyes flashed with anger and frustration. "Good evening, Leigh. We haven't had a chance to chat tonight."

"Why would we chat?" Christian raised a brow. "We are hardly friends."

Ware gritted his teeth and his jaw hardened. "Because we are civilized men."

"Speak for yourself," said Christian. "I have never made such a claim."

The man swallowed, clearly uncomfortable with the encounter but at a loss as to how to remove himself from it.

"Miss Crenshaw does not seem to find favor with you," said Christian. "Do you anticipate that she will accept your offer?"

Ware's eyes widened in surprise.

"Come now, I know you have offered for her."

"How do you know that?"

"There are no secrets, Ware. You are a fool if you think there are."

The man swallowed again, his lips pressing together to form a thin line. The urge to tell Christian to leave off was written all over his face, but he was too much of a coward to do it. "She will, once we know each other better."

"Prepared to win her over with your charm, are you?" When Ware's scowl only deepened, Christian added, "No? Your wealth? Oh, I forgot. You have nothing." Mineral rights notwithstanding.

"What do you want, Leigh?" Ware gritted out.

"Violet Crenshaw."

Shock registered on the man's face, making him blanch, before his eyes narrowed and he leaned forward with a ferocity on his face Christian had never seen there before. Desperation pushed men to desperate measures. "Leave her alone. She is mine."

"She will never accept you."

Ware grinned, momentarily alarming him. "Then I shall have to arrange it so that she has no choice in the matter."

Anger immediately began to roil within him, but Christian forced a bored smile. "Then you had better go catch her. I saw her being escorted toward the terrace."

The grin fled Ware's lips, and he hurried off in that direction.

Christian stood for a time, pondering the viscount's meaning. He clearly intended to compromise her in some way. The idea shouldn't horrify Christian so much, since his own plans had briefly wandered down that path, but the thought of Ware being anywhere near her was unsettling. At least when Christian had considered it, he had planned to give her so much pleasure she could not think straight. Ware, selfish boar that he was, would not be as considerate.

A door slammed behind him, and Hereford hurried out, his face a mask of anger as he stormed toward the front of the house without looking in Christian's direction. Intrigued and concerned, because that room was one of the few places Violet could have hidden herself, he slowly made his way toward the salon, the pain in his ankle from chasing Ware making his limp more pronounced. Just as he reached for the door, it opened and he found himself face-to-face with Camille, Hereford's duchess.

"Good evening, Your Grace." He gave a short bow.

Startled, she tried and failed to smile, murmuring a greeting under her breath as she turned and hurried after her husband. Christian glanced inside the room, expecting to find the salon empty, but Violet stood in the middle. Wearing an ice-blue gown that hugged her figure, she was as lovely as he had ever seen her. The moment their eyes met, a frisson of electricity moved through him, drawing him to her with the same invisible current that had moved between them ever since he had first laid eyes on her.

It was time to put his plan into motion. Thanks to Ware, he knew just what to say to her. Stepping into the room, he closed the door behind him.

Chapter 4

*The stakes were high, but Rose was prepared
for the game. One kiss would not alter the
course of their lives. One weakness did not a
sinner make.*

V. LENNOX, *AN AMERICAN AND THE
LONDON SEASON*

The Earl of Leigh came into the salon as if her salacious imagination had conjured him. Dispassionate and casual, he walked with a smoothness that belied his slight limp. His rich, dark hair curled a bit near his collar, and the eyes she knew to be gray were darkened in the low light of the room. Violet was too stunned to react as he closed the door behind him. Logic told her that it would be best to exit the room through the opposite door because being caught alone with him could be disastrous, but her burgeoning fascination with him kept her in place.

"Good evening, my lord," she said, forcing her voice to match his calm exterior. The truth was that her heart had started pounding the moment she set eyes on him, and her palms were sweaty.

"Miss Crenshaw." He inclined his head while holding her gaze.

Had she thought him dispassionate? His eyes were anything but that. The expression within them roiled with an intensity that held her rooted in place behind a sofa. And then he smiled. A tiny upward tilt on the left side of his mouth that promised wicked thoughts were accompanying it. Or were those wicked thoughts merely a reflection of her own? Her fictitious heiress, Miss Rose Hamilton, was known for coveting Lord Lucifer's distinctive smile. Violet simply had to work harder to separate herself from her character.

Coming to a stop, he left the length of the sofa guarding the distance between them. His powerful, gloved fingers flexed around the hawk's head grip of his cane. Butterflies came to life in her belly as they usually did when he was near. It was why she was always so atrociously sharp with him, she realized. She had been fighting her natural attraction to him, because it had been unfaithful to Teddy. A man who it seemed had little faith and had hardly deserved hers. Now that her relationship with her fiancé was over—she'd worry later about why it had been so easy to let him go—she didn't have to feel guilty anymore.

"I feel that I owe you an—"

"Hereford left rather—"

They both began at the same time, and then paused, awkwardly assessing the other. He inclined his head, indicating that she should speak first.

"I am glad to have a moment in private with you. I want to apologize for my short temper on our previous two meetings."

He didn't respond right away and simply continued to watch her as if he were trying to read her expression. His perusal drew a nervous smile from her. Another thrill of awareness shot through her belly when his gaze darted to her lips. He found her attractive at least. "I have no good reason for my behavior, except that I was angry with Roth-schild and perhaps a little unsettled . . ." She swallowed thickly to stop herself from saying more. Saying more when less would do had always been her downfall.

"Unsettled?" He prodded.

Giving her head a quick shake, she said, "Unsettled to find you in my home unexpectedly."

She would not tell him how he was the most handsome man she had ever laid eyes on and that alone was enough to fluster her. She would not. Being around him made her realize how unworldly and inexperienced she really was when it came to men. Her infatuation with him was nothing like the sloppy kisses she had exchanged with Teddy. They had been experiments, while her thoughts for Lord Leigh bordered on incinerating passion.

A grin curved the perfect bow of his lips. "No apology is necessary. You were right to be unsettled by my presence in both cases." He looked at her as if he knew the truth. Perhaps the blush staining her cheeks had told him as much. "Besides, I did say that I enjoy fireworks." A subtle challenge flashed in his eyes.

Those simple words made something clench deep inside her. Something visceral that hovered on the edge of painful longing. He liked their verbal sparring. He had seen her at her worst that day, and he had approved of her. She didn't really know what to do with that. Almost everyone she knew disapproved of any sort of display of emotion. Teddy had frowned and changed the subject when challenged. Lord Ware would certainly disapprove of her sometime wayward tongue.

Her cheeks burned hotter, and when she glanced down, she noticed she had been worrying the length of a silken thread that had broken free from the sofa. When she dared to glance back up at him, his grin had fled to be replaced with concern.

"Hereford did not seem particularly pleased when he left. I hope he did not upset you."

She only debated for a moment how much she should tell him. Despite his reputation, he was a good friend of the man who would soon become her brother. He was also the only one outside of her immediate family who knew that Rothschild had followed August to that ship, and there had been no hint of gossip about it. If Rothschild trusted him, then so could she. "It isn't me that I'm concerned about. It's Camille. He treats her poorly, and she has no recourse."

"No recourse?" he asked, dipping his head infinitesimally. She likely wouldn't have noticed had she not been so attuned to him.

"No, at least not here, not so far away from home and everything she knows. She belongs to him, and the fact of the matter is that he can do with her as he will and hardly anyone would intervene. He treats her like a rebellious stepchild—withholding her visitors, keeping her locked inside—and he is well within his rights to do so. It all seems so grievously unfair. She is a lovely person who has a wealth of affection and warmth to share, but it is all wasted on him. He only cares that she brought him money." She stopped, realizing that she had said far too much to someone who was essentially a stranger.

He took a breath, and his chest rose on the inhale. Had she noticed how broad his shoulders were before? She must have. He wasn't overly brawny, but his lean physique was solid and strong. His chest and shoulders were thick, and she didn't think it was from padding.

"It is the way of Society marriages." His voice was soft, but strong. "It seems as if you do not prefer such a marriage for yourself?"

"I don't care a whit for Society. I think people should only marry someone who can offer them some bit of affection. I am not so naive that I believe in the sort of romantic love and devotion that Miss Austen touts." Though what August had found with the duke seemed very close to that sort of love, and if she was honest, she actually wouldn't mind very much if she found that for herself. But that was far too complicated a subject to discuss with Lord Leigh, a man she should not be talking to at all, much less going on and on like she was. "But there should be some sort of mutual respect and consideration."

"Affection is important to you." His gaze dropped down to her mouth.

She licked her lips and then pressed them together to stifle the nervous tick. "Affection is important to everyone. People are much happier when they are in family units where they are supported and valued. It has been proven to be true."

He grinned, an attractive dimple forming in his left cheek. "You are a bluestocking like your sister."

"I read for information as well as entertainment if that's what you mean." She was aware of the way her shoulders stiffened and her voice hardened, but seemed to be able to do nothing to control her reaction to him. *Bluestocking* held all sorts of negative connotations. She knew she wasn't worldly enough to have someone like him return the depth of her attraction, but she wouldn't have him believing her interest in knowledge to be a mark against her.

His grin stayed in place. "That is exactly what I mean, Miss Crenshaw. It is a trait I admire in anyone, especially a woman who courts scandal by the very admission."

Her gaze flicked back to his, unaccountably pleased by the compliment. She fought the rather inappropriate urge to giggle. To laugh would have ruined a perfectly fine moment and reminded him that she wasn't yet twenty, and likely far too young for a man of the world like him.

Not that it mattered if he returned her attraction. Her interest was purely in the vein of exploring Miss Hamilton's feelings. She had no intention of involving herself with an English lord.

"Thank you, my lord."

He inclined his head again, but the grin regrettably faded as he asked, "Have you found this affection with your own fiancé?"

The question was so unexpected, she could only say, "Pardon?"

Shifting, he leaned a hip against the back of the sofa, making her realize how much taller he was than her. He still towered over her by a head, even though the shift should have cost him a couple of inches. He was deceptively larger than he appeared. "Forgive me for asking. It is none of my affair, but I find myself concerned for you. Rothschild once mentioned something about an American fiancé. I believe the man was your initial reason for refusing Rothschild. I simply wondered if you had found this affection with him."

"Oh . . ." She really should not tell him about Teddy. "I thought I had, but apparently not. He wasn't the man I thought he was." Why couldn't she control her tongue? Any hope of appearing the sophisticate with him was gone.

"Indeed?" He raised a brow.

"Our betrothal has ended." It was simply too embarrassing to admit that her own father had paid Teddy to leave her alone, and he had accepted.

"Ah, that explains it, then."

"Explains what?"

"Ware." He said the name as if that clarified everything.

"Lord Ware? What about him?" The hair on the back of her neck stood up in warning.

"I should not gossip. I have been told it leads to terrible consequences."

Before she knew it, she was in front of him, her hand on his forearm. His muscle flexed beneath her touch, again making her realize how much strength he held contained within his deceptively dispassionate exterior. Both of their gazes locked on the touch, prompting her to quickly retract her hand, drawing his gaze to hers. He seemed quite serious now as he searched her face, though she couldn't have said what he was looking for.

"Please. If it concerns me, then I want to know."

"He believes that he will marry you." They were so close that his breath caressed her temple, and she caught a faint trace of scotch and the hint of tobacco.

"That isn't true. He hasn't proposed or even asked my father." Had he? Knowing her parents' past behavior, she wouldn't be shocked if he had and they hadn't told her, but she would be deeply hurt. Her parents had the duke as an almost-son-in-law. They might want another nobleman in the family, but there was no pressing need to force another marriage. However, the dread in her belly warned her otherwise.

Lord Leigh did not say anything. His penetrating gray eyes simply held hers. It was almost as if he knew more than he was saying. He would have no reason to lie about this. Why would he, knowing that he would have to answer to Rothschild if he did?

"What did he tell you?" she asked.

"That he intends to have you, and he can arrange it so that you have no choice in the matter."

Her blood turned to ice water, and she might have swayed on her feet. His hand moved to her rib cage to keep her balanced. He was warm and strong, and she imagined him touching her for a different reason. This was improper, and she should immediately step away, but she couldn't.

"There was also some mention of mineral rights," he added.

Oh God. With August's marriage, Crenshaw Iron would be permitted to open a division in London. The necessary approvals were already winging their way through Parliament, pending her marriage to the duke. Papa would logically be seeking resources for that. But would he sell his own daughter for them? Violet knew the answer to that even if she didn't want to believe it.

"You didn't know."

She shook her head, but it wasn't as if she hadn't suspected. She simply hadn't wanted to believe. She had thought that perhaps the duke had been a stroke of luck, that he had approached her parents and they had been beside themselves with joy. But it was so much worse than that. Her parents actually hoped to sell both of their daughters. Even if she was able to convince Papa that she would not marry one of her suitors, would Lord Ware take matters into his own hands? He could easily seek to have her alone, to have someone find them. Would she be strong enough to face the scandal and accompanying repercussions against her family if she continued to resist marriage after that?

"I didn't want to believe," she said.

His grip tightened slightly on her rib cage. The pressure caused a pleasant tingle to work its way over her skin. His hand felt so strong and sure that she wanted to lean into it.

"What will you do?" he asked quietly.

His irises were rimmed in a darker color, though the light was too low to tell if that color was blue or a darker gray. He seemed so earnest and concerned for her that she covered his hand with her own. That simple touch thickened the air, and heat swirled between them.

"I'm not certain." And she could hardly think with him so close. Her heart pounded a frantic beat as her body kept wanting to sway into him. The effect he had on her was an immature infatuation, but she wanted more of it.

"If they disregard your feelings on the matter, then you only have two choices."

"Run away." She sounded a bit breathless.

"Yes." Was it her overactive imagination, or did he sound breathless, too?

When he didn't say anything else, she prodded him. "Or?"

"Marry someone of your own choosing."

Surely, he didn't mean him? No, she was imagining the connotation. "I-I suppose that might work, only there is no one that I want to wed. As I mentioned, I believe that a couple should have a mutual fondness and respect for each other. I could hardly escape one doomed marriage to rush into another one. It wouldn't be wise."

His lips thinned in what seemed to be disappointment. Had he really meant to propose to her? "Then it appears you have found your solution," he said.

Was he right? Had it already come to running away so fast?

"Do you have a means of supporting yourself if you choose that option?"

Would her parents truly cut her off? God, if she ran, she would certainly have to be prepared for the possibility. "Yes . . . I have a small stock portfolio that my brother controls for me. He would allow me to have access to it, I'm sure."

"How small?"

"I get quarterly statements." But the truth was she hardly examined them closely. "I believe around twenty thousand dollars."

"That's rather significant," he said, and his confidence gave her hope. Perhaps it would be enough. "But what if your brother sides with your parents? He could hold on to the stocks."

"He wouldn't, but I also have a small home in Manhattan left to me by an aunt. It generates an income."

"Or you could sell," he said.

"I suppose." Though she wouldn't want to. Aunt Hortense had been her father's eldest sister. Unmarried, she had held a particular fondness for Violet, an affection Violet had returned. Many happy hours had been spent in her home. "But all that will come later. I have a small amount of cash to get me by in the short term should I leave."

"I could help you." His eyes were resolute but also tender with understanding.

"Thank you, but I don't think such an extreme measure is necessary just yet. I'll need to have a conversation with my parents to clarify things."

His hand fell slowly from her waist. Despite herself, she felt at a loss when he did so. Instead of letting him go, she followed, covering his hand with hers when it came to rest on the back of the sofa. He stared down at their gloved hands, and she smiled, folding her fingers around his and giving them a squeeze.

"I appreciate your concern."

Still watching where her hand rested on his, he said, "I do not know your parents well, but I do not believe they will be swayed away from their purpose."

She could not seem to look away from the contact, either. As she watched, the pad of his thumb brushed gently across the base of hers in a slow back-and-forth motion that could be clearly felt through their gloves. A delicious shiver ran the length of her spine while heat pooled in her belly. She stared for so long that it seemed indecent, so she looked up into his eyes. He caught her, like a spider catches a fly in its web. Only she had no wish to get away. She liked being the object of his focus.

What if he asked for her hand instead of Ware? Would she be so quick to refuse him, or would she entertain the idea and allow him to court her? She knew the answer when excitement swirled within her. Perhaps if they kissed once—a chaste brushing of lips—then she could put it down as research for her poor Miss Hamilton. Neither she nor Violet had ever kissed a rogue. Teddy certainly didn't count in that regard.

Without making a conscious decision, she leaned forward, swaying toward him. He stayed where he was, but his swift intake of breath made her pulse quicken. Before she could stop herself, she raised up on her toes and pressed her lips to his. They were surprisingly soft and warm. She didn't particularly like scotch, but tasting it from his mouth would surely be divine. His heart pounded beneath where her hand had come to rest on his chest, indicating he was as affected as she was. A surge of exhilaration rushed through her veins, making her bold. The very tip of her tongue touched his bottom lip, drawing a sound from deep in his chest. His lips moved, parting beneath hers as his hand came back to her waist to hold her steady.

The sound of heels rushing against the carpet in the next room had her pulling back and turning in time to see Lady Helena March hurry through the door adjoining the salons. "Violet!" Her blue eyes were widened with concern when she saw them. "There you are."

Violet had no idea how badly the scene appeared. It was very likely the woman knew exactly what they had been up to. Still, Violet couldn't resist turning back to gauge his expression. The wanton desire she saw reflected in his eyes made the coil of pleasure in her belly clench tighter. He wasn't touching her anymore, but the imprint of his hand still warmed her.

"Lady Helena." Violet smiled, trying to appear nonchalant but knowing she probably failed. "Lord Leigh was showing me the . . ." She cast about for something, anything to focus on. "The Titian," she said, referring to a painting on the wall near them.

"Good evening, Lord Leigh," said Lady Helena, her eyes narrowing in censure.

"Lady Helena." To his credit, he inclined his head as if nothing untoward had happened. "If you both will excuse me." He offered no other explanation as he turned and left the room.

Lady Helena waited until the door closed behind him before she said, "Dear, I feel I must warn you about—"

Violet held up her hand. "There is no need. Believe me, I understand how foolish it was to be alone with him." And yet, a tiny but reckless part of her didn't care. If Lord Ware had planned to compromise her, then why shouldn't she kiss whomever she wanted? Perhaps finding her compromised by someone else would make him leave her alone.

Lady Helena smiled in understanding, her eyes shining with kindness and a hint of amusement, which reminded

Violet why she and August had befriended the young widow not long after arriving in London. She had taken them both under her wing, helping them navigate the often intricate and hazy rules of Society.

"I didn't mean for it happen," Violet elaborated, though she had.

"No one ever does when it comes to rogues."

Violet laughed. "He told me some disturbing things about Lord Ware."

"Tell me." Lady Helena laced her arm with Violet's, and they slowly walked back to the ball as Violet explained.

"It seems your parents are determined to make a match?" Lady Helena asked when she was finished.

"Yes, so I'll have to speak with them. I do not wish to marry now."

Lady Helena nodded. "In the meantime, please do look out for yourself. You cannot be alone with a man. I have never known Lord Leigh to be in search of a wife, but stranger things have happened, particularly when fortunes are involved."

"You don't trust him, then?" Violet had not been able to find out very much about him, because he seemed to be someone no one spoke about in polite company. It appeared to her that he hovered along the edges of Society, attending social events, but notably absent in some of the more respectable drawing rooms.

"Well . . ." Lady Helena's brow furrowed. "He has a reputation . . ." She smiled at someone walking past and lowered her voice. "He is known for eschewing polite company in favor of that gaming hell and less acceptable companionship. I cannot speak to his thoughts, but if he set out with marriage in mind, he wouldn't go about it in the conventional method."

"And you do not believe he would make a suitable husband?" That much was obvious from Lady Helena's tone.

Violet couldn't figure out why it mattered, but it did. Her breath lodged in her throat waiting for her conclusion to be confirmed.

Lady Helena smiled, but there was a strange sort of sadness in her eyes. "Who is to say what makes a good husband? I think the bigger issue here is that most people in this room would say he is unsuitable, and that would have a profound impact on the social life of his bride. Why?" she asked, her eyes narrowing with speculation. "Are you considering him?"

Violet smiled and shook her head. By this time, they had reached the edge of the ballroom, and she found herself searching the crowd for him, but he wasn't there. She didn't think that he had meant to compromise her himself, but why had he told her about Lord Ware? What were his intentions?

"Ah, there you are, darling!"

Violet had to force herself not to cringe at her mother's voice. She needed some time to distance herself from her thoughts of Lord Leigh before coming back to reality. The moment went from bad to worse when she turned to see her mother approaching on the arm of Lord Ware. He appeared sulky and unhappy with a frown that was almost accusatory.

"I told you she was around here somewhere." Mother gave the man a playful swat on his arm, but her eyes belied her good humor. They reflected notable relief and perhaps even a tinge of disapproval. "Violet, darling, we were half convinced you had set sail for Greece or some other exotic locale," she teased. "But here you are speaking with the lovely Lady Helena. It's so nice to see you again, my dear."

"And you as well, Mrs. Crenshaw. Please do not be alarmed. I simply needed a moment to catch my breath, and Miss Crenshaw was kind enough to walk with me."

As the women continued their conversation, Lord Ware

moved closer to her and said, "Come take a turn around the ballroom with me, Miss Crenshaw."

She meant to refuse but couldn't come up with a suitable reason to reject him. As she was thinking, Mother said, "Of course she will. You two go and have a lovely time. Leave us older ladies here to hold up the wall." Lady Helena might have been in her late twenties at most, hardly old, but Violet had no chance to protest as Mother all but pushed them together.

Digging in her heels as he took her arm, Violet finally managed to find her tongue. "But, Mother, I shouldn't monopolize Lord Ware, and there are many dances I have promised to others."

"They will quite understand." Lord Ware gave her a stiff smile.

"You see, dear," said Mother. "Listen to Lord Ware. He knows better about these things than we do."

To refuse further would have been in bad form, but also, Violet was left reeling a bit from her mother's quick dismissal. As if she were perfectly happy to take his side in things. With a lump of dread in the pit of her stomach, she allowed him to lead her away.

Chapter 5

*Their meeting had been like a single
firework—bright and brilliant, leaving a
dearth of sound that amplified the silence.*

V. LENNOX, *AN AMERICAN AND THE
LONDON SEASON*

Violet's unease stayed with her the rest of the night, overshadowing any thoughts of her kiss with Lord Leigh. Her apprehension only increased on the carriage ride home. As usual, her parents were oblivious to her feelings. They were both in good spirits and said their good nights in the entryway before she hurried up to her bedroom.

Ellen, her maid, greeted her when she walked in. "Good evening, miss."

"Good evening, Ellen." Violet inclined her head as she tugged off her gloves. The maid had only been employed in the Crenshaw household since August had taken their shared lady's maid home with her to New York. Though Violet liked her fine, she still thought of her as a stranger. After such a harrowing night, she simply needed to be alone with her thoughts.

Ellen hurried over and began working on the line of hidden fastenings down the back of Violet's gown. After gently pulling it off over her head, Ellen set it aside before loosening the laces of Violet's corset. When she could take a deep breath, Violet said, "That will be all for tonight, Ellen."

"But the gown—" She indicated where it lay draped over the chair.

"You can see to it tomorrow. Leave it there."

"I could at least unpin your hair, miss."

"Thank you, but you can go on up to bed." Violet had already turned toward the mirror and begun pulling the pins out herself.

Ellen nodded but paused in her path toward the door. "Are you quite all right, miss?" A crease appeared between her brows. "You seem a bit pale."

Violet shook her head, having worn her calm facade for as long as she was able. "I-I'm only tired, I think."

"Did you eat something that disagreed with you? I could fix you a tonic. In my village, my aunt was known for making over a hundred different ones, all guaranteed to cure a different ailment."

Violet gave her head another shake. She hadn't been able to bring herself to eat more than a couple of bites at the late supper served at the ball. "Thank you, Ellen, but I think rest is all I need."

The girl nodded again and bid her good night before hurrying out the door.

Violet finished her hair and quickly changed into her nightdress and dressing gown. Her brain was moving too fast to even consider sleep, so she ended up pacing around her bed. She wished August was here, while at the same time feeling annoyed with herself for wanting her sister. August had been the one to try to save her a few weeks ago when this marriage talk had started, while Violet had assumed that her supposed engagement to Teddy would solve her problem. She would be twenty soon. It was time she started taking responsibility for her problems.

With that in mind, she tightened the belt on her dressing

gown and marched down the corridor to Mother's suite of rooms. She would find out in no uncertain terms if Lord Ware was the man her parents intended she marry. If he was, then she would figure a way out of it on her own.

There was no light coming from beneath the door. Perhaps she was still talking with Papa. Violet hurried down the stairs and to the drawing room. The door was cracked open, and light spilled out over the rug. The murmur of Mother's voice, followed by Papa's, had Violet slowing to a stop before they could see her. Checking that the hall was deserted, she leaned in to listen.

"You worry too much, Griswold," said Mother. "Violet is the good one. She is placid and well-mannered. She will come to see that Lord Ware is the best choice. She trusts us."

"I know you are right, my dear. I suppose I'm simply feeling softhearted. She isn't even twenty, and she'll be leaving us. First August, and now Violet who will be left here all alone."

"She'll hardly be alone. August will be near, and with the new office in London, we can stay here for months out of the year if we want."

Whatever Papa answered was lost to the roaring in Violet's ears. This was really happening. The marriage plan was starting all over again, and they had chosen Ware. She shouldn't be surprised. Not one bit. And yet, she had hoped . . .

Turning, she hurried as quickly as she dared back toward the stairs. She was in no state to talk with her parents about this tonight. She was too upset, and anger never led to good decisions. As she passed the table with the silver tray that held their daily correspondence, her name written in a bold hand caught her eye. The letter must have arrived in the hubbub of preparing for the ball earlier in the day. Her hand visibly shook as she picked it up. A quick glance at the return address confirmed what she had already known; it was from the publisher in New York.

Rejection or acceptance?

She swiped the missive as if it were a secret letter and hid it in her skirts as she hurried up the stairs. The last thing she wanted to do was share this letter until she'd had time to absorb the contents. Locking her bedroom door behind her, she settled herself on the bed. The long-awaited letter trembled in Violet's hand, and a portentous chill swept over her skin. Once again, her future awaited in a letter. Taking a deep breath, she tore into it, her gaze skimming over the words haphazardly, reading it in discombobulated phrases.

Thank you for your submission.

. . . interesting and revealing . . .

We regret to inform you . . .

. . . readers prefer serious and prudent topics . . .

. . . writing shows promise . . .

. . . consider submitting a manual regarding women's interests . . .

They didn't want her book. The paper slipped from her fingers and floated lightly to the floor. Unlike Teddy's rejection, this one cut her deeply. Perhaps it was because they were rejecting not only her manuscript, but who she was. They wanted her to write books about etiquette or dinner parties. Nothing serious. Nothing real. Nothing that mattered to her.

Her parents wanted her to host dinner parties and show Mrs. Astor that they were very much worthy of her guest list. Again, nothing serious or real. If they had their way, she would live her life as an ornament. She would be pretty and mild and never utter a word that would cause anyone the slightest discontent.

For the past few years, she had suffered under the illusion that both were possible. That she could somehow be what they wanted while also holding on to the thread of who she was. But an impasse was ahead. She could choose herself, or she could lose herself completely. Both were not possible.

*   *   *

The next day dawned dark and dreary, pushing the afternoon garden party that had been planned indoors. Violet had to fight to find any sort of enthusiasm for the gathering. With the exception of a few guests, it was an entirely different set of mothers and daughters than those who had attended the small gathering Mother had held two days prior. Now that the news of August and Rothschild's romantic escape had begun to leak, the Crenshaws were more popular than ever, and Mother couldn't have been more pleased. Violet, however, simply wanted to be left to wallow in the ache of rejection.

Had the manuscript been badly written, or had it been rejected because she was a silly woman who couldn't possibly write anything of interest? Had the subject matter been too provocative? A lighthearted look at the eccentricities of New York's elite could be problematic, but Violet had kept it witty and good-natured in the hopes of overcoming that. Apparently, she had failed. Perhaps Mrs. Graham had only been exceedingly polite in encouraging her writing. She had been paid well by Papa to tutor both Violet and August. It wasn't outside the realm of possibility that she might have exaggerated her enthusiasm. But August had read Violet's work, and she wouldn't lie to her . . . would she?

These questions and more plagued her throughout the afternoon. By the time everyone had gathered in the entrance hall to pull on capes and gloves, she was ready to spend a few precious hours alone in her room in the company of Jane Eyre.

"It was lovely to see you again," said Lady Alfred.

Violet shook herself from her reverie and made her smile especially bright. "And you as well. I look forward to seeing you again at the Worthingtons' ball."

The woman nodded, already turning her attention to Mother, when her daughter, Lady Beatrice, screeched, "My pin!" She patted her chest in a display of dramatics as she searched for it. "I have lost it!" Lady Beatrice had made a point of showing everyone the gold-encrusted emerald she had recently inherited from her grandmother. It had likely been left in the drawing room, having been neglected after being passed around.

"I'll go find it for you." Violet was quick to volunteer before Mother could call out to a footman. Perhaps by the time she returned the crowd would have thinned and she would be spared an endless round of pleasantries.

She stepped into the drawing room and pulled the door behind her for a moment of welcome silence. The emerald bauble winked from its abandoned position on a table across the room. Retrieving it, she sank down onto a sofa and closed her eyes, happy for a moment alone. The headache she had awoken with thanks to her tears and fitful sleep the night before was pounding behind her eyes, but it seemed to lessen each time the front door opened and closed as another visitor left. Perhaps she would plead a headache tonight and forgo the theater outing her parents had planned. It would give her time to think of what to do next.

"Good afternoon, Miss Crenshaw."

Her eyes flew open at the sound of the male voice. Lord Ware stood before her. She noticed immediately that he was between her and the closed door. "What are you doing here?"

He smiled pleasantly. "I arrived a little before your party ended. Mrs. Crenshaw had the footman show me to the salon." He indicated the open door leading to the adjoining salon.

Mother hadn't said a word about his arrival, but they'd had guests. Anger threaded with a tiny bit of fear churned within her as she rose to her feet. He didn't appear threatening, but she didn't like the fact that she was alone with him. He knew that it was improper, and yet he had approached her. Was Lord Leigh right? Was Lord Ware planning something inappropriate?

She almost forced a smile, but then she stopped herself. Why force it? She didn't particularly like him, and it would be prudent that he knew it. Some instincts were difficult to deny, but not this one. Narrowing her gaze at him, she said, "You should return to the salon. I'll be with you as soon as I see my guests out."

He stiffened in surprise, but he didn't move. "Actually, I am happy to have a moment alone. Without your mother. There's something I want to speak with you about."

Surely not a marriage proposal. She edged away. "What would that be?"

"Your behavior last night was very naughty, Miss Crenshaw. Lady Helena said that you were with her, but I saw you leave alone. A lady should not be unescorted at a ball, especially in untraversed parts of a house."

"Well, I am hardly a lady," she snapped. It was terrible of her, but she couldn't stand the idea of being berated by the likes of him. The cut of his gaze scraped along her jaw and down to her bosom, making her long to cross her arms over her chest to hide herself from him.

"No, not yet, perhaps," he said. "But you will be."

There was such dark promise in those words that a chill whispered down her spine. Last night, Hereford had been so cold with Camille, his words like ice. She had no doubt that similar behavior would be in store for her if Lord Ware was her future.

"And how is that?" she asked.

He gave her a bland smile. "I understand that you were brought up in a different way, but we do things otherwise here. There are . . . tutors, if you will, women we can hire to make certain you learn what you need to know."

It sounded as if he intended to give her etiquette lessons and comportment tutors. Her heart pounded so hard that she could hear it in her ears. On a whim she said, "You should know that I intend to pursue a career as a writer." There. He couldn't tutor that out of her.

He laughed, but it lacked warmth. "There will be plenty of time to discuss the future, when it comes to it."

"But there will be no future without my writing. I want to be clear on that." She watched his Adam's apple drop as he swallowed. If she could make him understand that, then perhaps he would take his interest elsewhere.

"Respectable ladies do not participate in a trade. Ladies may indulge in hobbies, of course, but they always, before anything else, conduct themselves respectfully."

"And what happens when I am less than respectful?"

The corner of his mouth pinched as if the very idea of it caused him some sort of pain. "Then you will be corrected, until you understand your error. But never fear, Miss Crenshaw, you are intelligent for a woman. I have no doubts in your ability to catch on quickly."

Her stomach dropped as she imagined this conversation playing out ad nauseam in the years to come. In that moment, the only thing she knew for certain was that she would never marry Lord Ware or anyone like him. She shook her head. "Then I am afraid there is no need to continue our relationship. I will not give up my aspirations."

The pleasant mask slipped, and his eyes hardened. "You have been promised to me."

She tightened her grip on the pin so hard that it unfastened and gouged her palm. Startled, she glanced down at the tiny pinhole of blood. The red shone bright against the white of her palm. In that moment, that's how she felt. A tiny bloom of insurrection in the midst of conformity. What hope did she have of escaping?

Lord Ware clucked his tongue. "You have injured yourself. Let me help." He stepped forward, but she moved away, Lord Leigh's warning from the night before prominent in her mind.

"That isn't true. My parents would have told me—" She

stopped talking abruptly because his smile was back, but it was menacing now, or perhaps that was only her perception.

Shaking his head, he said, "Our future has already been decided. The contract is finished. You are mine for all intents and purposes. I had hoped to wait a little longer to tell you." He shrugged and reached for her.

She was too stunned to dodge him. As his hand closed over her shoulder, her gaze went to the door where voices were coming closer. He heard them, too. He turned his head toward the sound, and his free hand closed on her other shoulder, pulling her against him. When his gaze met hers, she saw anticipation tinged with triumph as he tried to kiss her. He meant for them to be found. He meant to take all of her choices away.

Hot anger swept through her. Before she could even consider what she was doing, she stomped on his foot. He yelped and loosened his grip so that she was able to swing out of his grasp. Without looking back, she ran to the salon door, slipping through as the drawing room door opened. Hurrying through the empty salon, she made her way to the hall and front entry to find it deserted save for the footman stationed at the door. Composing herself and noting her flushed cheeks in a hallway mirror, she hurried to the drawing room to see Mother, Lady Alfred, and Lady Beatrice speaking with Lord Ware. He seemed unaffected except for a swath of red sitting high on his cheekbones.

"Here!" Violet kept her voice light and held the pin aloft as she floated into the room. "It led me on a merry chase, but I found your grandmother's pin."

Lady Beatrice squealed with delight and hurried over to retrieve the pin. Lady Alfred offered her appreciation, and Mother said, "Look who has paid a call. Lord Ware. Aren't we so pleased to see him?"

Violet managed a benign nod, but she couldn't bring herself to look at the man again. She could feel his gaze boring into her. The next several minutes passed in a blur as she walked the mother and daughter to the door and bid them goodbye. Lord Ware had stayed in the drawing room with Mother. When the door closed behind the duo, Violet eyed the stairs with longing, but before she could decide if she could chance hiding in her room, Mother emerged.

"Come join us, Violet."

Stiffening her spine, Violet said, "I have a headache, Mother. I think I should lie down."

"And leave our guest?" Shaking her head, she closed the distance between them and lowered her voice. "I don't have to tell you that Lord Ware has come to see you, not me."

"I am aware of that, Mother," Violet said between clenched teeth. "I do not wish to see him."

"Why not?" Brows close together, Mother put her fists on her hips. "I say, Violet, you have been short with him ever since he expressed the slightest interest in you. It's a wonder he wants to court you at all."

"I wish he wouldn't. Do you know that he accosted me in the drawing room? He grabbed me, and I think his intention was for us to be found together. You know what that would have done to my reputation."

Mother shook her head. "You seem unharmed to me, and the man is fairly besotted with you. Anyone can see that."

As if that excused his poor behavior. The man was willing to ruin her to get what he wanted. The fact that she wanted something else wasn't even a consideration to him. What made it worse was that her own mother supported him over her. Violet didn't know what to do with that. She felt lost and alone. "I do not trust him, Mother. He has made it clear that his intention is marriage."

"And that's a bad thing? Violet, Lord Ware would be a fine husband. You make it sound as if he plans to compromise you and leave you ruined. His intention is marriage; that makes his purposes honorable."

Violet stared at her mother. The woman appeared so

perfectly reasonable in her earnestness that Violet had a vague attack of self-doubt. Was she overreacting?

No. She wasn't. He had wanted to force her hand without regard to her feelings on the matter. That was unforgivable. The fact that her mother didn't agree was heartbreaking. Swallowing against the lump that had risen in her throat, Violet said, "I have to go lie down, Mother. I really do feel unwell."

The frustration on her mother's face changed to concern as Violet raised a hand to her aching head. Her mother didn't want to relent—the battle of care versus pressing her case for Lord Ware waged clearly on her face—but she finally nodded. "Go lie down. I will express your regrets to Lord Ware."

The pounding in Violet's head was nearly unbearable as she hurried to her room. She had to run away. There was no other choice. It was now obvious that her parents would refuse to see any bad in Ware, and that Ware himself would do exactly what Lord Leigh had warned her he intended. What would have happened had she not been able to escape his grip this time? Lady Alfred would have seen them together. It was possible that Violet would have escaped total scandal because they had only been alone for a few moments. However, now that she knew what Lord Ware was capable of, how long before he tried to maneuver it so that they were alone again?

She couldn't risk it. She would die if she had to marry him, which meant she had to leave. Suddenly, her hastily thought out solution for Camille didn't seem so outlandish. The Lake District boardinghouse would be her refuge for a few weeks, or until she could make her parents understand that she would not marry him under any circumstances.

Chapter 6

❧

*Lord Lucifer failed to realize he was being
ensnared in a trap of his own design. A cynic
rarely had a fair grasp on reality, though the
same could be said for an ingénue.*

V. LENNOX, *An American and the
London Season*

THE NEXT DAY

Montague Club took up nearly half a block on a pleasant street in Bloomsbury. The expansive white marble address had once served as the very lavish residence of
the late Earl of Leigh's mistress. While the earl had kept a
home in Belgravia, rumors were that he had rarely resided
there, preferring to live with his mistress and their three
children—Christian's half brother and half sisters—until
an aneurysm had killed him at the age of forty-six. Sometimes Christian liked to have a scotch in the club's lounge
and imagine his father roaming the halls of his beloved
home in a rage over what it had become. Most days, however, he tried not to think of him at all.

Today was not one of those days. Christian could hear
the fool in the laugh of a drunken gambler upstairs and in
the belligerent shout of the man standing across from him
in the basement's fighting ring—the dungeon, as it was

known by most club members. It was where the club held
its most important matches. Not the ones for sport, but the
ones for money and notoriety.

The ones that mattered.

Christian's knuckles ached from the blow he had delivered to the brow of James Brody. The man swiped a palm
over his eye, smearing a crimson streak of blood across his
forehead.

"Ready to pay your penance, or do you need more en-
couragement?" Christian taunted. They had been at this for
at least a quarter of an hour, perhaps longer.

Shirtless and heaving with the same exhaustion weigh-
ing on Christian's shoulders, Brody said, "I owe you nothing, Leigh. Wilkes broke the rules all on his own, because
he's a bloody coward."

"Wilkes is your fighter. You are responsible for him. You
sent him to the fight with Rothschild. You guaranteed his
participation. The spikes he put on the bottom of his shoes
could have been deadly. He's paid for that crime. Now it's
your turn. You need to oversee your fighters better."

The match between Wilkes and Rothschild several
weeks ago had been the highlight of the year. Wilkes had
cheated when it had been obvious he would lose and had
almost maimed Rothschild with the steel spikes. The police
had come near the end of the fight, sending Wilkes fleeing
into the night. While Christian and his brother had eventually found Wilkes and forced a rematch, it had taken them
this long to track Brody down.

Brody's answer was to let out a growl as he charged
Christian. Christian feinted to the right, mindful of his
lame ankle, and pushed off on his other foot, swinging a
punch that landed in the man's gut. Brody groaned but was
too angry to stop. He swung, landing a blow to the side of
Christian's head, and while he was dizzy, Brody dragged
him to the ground.

Christian nearly laughed at the move. It was widely assumed that because of his ankle, he was not able to hold his own. He had disproven that theory numerous times, but there was always a new man waiting to underestimate him. While it was true that his balance wasn't the best while upright, Christian was a master when it came to grappling. He had beaten men twice his size, simply because he knew how to manipulate limbs and how far to stretch joints before they popped. It took him less than a minute to gain the upper hand and have Brody on his front, his dominant arm stretched behind him at an awkward angle, ready to crack at Christian's command.

"I yield! I yield!" Brody yelled, his voice threaded with panic. "I'll pay!"

"You might have saved us the trouble and come to that conclusion earlier." Christian let him go and rose to his feet, winded from the fight. Brody pounded on the ground with his palm and then followed at a slower pace, wiping the blood that had trickled into his eye.

"Bloody bastard," Brody mumbled.

"No, that's me." Christian's half brother and his father's notable bastard son, Jacob Thorne, stood next to the fighting ring, arms crossed over his chest and a proud smile on his face. The three of them—Christian, Jacob, and Rothschild—owned shares in the club and organized bareknuckle boxing matches at venues across London.

"Fuck the both of you." Brody spat out a stream of blood that landed on the packed earth floor, before climbing between the ropes to retrieve his shirt from a servant who stood waiting with a towel. Brody's two companions stood nearby, helpfully held back by the club's hired men.

"Let them go," said Jacob. Brody's men made a show of straightening their attire as if they had been very put out by their restraints. "If you'd kept your fighters under control, then this wouldn't have happened," Jacob taunted Brody.

The man shrugged into his coat and threw back some choice words as he was escorted up the stairs. Their men would see that he paid what he owed before he left. Brody liked to give them a hard time, but he was generally an honorable man; well, as honorable as criminals ever were.

The door had barely closed behind them before Webb, Christian's secretary, hurried down the stone steps. "The Crenshaws' maid has returned to see you, milord. She claims to have new information."

Christian's heart slammed against his rib cage. Run away or marry someone of your own choosing. Perhaps she had made her decision. He had already been informed that the Crenshaws held a house party yesterday, which Ware had attended briefly, and that her parents had gone to the theater later that night sans Violet. Unfortunately, no one had heard what went on between Violet and Ware, but their betrothal hadn't been announced yet, which was good.

"See that she is comfortable and given refreshment." Christian grabbed a towel and ran it over his face and chest, silently lamenting the fact that he would have to meet with the maid before his bath. But she had likely slipped away while on an errand, so this could not wait.

"This the maid you hired for the Crenshaws?" asked Jacob, the humor he found in the situation evident in his voice.

"The Crenshaws hired her. I am merely paying her for information," said Christian as he put on his shirtsleeves. Although he and his brother had once had a difficult relationship, they had grown close over the years, and Christian had shared his plan with Jacob.

He snorted. "If I recall correctly, you gave her false references so that they would hire her."

Christian grinned, shrugging into his coat. "Never let it be said that I don't do my part to help the less fortunate souls in our fair city. The girl would have gone to the workhouse had I not given her references and instruction."

"One day, dear brother, you will come across a situation you cannot manipulate or control." His brother's brown eyes glowed with amusement.

"Perhaps." Christian agreed. "But not today."

Jacob laughed and clapped him on his back before leading the way up the narrow stairs. "I am glad to see you in better spirits today. You've been grim ever since the ball."

"You know how dealing with Ware sets me on edge. The man is a snake."

They made their way through the rooms of the club, nodding at groups of men who greeted them as they passed. Christian and his half brother were nearly identical in every physical way except their coloring. Jacob took after his mother with his golden brown skin and dark eyes. Christian was paler and had his mother's gray eyes. However, they both had their father's solid build, coming in at a couple inches over six feet with wide shoulders, along with his blade-straight nose and high cheekbones. They attracted attention when out in public, even more so in their own club, so the trek upstairs was tedious.

Finally, when they had broken away from the crowd, Jacob asked, "You're confident that you can take the heiress away from him?"

Christian smiled again. "From Ware? It will be no contest. The bigger issue is that our heiress seems to have lofty ambitions."

"Such as?"

"She doesn't want to marry yet. She wants to pursue a writing career." Or that is what the maid believed.

Jacob gave a low whistle as he shook his head. "That family doesn't produce biddable females, do they? What will you do?"

"Show her that I can give her what she wants."

"That easy, huh?" Jacob raised a skeptical dark brow.

"Women are simple, brother. There's no secret to controlling them. Keep them well-bed and well-fed, and they tend to do as you ask."

His brother threw back his head and laughed. "God, I hope she marries you."

"You say that as if it will be a bad thing." Christian frowned.

"On the contrary. It will prove to be highly entertaining."

"She will." Christian was a bit foggy on the details, but he knew that marriage to her would be amusing.

Not only would marrying the Crenshaw heiress allow him to restore his beloved Blythkirk, but the money from the marriage would be the final nail that shut his father's coffin for good. The earl had willfully left Christian penniless, leaving all his liquid assets, along with the Bloomsbury house, to his mistress and his children by her, which included Jacob and his two younger sisters. This marriage would bring more money to the earldom than it had seen in centuries.

As if his brother could read his thoughts, he asked, "What happens if you go through all this trouble, marry her, and Crenshaw refuses to give her a settlement?"

"I doubt that will happen. He'll want his daughter to live in luxury."

"But if he does? You'll be saddled with a wife and very little else."

Christian shook his head, having already considered this. Speaking with her that night at the ball had cinched his plans. "She has funds in her own right. Stocks that her brother manages, and a house in Manhattan, inherited from an aunt. The proceeds from the sale alone will be enough for Blythkirk." Admittedly, less than he wanted, but he would be satisfied. Violet herself would be a prize.

Jacob was still laughing as he pushed the door open to Christian's study. Ellen Stapleton stood wide-eyed near the window, looking like she had half considered jumping out of it. She had been anxious and nervous from the start, making Christian wonder if he had chosen correctly at least half a dozen times. But she had been the only one he had found who spoke with a soft accent, possessed the manners necessary to pass as a fledgling lady's maid, and was willing to spy for him. A rare pang of conscience made itself known, but he pushed it down again. Wasn't it Lyly who wrote, "The rules of fair play do not apply in love and war"?

"Do you have information for me, Stapleton?" he asked, when her eyes became even wider as she looked over his appearance.

"Y-Yes, milord." She swallowed. "Miss Crenshaw pretended to be ill last night to avoid the theater outing with her parents."

"Pretended? Are you certain?" If she were to fall ill . . .

"Yes, milord. I do not know what happened, but she doesn't seem very pleased with her parents. She pleaded a headache but has spent her time pacing around her room."

"No one knows what happened?" he asked, finding it difficult to believe that there wasn't some gossip belowstairs about the cause of her distress.

The girl shrugged. "Not really, no. There is some talk that a marriage has been decided for her."

He let out a breath. Everything seemed to be going forward as he had assumed it would. Her parents must have approached her with Ware as a potential bridegroom, and she had balked. Good. Perhaps she was plotting now and ready to make a decision. Run away or marry someone else. Either way she decided, he would be ready. "And did something else happen?"

Stapleton nodded, her cap sliding to an awkward angle on her head. "Yes, milord. This afternoon she went out to visit Lady Helena March after her parents had left for an engagement. She had pleaded another headache, but she left soon after they did. Her visit was short, and she was back home within the hour, but I thought it interesting that she took with her a Gladstone bag. Said she was taking a few things to donate to Lady Helena's charity. While she was gone, I checked her room, and a few items of clothing were missing, namely a traveling dress."

"What else was missing?"

"Some personal effects from her dressing table, milord."
She blushed and added in a very soft voice, "Undergarments."

Miss Crenshaw planned to run away. He tried not to
smile openly, but it was difficult. To be certain, he asked,
"Did she return home with the empty case?"

"No, milord, she did not have it when she returned."

Perhaps she had left the bag with Helena, or perhaps she
had left it somewhere else entirely. He had to figure out
when she was leaving. Turning to his brother, he said,
"Have Dunn and Sanford watch the Crenshaw residence. I
need to know the moment she leaves." The men had been
driving by to keep an eye on the place, but he needed to
know the very moment Violet left again, or he would risk
missing her.

Jacob nodded and left to see to the task. To the girl,
Christian said, "You have done well, Stapleton. When she
leaves again, come here immediately and bring any of your
personal possessions. You likely won't be going back."

She nodded and fidgeted with the hem of her apron.
"And the reward we spoke of?"

"Of course, and you and your young brother have a
place in my household for life." Walking to the safe behind
his desk, he unlocked it and withdrew two coins, pressing
them into her hand. "For your troubles today. Remember,
come here directly when she leaves again. You must be
gone if she is ever reported missing. No one can question you."

She nodded again. "Yes, I remember, milord." Pausing
as if uncertain, she added, "You will not see her come to
any harm? Like you said?"

He smiled. "My plan relies on her being safe and bliss-
fully happy." It was the only way to ensure that she would
choose him over running away.

Chapter 7

Rose believed herself capable of all manner of resourcefulness, but sometimes to struggle meant to draw the bindings tighter.

V. LENNOX, *AN AMERICAN AND THE LONDON SEASON*

From her seat beside Violet in the carriage, the Honorable Mrs. Harold Barnes glanced dubiously at her from beneath the brim of her hat. The look clearly asked, *Are you quite well, child?*

Violet was not well. She was a mess of doubt and confusion held together by the power of her corset and sheer resolve. Today was the day she was running away, and she was not at all confident in her plan. Suppressing yet another nervous giggle, Violet gave her chaperone what she hoped was a bland smile.

The woman's brow drew together in puzzlement. "Are you certain that you are feeling up to attending this lecture?"

"Oh yes, I'm quite well, thank you. I believe that whatever ailed me the past couple of days has gone." She had at least recovered enough to stop wallowing in self-pity and plan her escape.

Lord Ware thought he could force her hand, and her parents seemed very happy to allow him to do it. Well, she would not go willingly to that fate. She would follow August's example and chart her own course. Perhaps that was the problem all along. Violet had gone along with things to keep the peace and make her mother happy until she had stopped asking for the things she wanted. She had been too willing to compromise. Not anymore. From this day forward, she would take control of her life.

The rejection letter had solidified one thing for her. She would not be an ornament who wrote books that told women how they should behave like ornaments. Beyond that, she didn't know what the future held.

Mrs. Barnes gave a brisk nod, the ungainly ostrich plume on her hat threatening to topple the whole thing from her head, but she continued to regard Violet with the occasional arch glance as the family carriage took them to the British Museum.

Violet could not blame the woman for being doubtful. Before they had left, Violet had rushed to her mother to give her yet another hug. Before that, Violet had stolen into Papa's study to tell him goodbye. He, too, had given her much the same look that Mrs. Barnes was giving her now. Despite the fact that they were trying to marry her off, Violet did not hate her parents. She loved them very much, even if they were misguided. She genuinely wished they would understand, but they wouldn't, which is why she had decided to take this drastic step. Perhaps a bit of time apart would help them understand her stance.

Yesterday she had written two letters. One had been privately dispatched to the mistress of the boardinghouse in Windermere notifying her of her planned arrival. The second had been left hidden in her armoire to be found after she had time to get away. She didn't want her family to worry overly much. It explained that she had taken her savings and would be safe. In fact, she had enough savings from her allowance to live very comfortably for a year or two, three or four if she economized and had her brother,

Max, sell the stock shares he held in her name. Last night, she had sewn half of her savings into the lining of her coat, while the other half was wrapped in linen and stuffed in her boot. A tiny portion had been put into her handbag for traveling expenses. She would be fine.

Lonely but fine. Dear God, what was she doing? August and Max were probably in New York by now. She would not see them for months at the earliest. Her parents would be so angry with her that they probably wouldn't speak to her for a long time. Possibly a year or more.

What if Rothschild refused to allow August to associate with her now? What if by leaving she was consigning herself to a fate of eternal spinsterhood and social exile?

"Miss Crenshaw? Are you quite all right?"

Violet opened her eyes to the ostrich plume dangling in her face as Mrs. Barned leaned over her. "I'm fine." Her voice was hoarse and weak.

"You are as pale as parchment," the woman proclaimed. "We should get you home at once. You're still poorly."

"No!" Her voice was a bit too loud, causing Mrs. Barnes's thin eyebrows to nearly disappear into her hairline. "No, that won't be necessary," she said in a calmer tone. "I've been home for days already, and I felt fine after visiting Lady Helena's yesterday."

"All right," said Mrs. Barnes. "But we are going to get you home directly after."

Violet nodded. The lump in her throat was not allowing her to say anything. The poor woman didn't know that Violet would be gone before the lecture ended. She planned to slip out during it with the excuse that she felt unwell, while convincing the woman to stay in her seat. That would give her approximately an hour at most before the woman began to look for her. Then she would leave and hire a carriage, which she would direct to take her to Lady Helena's where she had hidden her portmanteau the day before. Lady Helena wasn't home, so Violet would simply pick it up from a servant and then head toward King's Cross. She would have to hurry to make the twelve thirty train to Manchester, but it was possible. If she missed it, there would be another at two forty-five.

And if Violet believed deeply enough that all of that would work out flawlessly, then it would. She nearly groaned at the tenuous nature of her plan but managed to hold the sound back to spare poor Mrs. Barnes. Dread settled like a lead weight in her stomach.

You can do this, Violet.

She could, because she was prepared. She had spent her time in solitude poring through newspapers and books and writing directions for herself that planned for all sorts of contingencies. Train canceled? She had another route written down. A delay? Then she knew the major towns along the route and could arrange accommodations. If someone wondered why she was traveling alone? Well, she was a governess on her way to her first family in Windermere. She even had a lovely letter of introduction that explained everything, should it be needed. So while she was anxious, she was also prepared.

She was almost twenty years old. It was high time that she stopped waiting for others to solve her problems. With resolve straightening her spine, she forced what she hoped passed for a pleasant smile and offered her hand to the groom when he opened the carriage door. Together, Violet and her chaperone hurried into the museum beneath a sky that was horribly gray.

They barely had enough time to get themselves to the crowded room before the lecture began, which was a blessing, because Violet could not engage in polite discourse any longer. Her mind was whirling with her plans. Only a handful of seats remained near the back of the room, so they quickly settled themselves there. Egyptology was of particular interest to Mrs. Barnes, being the one subject the woman could talk on for hours—aside from idle gossip. It was no time at all before her complete focus was on the lecturer at the front of the room. A sarcophagus was displayed to his left, and when the speaker gestured to different parts of it as he discussed them, the older woman raised a pair of mother-of-pearl opera glasses to her eyes.

Violet's heart was pounding too loudly for her to pay attention to the man. She forced herself to count to five hundred, and then she leaned over. "I have to step outside the room. It's rather stuffy." She knew she didn't have to force herself to appear unwell; the color had probably leached from her face all on its own.

Mrs. Barnes pulled the glasses far enough away to glance over, clearly torn between following her charge out and staying to hear the entire lecture. Violet smiled and put her out of her misery. "Please stay." A lump rose in her throat at the lie she was about to tell, forcing her to swallow before she could finish. "I'll be only a moment."

The woman nodded once and brought the glasses back to her eyes. Violet did not waste any time on relief. She rose and forced herself to take measured steps to the door. A museum steward quietly opened the door for her, and she hurried through it. She kept up her pace all the way to the entrance of the museum. Only when she stepped outside did another wave of doubt sweep over her.

What are you doing? Your parents will never forgive you for this. You'll cause a scandal, and then where will you be?

No. She could do this. If she let the risk of a little scandal dictate her future, then how would she ever manage the ramifications of her novel? Its content, with its scandals and slightly biographical characters, wasn't precisely of the Austen variety. Besides, she would face censure if it meant avoiding a husband like Lord Ware.

Stepping between a pair of columns, she hurried down the stairs. The moment she cleared the overhang, a fat raindrop fell right in the middle of her forehead. Luckily, she had prepared for rain. Opening her umbrella, she proceeded toward the gates and in the direction of the hansom cab stand they had passed on the corner. True, respectable ladies did not ride in hansom cabs, especially alone, but she was a governess now. Miss Emily Smith, to be precise.

Her umbrella was black to match her boots, and she had chosen one of her darkest afternoon dresses, since it would have to make do as a traveling dress for a time. The skirt was vertically striped in charcoal and gray with a smart charcoal coat. It was likely too stylish for a young governess, but it was the best she could come up with.

A single hansom waited at the stand on the corner, and her heart gave a little leap of anticipation. She had made a plan and was following it through. She could do this. Except when she was little more than fifty feet away, the driver climbed up onto his back perch and picked up the reins, making a clicking sound with his mouth. The horse jolted into action.

"Wait!" She called out to no avail. The driver spared her a quick glance as he went past her, his eyes wide and focused as if he were late for something. It was a little dark with the gray clouds overhead, making it difficult to see inside clearly, but it didn't appear as if he had a fare. "Damn and blast," she muttered to herself, smiling as she realized she could say the expletive without anyone reprimanding her. This was true freedom.

She couldn't savor the moment, however, because she had to get away from the front of the museum. If Mrs. Barnes came looking for her, and a helpful person mentioned she had stepped outside, then she would be caught, and this would all be over before it had even begun. The heels of her boots crunched over the bits of gravel that had loosened. The sprinkles of rain became a nearly constant drizzle: a warning that more would be coming soon and that she should find refuge. Turning the corner, she hurried down the street lined with townhomes. Bloomsbury was a middle-class area with pockets of wealth, so not everyone owned a carriage. There must be another hansom stand somewhere nearby, or perhaps she could hail one.

Ahead, a single carriage was parked along the curb, and a few pedestrians—all middle-aged men—strolled on the opposite side of the street. Perhaps she could ask one of them where the next stand could be found. The idea filled her with some trepidation, as a lady did not simply approach strange men on the street. Would a governess? She didn't know for certain, but probably not.

Before she could decide whether or not to cross to them, the carriage door swung open, and a masculine leg stepped out. It was encased in trousers made of a fine gray stripe. There was nothing about it, except for the fact that it was long and lean perhaps, that should have made her heartbeat trip over itself. But it did, and then the man stepped out completely. Her heart took off as if it were being chased by wild horses.

Lord Leigh stood beside the carriage, his gaze halting her in her tracks. What was he doing here? Would he thwart her plans? Tell her parents? A quick glance at his carriage confirmed that it was not marked with his family crest.

"Miss Crenshaw," he called, raising his voice only slightly to be heard across the distance. His coachman, dressed all in black instead of livery, continued to stare straight ahead as he had obviously been trained to do.

"Lord Leigh." She walked closer with caution. "Strange to find you here."

The corner of his mouth ticked up in that way that she had begun to associate with him. "Perhaps I could say the same for you."

It was true. He was the one allowed to traipse about town as he pleased. She was the one who had broken with decorum. She didn't know what to say to make him not suspicious.

As if he sensed she might run—and she very well thought

she might—he said, "Montague Club is only around the corner." He nodded toward the other side of the museum. "I was leaving, on my way out of town actually, when I thought I spotted you."

"You always drive in an unmarked carriage?"

"Not always. This one belongs to Montague. All of our carriages are unmarked. It makes it more discreet when a member has indulged too much and needs to be driven home."

He stood there with his silver-tipped cane and smart frock coat, making sense, but something in the back of her mind warned her away. He was dangerous for her. She knew that because he was a lord and she was interested in him in a way that no man had ever interested her. That alone was enough. But she had gone the extra mile and kissed him. A single moment of indiscretion that would be burned into her memory for eternity. Heat stained her cheeks just thinking about it.

She was leaving. He was not for her.

"It is good to see you." She gave him a curt nod and continued on her way.

He had other plans and stepped in front of her, heedless of the drizzle wetting the shoulders of his frock coat. He really was quite broad up close. How had she already forgotten?

"You shouldn't be out here all alone."

"I am fine." She hated how there was a slight quiver at the end of that statement.

There was a brief pause in which his gaze narrowed on her, and she imagined the gears of his mind churning, the pieces of machinery clicking into place. "Run away or marry," he whispered, and then his eyes widened in sudden clarity. Louder, he added, "You're running."

There was no reason to deny it. Out here in the rain on the sidewalk all alone, it was hardly a secret. "I was, but you have hampered my progress. Good day, my lord." If she got herself to the train station quickly enough, then it wouldn't matter if he found her parents or not.

She attempted to go around him, but he moved with her. "Where are you going so fast in the rain?"

"I have to find a hansom cab to take me to the train station—" She bit off her words before she could tell him more.

"Let me drive you."

She was immediately grateful for the offer, which made her pause in accepting it. Wasn't she supposed to be doing this on her own? Proving to herself that she could solve her own problems? Could she trust him?

"It would hardly be proper to be seen with you alone in a carriage."

"That is true, but who will see you? The shades are drawn." His argument was entirely too reasonable. A quick glance confirmed that the windows were blackened by the lengths of heavy cloth. The rain had transformed from a near-constant drizzle to a very constant drizzle. She shifted her umbrella so that it shielded him as well.

His eyes flared subtly, as if he were surprised by the move. Though they were not standing any closer, the shelter of the umbrella stilled the air around them, bringing an immediate sense of intimacy to their discussion. "You would take me to King's Cross Station?"

"Of course."

"You would ensure that no one saw me alight from your vehicle?"

"Yes. There is an alley nearby. My coachman can walk you to the entrance if you prefer."

"And you would not tell my parents of my escape?"

"Certainly not." He appeared offended she would ask.

Still she felt suspicious. "Why would you do that?"

"I told you I would help you." He grinned again, giving her a glimpse of his white teeth. Strange, but somehow that seemed very intimate as well. She had hardly ever seen him smile with teeth visible. The fact that he was showing that smile to her made a very pleasant sensation tighten in her belly. It softened his good looks, making them appear less forbidding but somehow more beautiful.

"Why?"

"Because I would despise it if you were to marry Lord Ware."

"Why?" she asked again.

His smile widened and he shrugged. "Because I do not care for the man, nor do I care for the idea of him attaining you."

She laughed at his honesty. She had sensed a tension, perhaps even a rivalry, between the two of them. If his help was given to simply thwart Lord Ware's plans, then she trusted it more, but she would still tread warily with him, especially since it was her own reactions to him she didn't trust. "All right, then, but I will not tell you where I am going."

He held up a hand. "Understood."

"I will allow you to take me to the station. However, I need to make one stop first."

"I am yours for the day."

Chapter 8

Upon occasion the simplest way forward was the right path, even if it was littered with temptations.

V. LENNOX, *AN AMERICAN AND THE LONDON SEASON*

After telling Peterson, his coachman, to take them to Lady Helena March's townhome in Mayfair, Christian joined Violet in the carriage. Shaking the rain off her umbrella, he cast one last glance along the street to make certain no one watched them, before closing it up and settling himself across from her. She smiled her thanks and laid the umbrella on the floor.

Taking her had been almost too easy. Either her parents were incredibly naive about the lure their daughter presented, or they seriously underestimated her independent spirit. Probably both. As she settled her skirts around her legs, her scent washed over him. Though it was mild, he detected the sophistication of a French perfume. It was the same scent she had worn at the ball when she had kissed him. Despite his intentions to not allow his thoughts to go in that direction, his gaze drifted down to her lips. He had thought of that innocent kiss much more than he would have liked. Her inexperience had been obvious, but something about the kiss had hastened him to arousal quicker than he had anticipated.

Her lush mouth tipped up in a smile, and her brown eyes held a soft golden tint as she observed him. Her pale and flawless complexion glowed with health. She was as fresh and pure as a daisy in a field of manure. That meant he was the manure. No, worse. He was the loutish farmer who would crush her beneath his boot. She deserved better. Guilt dared to raise its unwelcomed head.

"You're scowling." Her voice was soft with just the right amount of husk to rake over his senses. The skin on the back of his neck tightened in awareness. "I fear I've inconvenienced you."

"No, you haven't." His gaze dropped to the attractive curve of her bosom before he could stop it, forcing him to drag it back up to her face. "I do not mean to scowl. My face does that from time to time."

She laughed. "I have noticed you rarely smile." All serious with concern now, she added, "Is it because of your leg? Does it pain you?"

No one brought up his limp, not ever. It wasn't discussed in polite circles. He had almost decided that most people assumed the cane was a mere accessory. She was a decidedly outspoken woman. Her question reminded him that the rain had made it ache a bit, so he stretched it out, his calf brushing her skirts in the process. She did not move them away as propriety dictated. "It is because I am an earl and looking serious is part of the title."

"Being an earl sounds tedious and tiresome." She smiled again, settling back into her seat as the carriage turned a corner. "Thank you very much for the ride. I'm not sure I can ever repay you, considering I am leaving town for the foreseeable future, but if you ever have need of me, I assure you I will be happy to assist you in any way."

The coil of desire that seemed to always possess him in

her presence made itself known, tightening deep in his gut. A vision of her on her knees in the carriage repaying him ran through his mind. She was entirely too naive to have meant those words the way his body had taken them. A quick glance at her innocent face assured him that he was every bit the lecher in this scenario.

He would not seduce her innocence away from her, not until they were married. That flicker of guilt returned, putting a fine edge of pain on his desire for her. The gossips would have told her that he was not some bastion of virtue. She must know that men like him were to be avoided. He had even heard Lady Helena warn her away. She should have run from him, or at least made him chase her down the pavement, forced to prove his good intentions. But no, she had put her small hand in his and allowed him to help her into his carriage. The wolf leading the innocent astray.

"A gentleman never requires payment from a lady for a good deed." His voice came out like gravel, forcing him to clear his throat. Christ. They had been in the carriage for only a handful of minutes. How would he survive days with her on the trip to Scotland?

"Nevertheless, I don't aspire to charity." She leaned over and pulled the thick curtain back to peek out at the museum as they passed the front. "I hope to repay my debt."

"Who are you running away from today?"

"My chaperone," she answered a bit absently as she scoured the courtyard, which was all but empty as the rain came harder. "She doesn't seem to have noticed my absence yet." She gave him another smile as she let the curtain drop.

"Something must have happened since I spoke with you at the ball to send you running. Did Ware propose?"

"Not to me, no, but my parents have already accepted on my behalf."

"Did you speak to them, then?"

She shook her head. "There's no need. Past experience tells me it won't work to change their mind, and I didn't want to give them any hint of my plans to run away."

He nodded at her sound reasoning. "You should consider going directly to King's Cross. If you make a stop at Lady Helena's, you could be seen or potentially delayed. The moment your chaperone notices you missing, she can have people out searching for you. If anyone sees you on the street, or even if Lady Helena herself sees you, then it might be too late to leave." The truth was that he was worried she would encounter Lady Helena and the woman would talk her out of leaving. If she found out that Violet would be in his company, then there would be no question of the woman allowing her to leave with him.

"Lady Helena is not at home, so she won't see me. She was leaving early this morning for her cottage in the country. I already let her know I would retrieve my things today. Unfortunately, I'll simply have to take the risk of someone else seeing me."

He hid his relief. "Your bag isn't important enough to risk being seen. You can acquire ready-made clothing at a shop along your way. Actually, I would advise it. You need more common clothes to blend in with other travelers. As soon as it's known that one of the Crenshaw heiresses has run off, you'll be noticed in no time." She appeared very much the heiress as she was dressed now. "How many wealthy American women are traveling alone?"

For the first time she appeared to be in distress as her brow creased. "I am concerned about the state of my clothing, but there is no help for it. I'll arrive at my destination by the morning . . ." Her voice trailed off as she realized she let slip that bit of information. "I will arrange for more suitable clothing there. But I still have to stop at Lady Helena's. I've left something very important to me there, and I have to take it with me."

"What could be important enough to risk being found before you have even left?"

She seemed to wrestle with telling him. The longer she was silent, the more he wanted to know the answer. Finally, she sighed. "It's my manuscript. I won't leave it behind."

"Your manuscript?"

"I have written a novel. Don't ask me for details, because I'm not ready to share it, but I won't leave it behind. It's the only copy I have."

He nodded. "No, I won't, and I understand why you wouldn't leave it."

He was possibly the only nobleman in England who would be willing to allow her to pursue her writing. He was the only one who did not give a damn what Society had to say about it, because his finances were not reliant on his connections. The club's clientele were discontent younger sons, aristocratic cousins, merchants, and foreign money—all snubbed by the Society clubs. His cooperation was a rather large mark in his favor, if he could simply convince her.

"Thank you for understanding." Her gaze settled on him again. Her eyes were all things hopeful and good as she watched him, and then an eyebrow quirked upward. "How did you know that I was retrieving a bag from Lady Helena's?"

Naive, but not unintelligent. He would have to remember that about her. "Did you not mention it was a bag?" he asked.

"No, I'm certain that I did not." Her gaze narrowed.

He cursed inwardly. The last thing he needed was for her to find out he'd been all but spying on her. His conscience, long in its death throes, was once again pricked. "An assumption, Miss Crenshaw. Who would make a grand escape without a change of clothing?" He gave her what he hoped was a bland look.

She regarded him a moment longer and then nodded. "Forgive me. I'm too anxious."

She appeared so trusting of him that he had to fight himself to not confess to his own nefarious intentions. He looked away instead. "I did not know you are a writer."

"If my mother had her way, no one would ever know. Another reason why I must leave if I'm ever to pursue it seriously. It's why I'm going where I'm going." She took a breath, and from the corner of his eye, he saw her silently castigate herself for saying too much.

"Where? You've leased a quiet country home somewhere?"

She shook her head. "I won't say. It's best if you don't know in case you're ever questioned."

He fell silent as he considered her destination, curious now in spite of his own intention that she never reach the place.

"I noticed your trunk on the back of the carriage. Where is your destination, my lord?" she asked.

"Scotland. I have an estate there. Unfortunately, there was a fire there recently, so I've decided to go and oversee the refurbishment."

"I am sorry to hear that, but this is a happy coincidence. Perhaps we might share a train. I am going north myself, though not that far." She smiled again, all doe-eyed and happy.

Guilt churned in his stomach. "Perhaps we might."

Before he could say more, the carriage swayed as they turned a corner near Berkeley Square. "I believe we have arrived at Lady Helena's residence," he said as they pulled to a stop, and he peeked around the curtain at the row of elegant town houses. "I shall go in and retrieve your bag."

She was already moving from her seat and had the door open before the coachman was there. "Thank you, but no. If you don't mind waiting, I'll only be a moment?"

At her questioning glance, he nodded and watched as she hurried up the steps of the townhome. The door opened before she could even knock, and she swept inside out of his view. A large part of him wondered if she would come back. She was a very young woman on the verge of doing something outrageous. It would take only the slightest provocation to make her change her mind. How many women in her position would choose marriage to Ware over a future of uncertainty and social censure? Nearly all of them.

The oak and leaded glass door with its intricate ironwork stayed closed. His heartbeat counted out the seconds as he imagined her finding Lady Helena inside after all and the woman doing her best to talk Violet out of her plan. He had been a fool to allow her to go in. He should have insisted. His own guilt had prevented it. Perhaps he wanted her to escape his clutches. Perhaps he wanted . . . The door opened, and a relief like he had never known moved through him when she came down the steps bearing her portmanteau.

Her smile was so big as she climbed back inside that he found himself smiling, too.

"You came back."

"You doubted me?" Her teasing grin mocked him.

"Never," he said as the carriage lurched forward.

"Liar. You clearly have not been introduced to the Crenshaw stubbornness. Once we decide on something, it has been decided."

He could not help the laugh that escaped him. "Sadly, I have not been properly acquainted." Sobering slightly, he said, "I've been thinking of something and have a proposition for you."

"Yes?" Her brow rose.

"Let me take you north. In the carriage. We can avoid the train stations and travel in anonymity."

"Why?"

"Because where there are trains, there are telegram lines. Once it's known you are gone, a single wire is all it will take to find your location by train. You said it yourself." He indicated her clothing. "You are hardly able to blend in with your attire and accent. I bet you were even planning to travel first-class."

When she frowned, he knew he was right, so he pressed his case. "We can stay on the smaller roads. Give assumed names at inns. No one will know who we are. You will be gone without a trace, only to be found when you decide to be found." His heart pounded as he waited for her to speak.

"I . . . I suppose you're right. My father could send a wire, and some train official is bound to have seen me. But I'll be at my destination by the morning. Surely, it won't matter."

"I cannot say, Miss Crenshaw. Do you have a guard at your destination willing to stand between a father and his daughter? Do you think your parents will be calm enough to listen to you by the time they arrive to retrieve you to-morrow afternoon, because they will certainly set out right away once they know where you are."

Twin lines formed between her brows. "I suppose not. I thought I would have a few days before they found me."

"If we drive, it will take about a week or so to reach Scotland, less to your destination, I presume. This way would ensure you have more time, and no one who can identify you is likely to see you arrive. No train attendants or officials."

"Why would you do this for me? You were planning to travel by train. Surely, you don't want to be delayed."

He shrugged, hoping she didn't notice exactly how un-bothered he was by this supposed delay. "As you so help-fully pointed out, the life of an earl is boring and tedious. I need this little bit of intrigue. Besides, you'll be Roths-child's sister soon. What sort of friend would I be if I didn't offer my assistance?"

Her smile returned, but it was tentative. "Okay, let us do it." Nodding, her smile gained in conviction until it lit up her entire face again. "Let's drive."

His breath caught. If all went well, this woman would become his wife before the trip was finished.

Chapter 9

For the first time, Rose understood the danger before her. The difference between a man and a boy was as subtle as that of a wolf and a hound.

V. LENNOX, *AN AMERICAN AND THE*
LONDON SEASON

She was in a carriage alone with Lord Lucifer. The thought made Violet's lips twitch, but she managed to quell the smile. She could not, however, stop her errant gaze from going back to him far more than was prudent for her state of mind. After they had left London, he had tied back the curtains to allow in the light and had spent the past several hours reading over a few ledgers while occasionally marking entries with a pencil. As best she could tell, they were accounts for an estate, and they were of far more interest than her company.

The realization had made her feel dispirited. She was quite unworldly compared to a man such as him. He owned a club, had likely traveled extensively on the Continent, and had seen more of the world than she probably ever would. Why would he find her company of interest?

He had been gentlemanly enough as they had ridden through the streets of London. They had exchanged remarks on a couple of mutual acquaintances, discussed the

abysmal rain that had seemed to have fallen for days on
end and a few of the exhibits in the Egyptian room of the
British Museum. Her initial worry that he might have been
so willing to help her because he harbored some interest in
her had given way to disappointment, and then mild embarrassment that she had kissed him at the ball. To be fair, he
had kissed her back, but he had not so much as glanced
her way in the hours that had taken them far away from
London.

Perhaps he found her girlish attention tedious. He was
nearly a decade older than her. He had shallow creases at
the corner of his eyes that shone vaguely the few times he
smiled. Now that it was evening, his valet—had he been
traveling with one—would probably have given him a
stern look at the fine shadow that had begun to darken the
lower half of his face. His eyes were always serious. She
found that she liked that. He was the opposite of Teddy in
every way.

Teddy with his ready smile who was hardly ever serious
about anything. Teddy who sounded like a proper goose
when he laughed. Teddy who had allowed Papa's money to
sway his affections for her. A tender pang sliced through
her at that memory. She had never properly mourned the
loss of him, and now she knew why. It was not his loss that
she regretted. He had been a friend, and in her ignorance,
she had tried to make their relationship more than it
was. She had never once longed for a deeper connection
with him, nor had she ever sought out his touch.

Their kisses had been full of excitement because the
idea of kissing had been exciting. His boyish charisma had
been charming because she had wanted to be charmed. The
idea of marrying had been more appealing than the actual
state would have been because she had wanted control.

Control. The thought came from nowhere, but the force
of it made her sit up straighter. Yes, that was why marrying
Teddy had held any appeal at all. She had wanted to choose

her husband because she hadn't wanted her parents to do it. Even then, some part of her had known that she would not like their interference. Teddy had been the obvious choice. They had the same circle of friends, and he had made her laugh, but there had never been any sort of real attraction to him on her part. Not like with Lord Lucifer—er, Lord Leigh.

"Everything all right?" He glanced up at her and raised a brow. Had his voice become deeper in the hours since he last spoke?

She nodded. "Yes, fine."

He gave her a quick once-over before glancing back down at his work, then sighing at the lack of adequate lighting, he closed the ledger. "You are having second thoughts," he said, as he tucked the books into a leather satchel on the seat next to him.

"No. I am a little worried for my parents. They must know that I'm missing by now. I hope they find my note soon. I wouldn't want them to worry needlessly."

That brow rose again. "You left a note regarding your whereabouts?" He sounded alarmed.

"I merely told them that I had left of my own volition, and that I would not marry Lord Ware or anyone like him. I didn't want them to think that I had been taken away."

His shoulders relaxed, and he went back to casually perusing her face. Despite her best effort, her face warmed from his attention. What did he see when he looked at her? A girl running away from her troubles, or a woman taking control of her life? She hoped the latter.

"It is beyond me how you can fret for them when they would have fed you the wolves." There was a thread of steel in his voice.

"I love them very much." Something made him breathe in sharply through his nose. The word *love*, perhaps?

"Touching." His glance moved to the window where it was now almost fully dark, though the moon was bright.

"Did you not once love your parents, my lord?" She knew very little about his family. He seemed to have none.

Without looking at her, he said, "My father was more concerned with raising horses than children. My mother only sometimes remembers she has any offspring."

His mother was alive, then. Interesting. "I am sorry to hear that. Every child should have a loving family."

He glowered at her. She was certain now that he saw her as a girl running away from her troubles. Her heart sank in disappointment. "Yes," he said. "Look what a loving family has done for you."

"Touché." She inclined her head but refused to back down to him. "However, I have many good memories of my parents. They are simply misguided in their plans for my future. They can love me and still make mistakes. Both are possible."

His scowl softened slightly, though it was difficult to tell in the poor lighting. After a moment, he said, "We shall stop for the night up ahead. The last inn for a bit is in the next town, and if we miss it, God knows how long until we find the next one."

"But is it too soon? Can they find us?" She was suddenly afraid that her plans could come to an end before they had even begun.

"Not likely. They have no idea where to look, but we should leave very early in the morning. It is best to make good time tomorrow. We can discuss the route tonight if you like—you still have to tell me where I am taking you."

"Yes, I suppose I must tell you my destination. It's too late for you to back out of our deal now."

"Did we make a deal?" She heard a smile in his voice.

"Of sorts. Though we never settled on how I could repay you. Perhaps we can do that over a meal tonight." Her own words made her face flame hotter than it ever had before. They had sounded rather like a proposition. Who was this person sitting so casually across from an earl in his own carriage and flirting? She didn't recognize herself, but she liked this new person.

"Let us do that." That gravelly husk was back in his voice. It sent a thrill of anticipation right through her.

The White Horse Inn was a well-kept, picturesque establishment in a small village outside of Cambridge. Violet seemed to regard the thatched roof along with the white plaster and stone exterior with all the enthusiasm of a proper tourist, smiling and pointing out the weather vane with a metal horse perched on top. Christian smiled to himself as he ushered her through the misting rain and the front door. Traveling with her was proving to be an entertaining experience.

The innkeeper, a small, round man, seemed pleased to see them when they walked inside. He jumped to his feet and hurried around his desk to greet them. "Good evening, Lord . . ."

Before Christian could reply with a name, Violet offered, "Rochester."

He glanced at her with a raised brow, and she offered a gentle shrug.

The innkeeper gave a short bow. "Milord, would you be needing a room for yourself and your wife?" His smile was eager as he leaned forward. He was obviously pleased to be entertaining a nobleman. Christian had directed his coachman to leave the Great North Road some miles back to avoid the main coaching inns, so he doubted the quaint establishment had seen more than local gentry.

"I'm his sister," Violet offered.

The man stared at her, obviously surprised by her accent. Christian stood silent for a moment, having forgotten that they would need to navigate this particular issue with care. "Two rooms. I also need accommodations for my coachman." The innkeeper's pink-rimmed eyes had stayed wide in surprise, so Christian felt the need to add, "My sister has been abroad for some time."

"Of course, milord."

Glancing toward the dining area that featured a bar along with several tables, most of them occupied by young men, Christian said, "A private dining area for my . . . uh, sister and me to have a meal."

"Yes, milord." The man gave Violet a dubious glance as he led them to a small room off the main dining room. He bowed and fussed over them, helping Violet out of her cape, before seeing them settled at a small table. A maid hurried in and set the table for the two of them, and then they were left alone with a bottle of Bordeaux and a candelabra lighting the room. Rain tapped gently against the diamond-paned window.

Violet smiled at him, the light catching the pink apples of her cheeks. "I've never been to a proper English inn."

He gave her a bland smile and filled his wineglass very nearly to the top. "Have you not traveled outside of London?"

"Yes, but only by train. Even when our family traveled to Rothschild's estate in Hampshire there was no need to use the services of an inn."

"Then here's to your first night at an inn." He held up his glass in a mock toast before taking a swallow. "How lucky I am to share the evening with you."

Actually, a fit of conscience had been bothering him ever since they had left London behind. When they were found—if his plan worked and marriage resulted—there would be no escape from the gossip. She would no longer be viewed as the innocent and beautiful American heiress. It wasn't a terrible fate, but it bothered him more than he had anticipated. Christian had never despoiled an innocent. Married women, yes; widows, for certain; but never an innocent. But had her plan been successful and she eventually made it to her destination under her own guardianship, similar talk would have happened anyway.

"How old are you, Miss—?"

The maid chose that precise moment to barrel into the room bearing a tray filled with their dinner. Violet smiled, biting her lip to stop her laughter as the woman gave them a startled once-over.

"Your meals, milord." She quickly unloaded her burden, leaving the table laden with crusty bread, pots of butter, and a steaming platter of roasted lamb and potatoes.

"Thank you," said Violet.

The woman nodded, her gaze bouncing slowly back and forth between them.

"That will be all for now," he said.

She bobbed a quick curtsy and hurried out the door, no doubt on her way to the kitchen to report on the true state of their relationship.

Violet snickered when the door closed behind the woman. Gently yanking on the ends of each finger, she began the process of removing her gloves. "Now you've done it," she teased. "Imagine, a brother referring to his sister as miss and not even knowing her age. They will gossip about that for days."

He could not help but stare at the expanse of smooth, pale skin she revealed. His own skin tightened in awareness as he imagined that it would not be very long at all before those hands would caress him. They could be married in Scotland in a week.

"You realize they do not believe you are my sister?"

Her playful smile told him that she did. "Perhaps it wasn't the wisest persona to assume. When he believed I was your wife, I . . . well, I . . ." She blushed attractively, and her gaze dropped to the gloves lying in her lap. "It didn't seem proper."

"No, I suppose not. Perhaps we didn't think things through. Are you having second thoughts?"

"Not at all." Her voice was surprisingly strong in her conviction as she began to butter a slice of bread. "Staying was out of the question, especially knowing what Lord Ware was prepared to do."

The hair on the back of his neck stood upright. Something in her tone suggested Ware had indeed tried to further his pursuit of her. "He came to visit." It was not a question, but she nodded. "What did he do?"

She shrugged and focused all her attention on her task, sliding the fresh butter all the way to the edge of the bread. "He made certain to get me alone, just like you said he would. He wanted us to be discovered in an embrace."

Ice-cold water shot through his veins, followed by a wave of anger. "Did he hurt you?"

She glanced up, perhaps startled at the ferocity of his question. "No, but he was very aggressive. I managed to slip away before we were found." She placed the butter knife down beside her plate, and he noticed her fingers were trembling.

He reached over and covered them with his own. His breath hitched when she turned her hand over and gave his a gentle squeeze. "Did you tell your parents what happened?"

She frowned. "My mother didn't seem concerned. I'm not certain if she didn't believe me, or if she merely didn't understand what the fuss was about. It's not as if anything actually happened." Taking a deep breath, she withdrew her hand and covered her face. "Perhaps she's right. Perhaps I made too much of a fuss."

"Violet." She glanced at him in shock. Clearing his throat, he tried again. "Miss Crenshaw . . ." She stared at him as if somehow only seeing him now for the first time. He was not at all certain what the look meant. "If he made you feel uncomfortable, if he touched you without your leave, either of those are unacceptable."

She dragged her gaze from his eyes to his mouth in a slow and weighted caress. "Thank you," she whispered. Blushing again, she picked up her abandoned piece of bread and took a bite as she gave him an abashed smile.

When she swallowed, she said, "To answer your question, I'll be twenty soon."

Taken aback at the abrupt change in topic, he nodded and reached for the serving tongs to place lamb on each of their plates. "I am only eight years older than you." The fact made him feel slightly less the lecher.

"That's perfect for a brother. My brother Max is eight years older than I am."

"Perfect for a brother . . . What about a husband?"

She stilled. "What do you mean?"

He tried not to look at her as he moved the food around on his plate. His appetite for the meal had suddenly deserted him, while his appetite for her had moved to the forefront of his thoughts. The blood warmed and thickened like honey in his veins, but it was too soon for any of that. He didn't want to frighten her. "Perhaps it would be more believable and raise less suspicion if we present ourselves as a married couple, like the innkeeper assumed."

"Oh." She took a bite of a roasted potato and chewed it thoughtfully before saying, "Yes, I can see your point. I should have a different name. Something common."

"Jane, perhaps." He grinned and watched the blush return to her cheeks.

Her gaze tracked downward in embarrassment before darting over to meet his. "I've been rereading *Jane Eyre*. I hope you don't mind being Rochester. It was the first name that came to mind." He shook his head, and she added, "As long as you don't have a wife hidden away in an attic somewhere, I will be Jane."

"You are in luck, my lady. You are the closest thing I have to a wife."

"Good." She giggled, but it wasn't a girlish sound. It held the soft husk of her voice and raked pleasantly down his spine.

"Perhaps we should address your accent if you're to be presented as a proper Englishwoman."

"Oh yes, yes, we should. Actually, I have already been practicing. I should have used it earlier with the innkeeper."

"Let's hear it, then."

She nodded and took a drink of wine. Clearing her throat a few times like a singer preparing to belt out a lyric, she sat back from the table and squared her shoulders. "Good evening, my good lord. Would you be so kind as to pass the salt?"

Her face elongated with each syllable as if the words themselves were difficult to form and required the use of her entire face. Her voice had gone frightfully high as she skipped over the vowels, clipping the syllables with precision. The attempt was appalling.

She stared at him expectantly, and he tried to keep a straight face but failed. Laughter came tumbling out of him. She giggled, then snorted, and they both laughed harder. Shaking her head, she hid her face in her hands. "That was terrible."

He laughed harder, until his sides hurt. "I should not laugh," he managed to say.

"No. You should. I failed miserably." Her eyes were filled with tears of mirth.

This could be his life. Her beautiful face could be across his table every day. The thought was enough to steal his breath, because it was not at all unpleasant.

She would be his wife.

"Are you quite all right?" she asked. The warmth of her small hand covered his. Before he could stop himself, he turned his hand over so that his palm enveloped hers. Heat licked its way up his wrist. She felt it, too. Her eyes were dilated, and the air seemed to have thickened around them. His fingertips moved in gentle circles across her palm, seeking to draw more of her need to the surface.

"Is everything to your satisfaction, milord?" The innkeeper strode into the room, his gaze locked on the very unbrotherly way Christian was caressing her hand. She pulled her hand away immediately.

"Exceptional," said Christian, unable to take his eyes off of her. "We won't have need of you anymore tonight." He was annoyed at the interruption, but even more at his inability to keep his hands to himself. She would need time to become accustomed to him. Perhaps he was planning to take her choices away from her, but she still deserved a proper courtship, such as it was.

"Yes, milord. Your rooms are ready." He backed out of the room but stopped at the door. "When your sister is ready to retire, my girl Katie can assist her." There was no mistaking the disapproval in his tone or the sharpness of his gaze before he left them.

"We have scandalized him," she whispered. There was laughter in her voice. Where he had expected to see censure in her face, she smiled at him. "I fear he believes me to be a fallen woman."

"We have botched our first night out."

"We have." She gave him a grave nod before smiling again. "Luckily, we have several days yet to get it right."

"Does this mean you plan to tell me where I am taking you?" Not that he meant for her to arrive there.

"Yes, tomorrow morning."

Never had he smiled so much in one night. Life with Violet would not be dull.

Chapter 10

*He found her weakness without even trying—
a man whose confidence outweighed his ar-
rogance was a dangerous creature indeed.*
V. LENNOX, *AN AMERICAN AND THE
LONDON SEASON*

NEW YORK CITY
LATER THAT NIGHT

Maxwell Crenshaw raised his glass in yet another toast to his sister August and her new husband, the Duke of Rothschild. Rothschild stood with his arm proudly around his bride's waist. Any fool could see how happy the newlyweds were. Their obvious affection for each other had been on display in abundance on the ship. So much in abundance, in fact, that Max had encouraged a civil marriage ceremony as soon as possible after the three had arrived in New York. Not that the couple had needed to be persuaded. Max smiled, thankful that a situation that could have brought eternal unhappiness for his independent-minded sister had turned out in her favor.

The Crenshaw family home on Fifth Avenue was bustling with well-wishers. The three of them had arrived in New York only days ago and had put off organizing a small gathering of family friends as long as possible. The news-papers had immediately run stories about the couple, citing Society sources who had made the crossing with them and could confirm the grand match. More stories had run about the quick marriage with speculation running rampant about the need for such haste. As a result, when the couple had reluctantly announced that they would host an evening of celebration for close family friends, the line of people hop-ing to get inside was endless.

Max glanced at the clock on the mantel. There were still hours yet until he could excuse himself to return to his own home in Gramercy. He had another full day of meetings planned for tomorrow at Crenshaw Iron Works where he was overseeing operations in his father's absence. His un-planned trip to London to save August from this very same marriage had stalled many of his projects. But he wouldn't abandon the couple to face the throngs of gawkers alone.

"I say, Maxwell, your parents knew what they were do-ing when they took the girls to London." This came from Samuel Bridwell, industrialist and longtime friend of his father. Bridwell had married his daughter to the Duke of Hereford the year before, which, Max suspected, had pre-cipitated his own parents' marriage plans for August. From what August had revealed to Max, Camille's marriage wasn't a happy one.

Martin Van der Meer, another friend of his father's, said, "I hear England will become a popular destination this year." The older man raised his glass of champagne in a toast, smirked as if they shared some private conspiracy, and drained his drink.

Having just spent almost three weeks of his life trying to save his sisters from a fate similar to Bridwell's daughter, Max found it impossible to humor them. "I'm afraid you could be right. What a tragedy."

He took a swallow, the bubbles going flat on his tongue as he watched August smile adoringly at her new husband.

As the wealthy and socially hungry gathered around the happy couple, he wondered how many young women would be sold for a title without regard for their well-being. The floodgates had been opened, and the parents would point to his sister's happiness as reasonable justification for their own greed.

Bridwell arched a brow at him in consternation, and Van der Meer frowned, while his daughter Amelia gave Max a grin of approval. Young, unmarried, and with wealthy parents, her future would likely be in London whether she wanted it to be or not. "I, for one, don't understand the fascination with nobility," she said. "We have plenty of fine, upstanding bachelors here in New York." For all her innocence, her gaze narrowed in on Max with single-minded purpose.

Max felt the proverbial noose of matrimony tighten around his neck with that look. Clearing his throat, he said, "If you'll excuse me, I must go see to my sister." Without waiting for the group to reply, he tipped his head and made his way into the crowd. Amelia wasn't the first to allude to his unmarried state tonight, and she wouldn't be the last. But he wasn't yet thirty and did not feel the need to settle down with the responsibility a wife and children would bring him. That would come soon enough.

A footman approached him when he was a few steps away from reaching August and Rothschild. "Excuse me, Mr. Crenshaw, a wire has come for you." His face was tense, and he lowered his voice as he said, "From London, sir."

"Is everything well?" On instinct, he distrusted all wires from London now. The last had been pleas from his sisters to come and save them from their parents' treacherous arranged marriage plans, which had resulted in a mad dash across the Atlantic.

The man hesitated. "It seems urgent, sir."

He nodded and followed the servant to a little-used study in the back of the house. A messenger waited for him with the small yellow missive.

"Thank you," he murmured, his eyes already scanning the words as the messenger left him alone. The dread in the pit of his stomach grew heavier with each word. "Fucking hell," he muttered to himself.

Violet had run away, and no one knew where she was.

"What's happened?" asked August as she hurried into the room, Rothschild behind her.

"Why do you assume something's wrong?" he quipped.

"Telegrams from London at this hour are never good."

Max sighed and held up the paper for her. "A telegram from Papa. Violet ran away. They found a note in her room that claimed she would not be pressed into a marriage she didn't want. It gave no clue to her destination."

August grabbed it and skimmed it with Rothschild reading over her shoulder. He shook his head in disappointment. "Ware indicated his interest in her. I warned him away, but he must have pressed his suit," he said.

August glanced up at her husband and then looked at Max. "I married their duke. Isn't one nobleman in the family enough?"

"I don't pretend to understand them."

August shook her head. "It's my fault. I should have insisted that Violet leave with me."

"If anyone is at fault, it's me. I spoke with Papa, and he assured me that their only interest was you, Rothschild. He made it seem as if your offer was too good to pass up. I never thought they would try to force another marriage." Raking his hands through his hair, Max walked to the window that overlooked the small garden in the back of the house. "I always knew that he had a ruthless streak when it came to business, but I never realized that it would extend to his children. More the fool am I. We were stupid to leave her there."

"I may be able to help. I will send a telegram to my partners at Montague Club. They can find Ware and dissuade him from her," Rothschild said.

August worried the edge of the telegram with her thumb. "Papa can be very persuasive when he needs to be."

Rothschild shrugged. "Ware is a known coward, and Leigh already despises him from our days at Eton." He gave August's shoulders a gentle squeeze. "Perhaps it will delay things while we can return to England and find her. We can search train stations and ship registers. Someone will have made note of her passing through."

August nodded. "Once she knows I'm back in London, I'm certain she will attempt to contact me."

"No," said Max. "You both have business here in New York." Having recently discovered that he had inherited interest in a mining company, Rothschild had a series of meetings scheduled for the next week. "I'll go to London and look for her." It would also give him the opportunity to deal with their parents in person.

"But what of Crenshaw Iron?" asked August.

"What of it?" Max raised his brow at her. "You know that you're as capable of running it as I am." August had spent the past ten years of her life learning the ins and outs of the business right alongside him. Papa had already given her more responsibility in the company than many were comfortable with. If he hadn't allowed opinion to sway him from giving her even more, she would already be running it.

August shook her head. "I simply can't fathom her out there alone, and if our parents find her first, they may very well force this marriage. You stay. I'll go."

"And leave your husband here?"

August glanced up at Rothschild, who nodded. "Go if you need to. I'll follow quickly."

Turning her attention back to Max, she said, "That's settled, then. I'll go."

"No, I owe this to Violet." He did. He should have done more while he was there to make certain she was safe and this wouldn't happen. He had failed her once; he wouldn't do it again. "Had I not let them convince me that they had no plans for marriage for her, she would be safe and not left to face this on her own. This time I'll bring her back with me." He should have seen through their parents' assurances.

She frowned, still hesitant, but she nodded her agreement. "If you're certain."

"I am. Forgive me, but I need to leave to make arrangements. With any luck I can book passage on a ship leaving tomorrow."

SOMEWHERE IN THE ENGLISH COUNTRYSIDE

Doubts, along with the sensation of being alone in a strange place, had given Violet little peace last night. She had tossed and turned until her dreams had mixed with her worried thoughts, driving out any of the good humor left from her meal with Lord Leigh. Had she done the right thing in leaving home? Yes, she was certain that staying would have only created strife. However, she disliked the anxiety and pain that leaving was certainly causing her parents.

After giving her direction to Lord Leigh the next morning, she noticed that he seemed to retreat into the same aloofness that had plagued him yesterday on the drive from London. The silence between them wasn't tense, and for that she was grateful. Their shared laughter from the night before had created a more relaxed environment between them. However, she still found herself wondering what he thought of her. She should probably apologize for the kiss at the ball, but she was too afraid of his further rejection to broach the topic. He had held her hand briefly and laughed with her last night, but it would be folly to assume that he felt more for her.

While she was reasonably certain he found her pretty,

she really wanted to know if he found her admirable, someone worthy of his more romantic attention. Not that it
should matter. He was an earl and she was an heiress, and
that meant she would not choose him to placate her parents,
even if a small part of her revolted at that fact. There. She
acknowledged it. She didn't simply study him in the interest
of research. She admired him all on her own. Violet Crenshaw, not Miss Hamilton.

As he continued to work on his ledgers, she retreated
into her writing, which was the only thing that calmed her
when she had these anxious thoughts. It wasn't easy to
work on her manuscript with the constant jolting of the carriage, but she managed it for a bit, until she broke the lead
of the third pencil she had used that morning. Giving up,
she dropped the loose pages of parchment on the seat
beside her and stared out the window until she drifted off
to sleep. Her face pressed against the lush upholstery of her
seat back.

She awoke a bit later when the carriage moved over a
deep rut in the road, jarring her so that her forehead bumped
against the window. The farther they moved from London,
the worse the roads seemed to get.

"Ouch," she murmured and pushed herself away from
the glass.

"Careful, Miss Crenshaw." Leigh's voice, bored and
slightly distracted, came from his side of the carriage.

She rubbed the tender spot near her temple. He sat with
his legs outstretched, seemingly absorbed in the pile of papers on his lap. His calf pressed against her skirt, so she
leaned her leg slightly into the contact, simultaneously
aghast at how desperate she was for a scrap of affection from
him and exhilarated by the touch. A lock of hair had fallen
down over his forehead; it was almost black in the shadows
of the carriage. His brow was furrowed in concentration.
She wished that made him less appealing, but the more
unapproachable he appeared, the more she seemed to de-

sire him. No, not true. Last night when they had sat and talked and laughed, she had wanted him to be hers with every part of her being. The very idea of posing as his wife tonight filled her with an emotion she wasn't quite certain she recognized.

"Are you injured?" he asked and looked at her, likely prompted by her silence.

"No." She sounded like a petulant child and immediately regretted her tone.

His gaze swept her face as if he were determining on his own if that were true. The hint of a smile touched his lips when his focus came to rest on her eyes. The color encircling the gray was dark blue. His expression was earnest and searching, as if he were attempting to mine her secrets. As if she had secrets worth foraging for. A flicker, light as a butterfly, quickened in her belly at his attention. "You are an insightful writer," he said.

She stared at him, completely caught unaware by the compliment. "Why do you say that?"

She regretted the question as soon as it made him look away from her and down at the papers in his lap. *"Rose stared in growing horror at the scene before her. The couples twirled, light and gay in their movements, but hollow and numb in their hearts. Did they feel the poignancy of the music, or were they like figures in a music box, set to perform at the turn of a key but deaf to the soul of the melody?"* He read her own words back to her.

She knew he had her pages, and yet she still looked to the seat next to her where she had placed them before falling asleep. The black upholstery lay bare. "Give it back." Louder, she added, "How dare you?"

When he simply stared at her with a puzzled expression, she reached over and tore the manuscript from his grasp. He let it go so easily that she became off-balance and wobbled. His hand came out to steady her, but several loose pages fell to the floor.

"This is my work. My private work. You had no right to take it and read it." Her whole body felt hot and tight, as if her skin had grown too small for the anger and embarrassment contained within her. No one read her work except for August, and she had shown close friends a few selections, but no one ever read her unedited manuscript. The exposure she felt could only be compared to a stranger storming into her bath unannounced. It was as if she had been laid bare to him.

She couldn't stay in close confines with him another minute. She needed to have some distance between them. As her cheeks burned, she made for the latch on the door only to belatedly remember they were traveling down the country road at a fast clip. She stopped before she pushed the door open, but not before he asked in a panic, "What are you doing?" as he grasped her shoulder.

"I have to get out. I can't stay here with you."

He raised a fist and pounded on the ceiling of the carriage, as she took in gulping breaths. Had he read about Lord Lucifer? Did he know the man was him? Had he read the sinful thoughts Miss Hamilton had about him? Violet had written them too honestly and explicitly for publication. She had intended to go back and edit out some of the more wicked lines. They had been little more than girlish fantasies she had set to paper. Those lines came out to torment her now.

He was depravity and his name was Lord Lucifer, the dark angel himself come to earth to tempt innocents. Rose had never so wanted to be debauched as when he gazed upon her.

And this one: *She stared at his mouth, the sensual lips and pink tongue licking at the drop of honey, and she longed to feel him licking at her.*

Oh, dear God! Neither of those were ever meant to see the light of day. She had written the last one in a heated moment after coming home from a ball where he had eaten a honey-drenched fig.

As soon as the carriage slowed, she pushed the door open and jumped down, holding the papers to her chest. Then she walked as fast as she could down the country lane, heedless of the mud from the previous days of rain. All of her doubts rose to the forefront as she marched away from him. She had been an absolute fool to take this cross-country trip with him and, more specifically, to allow her infatuation with him to fester and grow. He was a spoiled aristocrat, believing himself above everyone and everything.

"Miss Crenshaw!" he called from behind her. She could tell he was outside the carriage because his voice wasn't muffled. "Miss Crenshaw!" His voice was much closer, prompting her to speed up her steps. "Violet!" This came from right behind her. In the next moment he was in front of her, prompting her to walk around him only to have him step in front of her again.

"Miss Crenshaw to you, my lord. I have never given you leave to address me by my first name. You know it is improper."

"This whole trip is improper," he quipped.

"Yes, it is. I don't know what I was thinking." Her foot slipped in a slick of mud, and he was there to catch her with his hands at her waist. Holding on to his arm lest she fall, she paused to regain her bearing, while keeping the manuscript tucked against her chest.

"Stop walking . . . please," he said when she tensed to step away. His voice was low and graver for it. "My apologies."

Staring at the serpent engraved on a brass button on his frock coat, she said, "While I appreciate your attempt to placate me, I doubt your ability to understand your transgression."

He didn't say anything for a moment and simply continued to hold her in this indecent way. His hands tightened on her rib cage, and while she knew that she should, she couldn't let go of his forearm. The heat and strength of him beneath her bare hand felt too strong and solid, a part of him that she wanted to explore. She stared at his gloveless fingers, long, graceful, and lightly tanned against the dark blue of her traveling costume. "I know that I have upset you, and for that I apologize."

His face was difficult to read, but he said the words with meaning. Unfortunately, she also knew that he had no idea how he had violated her privacy. "You are an only child, aren't you, my lord?"

Twin lines formed between his brows. "Aside from a bastard half brother and two half sisters . . . yes."

She tucked that bit of information away to dissect later. "Then you have never had to respect boundaries of privacy?"

The lines deepened. "You are angry that I violated your privacy?"

How could he not realize that? Sucking in a deep breath, she said, "Yes, of course I am. My writing is very private and personal. I am not yet ready to share it with anyone, much less someone I barely know."

Dropping his arms, he stood quietly before her, and she realized that she had hurt his feelings. "I thought we were friends."

"We are, but I wasn't ready to share that with you. August typically reads my work, and even she has not seen this yet. You had no right to assume that I would grant you unfettered access to everything."

When he didn't say anything immediately, she added, "You are like every other nobleman who has come to call during our time in London. You assume simply because of the virtue of your birth that I owe you pieces of myself that I am not ready to share. Who I am, my joys and pleasures . . .

I will not be forced to reveal more than I am willing to you or anyone else."

He let out a rush of air and pushed a hand through his hair. He had discarded his hat as soon as they settled themselves in the carriage earlier. "You are right, Miss Crenshaw. I assumed too much."

Her heart squeezing in her chest despite herself, she said, "It's not your fault. It's the way you were raised."

"It is my fault. I should have seen. My birth does instill in me certain privileges, but it is my fault for being blind to them."

Just like that, she felt her defenses lowering. Pleased with his answer, she smiled at him. "No one has ever told you no, have they, my lord?"

He grinned, revealing that tiny dimple in his cheek that sometimes made an appearance. "It happens. Occasionally."

"It should happen more often." She felt better about things. He wasn't beyond redemption, unlike Lord Ware, who thought he could simply weasel his way into what he wanted. And it didn't seem as if he had read her wicked lines, because he was not regarding her any differently.

"I shall endeavor to make it so." His grin stayed in place as he offered his arm to her. She accepted and walked back with him to the carriage. After helping her inside, he picked up the stray sheets of parchment that had fallen and handed the pages back to her. He held them as if they were precious and he was afraid of mussing them. That pleased her immensely.

She shuffled them back into the stack on her lap, all the while watching him covertly. The heat of his touch still lingering on her waist, she was besieged by a new and possibly more powerful sensation than desire. It swelled within her chest and almost caused a sigh to leach out of her. Was it adoration? Dear Lord, how would she survive this trip with such a feeling within her?

Chapter 11

❦

They traveled blindly, so propelled by that first explosion of love that one could almost pity them their ignorance of the reckoning ahead.

V. LENNOX, *AN AMERICAN AND THE LONDON SEASON*

They were husband and wife that night.

"Rochester." Christian gave the name to the sleepy-eyed innkeeper who greeted their arrival. They had traveled as long as they dared after sunset in an attempt to outrun the men who would most certainly be looking for them. The alarm must have certainly been raised by now, and all the larger coaching inns and train stations would have their names and descriptions. Christian hoped that no one had put together his departure from London with hers, but it would have been foolhardy to rule out the possibility. For that reason, they kept off the main road as much as possible.

The innkeeper nodded and ushered them inside. "Good evening to you, milord. My apologies to you and your wife." From the corner of his eye, he saw Violet grin and the apples of her cheeks redden. "I received no notice of your arrival."

Christian gave a shake of his head. "All's well, my good

man. My wife and I decided on a quick jaunt to visit an ailing aunt without the requisite travel arrangements."

The man kept nodding as if he understood perfectly and indicated they should follow him up the stairs. "You're in luck that we have accommodations for you. Will you be needing a meal? The kitchen has closed, but I am certain my wife can put together a cold supper for you."

They had decided that Violet would not talk if at all possible. Her attempt at a proper accent was one of the worst he had ever heard in his life. Instead, she put her hand on his arm to follow and nodded her head vigorously.

"Yes, and some warm water. My coachman will bring in our luggage."

Once he had led them to their rooms, the innkeeper left to bring their food. The rooms were humble and furnished with a small bed, a bedside table, and a washstand. One room had a small table with two ladder-backed chairs, which is where they took their meal. Over bread and cold chicken, Violet said, "Do you suppose that I might write to you, my lord?"

He nearly choked on his bread. Taking a sip of ale—no wine having been offered—he said, "Why?" It was a daft thing to ask. He should be encouraging her interest and not giving her chances to revoke her offer. The truth was that he had been off-balance ever since reading parts of her manuscript. It was plain to see that Miss Rose Hamilton was an amalgamation of Violet and her sister. But who the devil was Lord Lucifer? She claimed to not prefer lords, but someone had inspired such passionate words. He had planned to ask her, but after such harsh words, he knew that he should keep his mouth firmly shut on the subject.

"Because I will be in Windermere, and you will be at Blythkirk, and eventually London." She shrugged. "I've enjoyed our journey together. I think we might strike up a proper friendship if given the chance." She smiled, looking both shy and eager for his acceptance.

He had to look away, lest he reveal how much he wanted her. They could be very good friends. He could see that easily. She was charming and intelligent, with a sensible logic that belied her years. To be fair, she was not at all how he expected she would be. His interest before had been almost purely physical and mercenary—even then something else about her had appealed—but now . . . at some point during the past couple of days a fondness for her had taken root. He had no doubt that she would be a delightful and passionate lover, and that even their time spent out of bed would be pleasing.

"Or do you suppose it's wildly improper?" she added when he hadn't responded.

"It is wildly improper." He cleared his throat to soothe the husk in his voice. "We are both unmarried."

Glancing down at her plate, she said, "Does that bother you overly much?"

"It did not bother me in the least before." He paused, understanding before he even said the rest of the words how true they were. He meant them to be contrived, to add another layer to the foundation he was building, but they were absolutely true. "But with every day that passes, I find that the married state does hold some appeal."

She stared at him and blushed, a wave of color washing down her face. He would have bet his entire life that her breasts were now a pretty shade of pink. "I meant would it bother you if I write to you even though it is improper?"

He had known what she meant. His words had been intended to turn her thoughts toward marriage. They had succeeded, but unfortunately, they made his own thoughts turn to the fact that they were posing as husband and wife and there was a bed conveniently located behind them.

Christ. To bed her . . . He closed his eyes and drank deeply of his ale. One more week. The fall of his trousers pulled tight across his hips.

"Does it bother you?"

She shook her head. The pretty blush still stained her cheeks. "No, but then we know that I am prone to improper decisions." She smiled and waved a hand at the room, indicating the whole trip. "Besides, perhaps a little intrigue will dissuade some suitors from their pursuit."

Some would be repelled, but the worst ones would want her anyway because of her money. He wanted to tell her that marriage would solve her suitor problem, but it was still too soon. Instead, he said, "Then write to me, Miss Crenshaw, and I will write you back."

She smiled broadly, thrilled with his answer. Turning her attention back to her meal, she said, "Will you tell me more about Blythkirk?"

He stared at her fingers as she played with her bread, his brain still swimming in the arousal of the previous moment. He had never noticed before, but ink seemed to permanently stain the tips of the fingers that held her pen. "There isn't much to tell. It's a small estate compared to Amberley Park. It belonged to my mother's brother. When he died without issue, it was left to me. It was where I would go between terms at school."

"You wouldn't return to Amberley Park?"

"My father abhorred my presence there and I his. Blythkirk became a refuge."

She was silent, watching him with those all-knowing eyes that saw too much. He didn't know why he had revealed so much to her. His father was dead and buried. There was no need to discuss the bloody bastard.

"Your mother is still living? Where is she?"

"My father banished her to the Continent years ago, after she had taken one lover too many." Christian could still remember the terrible row they had had that night when his father had returned home to Amberley Park early. His mother had been packed off the next day, sporting a swollen jaw and red-rimmed eyes. Christian had never known the man she was cavorting with, except that he had been a commoner from one of the nearby villages. "She has never seemed inclined to return for very long, even though he's been dead for over fifteen years."

"I'm sorry. How old were you when she left?"

He shrugged. "I do not remember precisely. Five, perhaps."

She made a soft sound in the back of her throat and put her hand on his arm. The look she gave him was kind and filled with concern, without a hint of censure or mocking. "How often have you seen her since?"

"She has returned a handful of times for momentous occasions only to sweep out again to return to her life."

"Do you regard her harshly?"

He shook his head. "Not anymore." He had for a time. After all, hadn't he grown up under the wrath of his father's ire? Hadn't he managed fine, even while knowing that the man despised the sight of him and questioned his paternity? Couldn't she? But that had changed when the man's wrath had manifested in more physical consequences. Once Christian understood what it meant to have the entirety of that man's hatred centered on him in a physical way, he had forgiven her immediately. "My father was not an easy man. I think she was happier away from him. By the time he died, she had a life on the Continent, and there was no reason for her to resume her life here. Besides, Society would not have allowed her to return without bearing the brunt of their disapproval for some time."

"You miss her, don't you?"

He shrugged. "It is difficult to miss someone you barely remember being in your life. I suppose I did miss her early on." He remembered the feel of her arms around him and her soft bosom beneath his cheek as he cried about some childhood trauma, but as he had grown older, those memories had faded. He had never had a mother to deal with his adolescent concerns, so not having one had not bothered him.

"After my father's death, I learned about my half brother, Jacob, his mother, and his sisters. My father had arranged it so that while I inherited the properties and debts, they inherited the funds, along with their home in Bloomsbury. One day I went and confronted them. I was still a child in many ways." He remembered that day still. The surprised look on Thea's face, the way she had calmly shown him the door when he had said unspeakably rude things to her.

"What happened?" Violet asked, leaning forward.

"Dorothea . . . Thea, Jacob's mother, my father's long-time mistress, rightfully had me thrown out. I accused her of terrible things. I allowed my anger with my father to lead me, and thankfully, she understood that. I soon returned, and she allowed me in. Over time I came to know her very well. She helped me grieve and eventually supported my plan to begin the club with Jacob. She became important to me." He glanced down at his food, swallowing over the tender ache in his throat. "She died several years ago."

"I'm sorry that she is gone. She must have been a very loving person."

He nodded, and the words kept tumbling out of him. "Her father was a successful coal merchant outside of London. My father had dealings with the man, which is how he met Thea. She was the youngest of her family, and her leaving reportedly caused a rift between her and her father. He wanted her respectably married. But by her own words she loved my father very much and chose to live with him." Christian had never understood how the man he had known had been so different from the one of Thea and her children's experience.

"Do you suppose your father ever wanted to marry her as well?"

"I don't know. I do know that he despised my mother. Jacob and I are only separated by a few months. I can only assume that he was with them both and chose Thea. My mother didn't take this lightly. I know that he only married her because she arranged for them to be found together, thereby forcing the marriage. He always believed that I was someone else's bastard. I would have believed it, too, had the physical similarities not been so apparent. By all accounts he was faithful to Thea until his death."

"You do look very similar to your brother. Aside from your coloring, you could almost be twins."

"We both take after our father. It was the one thing that shocked Thea when she saw me."

"I would have very much liked to meet her, but I am glad to not know your father. He treated you poorly."

Christian could not help but stare at this strange and wonderful woman before him. Thea had been born the daughter of a merchant. Though her relationship with his father had elevated her position somewhat, she would never have been accepted in Mayfair ballrooms. No self-respecting lady would have dared to acknowledge her existence, much less meet her.

"I believe she would have liked you," he said with all honesty. Thea had liked anyone who was out of the ordinary, who wasn't afraid to forge their own path.

He took another drink of ale, guilt burning in his stomach. No matter how often he told himself that he was the better choice for her, he could not forget the fact that he was taking her choices away.

"Does it not strike you as odd that the villain of this story, your father by your account, would be the hero in the eyes of Society? His mistress and his wife would both be shunned," Violet said.

He nodded in agreement. "He was most definitely a villain."

"I rarely agree with Society's opinions."

"I am shocked." He teased her.

She laughed.

"I gathered as much in your dash from London. Have you always been rebellious?"

"Not really. Quietly rebellious, perhaps. I prefer things

to be calm and orderly, but not at the expense of what's right."

He grinned at that, wondering how many rebellious thoughts she harbored. At least he knew a few because of her precious Lord Lucifer. The burn of guilt faded into the ache of jealousy. Finished with his sparse meal, he pushed his plate away and held his tankard with both hands, reluctant to depart for the evening.

"How did you learn about your father's other family?"

Surprisingly, he did not find anything abhorrent about telling her. He had never spoken to anyone about his past so freely. "Ware helped."

"Lord Ware?" Her eyes widened.

"Yes. We both were attending Eton, and someone was spreading rumors, very true rumors actually, about the condition of my newly inherited estate. I tracked them back to Ware, and when confronted, he told me about Jacob, Maura, and Lilian."

"What did you do to Lord Ware?" There was the unmistakable gleam of bloodlust in her eyes.

"I beat him soundly, of course." More seriously, he added, "I didn't want to believe it, but there was hardly any reason not to. When I confronted my father's man of business, he admitted that it was true."

"Perhaps your father should have been outcast instead of your mother. He had an entire other family."

Christian could not argue with her logic. "But then the rules are different for women than they are for men. He kept his seat in Parliament and was invited to all the important events of the season. My mother would have been a laughingstock and relegated to only the lesser events, and only if she seemed suitably contrite."

She harrumphed and set her tankard down. "Sometimes I wonder why bother with the lot of them."

Despite the subject, he found himself smiling at her irritation. "Would you prefer to leave? Tour the Continent, sail around the world?"

"Neither of those are terrible suggestions," she said, relaxing her shoulders. "Especially if I can write."

And have someone make love to you at night, he added silently. Perhaps his quiet Miss Crenshaw was strong enough to not be bothered by the inevitable scandal of their marriage. She might even thrive because of it.

"Tell me more about Montague?" she asked, changing the subject. Her thirst for information about him was heady. He found he wanted to tell her everything.

"What do you wish to know? Jacob runs it with me, and a few years back the duke bought in."

Sipping her own ale, she smiled at him in a way that let him know she thought herself being very naughty. Anticipation rippled like sparks across his skin. "I have heard that all manner of deviousness takes place there."

He could not have this conversation with her. Not now. Not when they were all alone with a bed conveniently nearby. Shifting in his seat to find a more comfortable position, he said, "All stories are true, though perhaps slightly exaggerated."

"What about the room?"

There was no need to ask which one she meant. Tales of a special bedchamber at the club had been greatly embellished.

Dropping her voice even though they were alone and no one was likely to be listening, she asked, "The bedchamber?"

"What have you heard?" What would an innocent debutante be told about such a subject?

She shrugged a shoulder and dropped her gaze as if suddenly too shy to meet his. "Only that couples go in there to indulge in all manner of immoral and decadent behaviors."

Sometimes there were performances. Other times couples chose to go there alone or with a few companions. But there were accoutrements available for their pleasure. She glanced up at his silence, the interest clear in her eyes. They were dilated, and her lips parted as if to catch her breath. She would want to go, and he would take her there. He closed his eyes as he imagined using the silk cords to tie her hands to the bed. The way she would tremble with need.

"Yes, that much is true."

"Do you go there?" she whispered.

He stared at her, astounded at her brazenness and how appealing it was. "I have, yes." His voice was husky and thick with want. She blushed in response, and he knew that she was imagining such a scene. Was she his companion? "Would you like to go there?"

"I don't know how I would. As I recall, your club doesn't allow women." Her shoulders squared, and she looked at him in defiance. He noted that she had avoided his question.

"You are misinformed. We have women members. Although, admittedly, they are few and their reputations are nothing to speak of."

Her flare of indignation faded as quickly as it had appeared. "Oh." She paused, taking in a breath as if preparing herself for something. The way this conversation had taken so many twists and turns, he wasn't certain what to expect. "Do you recall when I kissed you?" Her gaze went to his mouth before settling on his eyes.

"Yes." His voice was almost unrecognizable. His cockstand would certainly be noticeable to her if she dared to look. It became apparent that he needed to immediately remove himself from her presence, lest he convince her to do something she would likely regret at this point.

"What do you remember about it?" she whispered.

He nearly groaned at the desire in her voice. "How much I liked it."

"You didn't think me immature?"

"No." Leaning forward, he let his fingertips rest on the back of her hand. She took in a little breath at the touch. He would be lying if he didn't acknowledge the way his own blood sped at the simple contact. "Was that your first kiss?"

"No."

Despite the fact that it was completely unwarranted, a flicker of jealousy flared inside him. "Your fiancé?"

"Yes."

The brute inside him demanded he find out who had kissed her best, even though Christian had hardly kissed her at all before they had been interrupted. "Why would a man who had held you and kissed you be so stupid that he let you get away from him?"

"My father paid him." Her voice was choked with misery, and her gaze had moved to his hand. She was embarrassed.

"Crenshaw paid him to leave off? To pave the way for Ware?"

She shrugged one shoulder. "I suppose that's the reason. Although, it's possible Teddy had already found someone else."

"He's a bloody fool." The vehemence of his tone drew her gaze back to him, and her eyes shone with approval.

"I think so, too." Her eyes dropped to his mouth.

Christ. He wanted to kiss her. To kiss her so hard and deep that she fell back onto the bed, splayed beneath him. His cock was so rigid that he'd merely push her skirts up, find the slit in her drawers, and slide into her. Only it wouldn't be that easy. She was a virgin, and he had to take her with care, not with mindless need. He needed to leave. Now. He wouldn't ruin her, not physically, without her agreement to marry him. It wouldn't be fair to her.

With a groan born from the frustration bearing down on him, he pushed away and rose to his feet. "We should retire for the night. We must leave at daybreak to stay ahead."

"Oh." Clearly disappointed and ashamed of that disappointment, she rose. "Good night, my lord."

Hoping she didn't notice the need coursing through him,

he gave a slight bow—as near as he was able—and hurried out the door of her bedroom. He waited until he heard her lock it, before going into his own.

The next two days were both fearful and wonderful. Violet was able to finish precious little writing. She was hopelessly distracted by Lord Leigh and spent almost the entire time in the carriage talking to him. They spoke of almost everything, from the terrible news of that poor German ship that had sunk off the Isles of Scilly to *Minor v. Happersett*—the Supreme Court case that had denied granting women the right to vote—to Lady Helena's charity. Much to her delight, Lord Leigh supported the idea that women should be granted the vote. He even believed that a woman should be allowed to find a place for herself outside the home, and he had donated to Lady Helena's charity.

While the charity had originally funded a home for foundlings and orphans, it had been expanded in recent years to accommodate the growing need created by women, many unmarried, working twelve- and sixteen-hour days who could not care for their own children. Lady Helena had confided to her that Society people sometimes found it disagreeable, as it could be seen to promote promiscuity. As a result, she was struggling to find funding. Violet and August had promptly donated, so it was heartening to know that Lord Leigh shared their sentiments.

Especially since Violet was fairly certain she was developing strong feelings for him.

It wasn't the same sort of tepid comfort she had found with Teddy. No, this was an all-consuming thing that swept in and took hold of her. A possession of sorts. It had started with physical signs: his electric touch sending sparks of heat along her skin, his scent making something deep within her long to be cosseted in his arms, the sound of his voice swirling inside her, stripping her defenses until she was a mass of need and longing. A smart woman would say this was the dangerous effect of a rogue. Even now she could hear Lady Helena warning her away. The woman would be correct to do so. Those were merely signs of passion. Those weren't what frightened her.

Violet was much more touched by what had come along with the physical manifestations. For one, he asked her about her life in New York. She told him about her friends, and Alabaster Court, their summer home in Newport. She told him all the little details about growing up that she had never spoken about to anyone. Her cat, Mittens, who had arrived one day in their back garden scrawny and missing patches of his coat, only to live the next ten years of his life in the luxury of her care. Teddy had never even known about Mittens, and she was certain he had never thought to ask about pets. Not only did Lord Leigh ask, but he listened.

He listened when she told him about the first time she had written a story and read it to her friend Amelia. Amelia had begged for another chapter to be written immediately. Lord Leigh had asked her what it was about and had listened as she had told him the story of the orphan girl who had learned she was a princess. Teddy had supported her writing aspirations, but he had never once asked her the contents of a story. It hadn't occurred to her to mind that lapse in a prospective spouse. Perhaps she still didn't, as her work was her own and would not be his; but after a lifetime of her work being disregarded by nearly everyone she knew, having Lord Leigh's undivided interest in her writing was a heady thing.

The depth of her newfound affection for him was so acute and sudden that Violet was certain it couldn't be real. Infatuation was often mistaken for love, wasn't it? That's what terrified her so much. She would act on her feelings only to find they weren't real. Worse, she would act on them only to discover that, rogue that he was known to be, he had played upon her affections. Despite her longing, she had come to the conclusion that she must be wise in the days ahead.

She would go to Windermere as planned, but she would write to him immediately. If he replied and their correspondence continued, she would propose that perhaps he might court her. She wouldn't come out and say it, of course. She would have to find some way to hint at it, to tease his thoughts on the matter out of him. If that went well, then she would gently, after the proper time had passed, propose they marry.

The very idea of it sent butterflies of doubt and anticipation swirling in her belly. She would have to marry at some point, and she did want a marriage for herself. Children and a home of her own had always been something she planned for her future. Of course, she had always assumed she would find a husband in New York, far away from this current madness. But now she could think of none better than Lord Leigh to be her husband.

No, she was getting ahead of herself. Marriage was not something she should be thinking about now. He could very well continue to Scotland and forget about her. They would start with correspondence, and she would simply wait to see how things developed from there. It was her own excitable nature making her imagine this lush and extravagant future between them. Only she seemed to have no control over her imagination. Every time she closed her eyes, she dreamed of him.

"You're not sleeping, Miss Crenshaw."

She grinned and opened her eyes to see him smiling at her from across the carriage. "No. It is impossible to sleep in this steel conveyance of torture."

He laughed, his eyes shining. "It is not quite dark yet, but I thought we should stop at the town ahead. The rain is heavier now, and Peterson tells me that the roads are becoming treacherous. We have made good time despite the weather."

"That sounds wonderful. Now if only they have a proper bath and hot water, it would be heavenly."

His eyes deepened. There was no other way to describe them. They darkened somehow and became more intent and serious. He had given her that same look several times now on the trip, and it never failed to make her breasts feel heavier and an ache begin deep within her.

"I will make certain of it," he said.

A naughty image of him joining her in the bath flitted across her mind. Did people do that, or was she being depraved? It hardly mattered; she could close her eyes and dream of whatever she wished with no one being the wiser.

"Come and sit with me." He shifted a bit to make room. "Allow my shoulder to be your pillow."

"I couldn't." But she was already moving. The seat was warm from his body heat. An inviting cloud of his scent enveloped her. Spicy with an undertone of woodsy. She wanted to bury her nose in his neck. She managed to only rest her cheek against his shoulder, and he slouched down a bit to help her get more comfortable. Their hips touched. She shifted slightly to ensure that her thigh pressed against his as much as it was able.

With a sigh of longing, she closed her eyes. Sleep wouldn't come, not with her stomach swirling in delight and her blood thrumming through her veins, but she would enjoy this moment as long as it lasted.

Chapter 12

❖

*Lord Lucifer had plotted well. Even if he
wanted to change course now, the scheme
drew breath all on its own.*

V. LENNOX, *AN AMERICAN AND THE
LONDON SEASON*

Christian knew that he had made the wrong decision.
That morning's conversation with Peterson mocked
him. They had been securing the horses while waiting for
Violet to emerge from the inn. The dark clouds in the sky
had promised another day of damnable rain.

"The turn off for the road to go north to Scotland is up
ahead. Do we take it, milord?"

Christian had glanced toward the inn's door to make
certain he wouldn't be overheard. "Yes. We go to Scotland."

Even then, his hesitation had been minute. Violet was
infatuated with him. It was obvious in how she looked at
him, and how she flirted even though she probably didn't
realize she was doing it. He had kept his hands to himself
as much as he was able, but she still sought him out. Her
fingers would brush his as they walked, or her hand would
rest on his arm at the table. Her eyes were dilated with a
simmering desire. She wanted him.

He would ask her tonight to become his wife. He should

have done it sooner, especially after their talk about the secret chamber at Montague. His only excuse for waiting was the guilt. It had been clawing at him with sharp daggers of accusation. His bold plan for coercion and seduction had been wrecked by his growing affection for the woman.

Now it had come to this. He would be forced into another half-truth. If they took the road north without her agreement, then one could argue it would be akin to kidnapping. However, he hadn't left himself much of a choice. The only solution was to take her north now.

Christian's hand fisted on his thigh as he resisted the urge to reach up and touch her where she lay so trustingly against his arm. This mad dash away from London had come to represent more to him than a means to an end. He was now seeing a glimmer of the sort of life he could have with her. There would be no more nights alone, no more of the interminable silence that chased him from Amberley Park. She could be with him.

But not if he ruined this. He was afraid. Afraid that he would ask and she would say no, perhaps not quite ready to commit herself to him because her feelings were new. Or that she might say yes, but want to wait to get married. He could argue the need for haste all he wanted, but he could not force her hand. The problem was that he very much needed her to say yes and be willing to marry in Scotland.

Her breath came in soft sighs. He closed his eyes as he listened, her scent rising up around him. He would propose to her tonight. If he could gain her agreement, then there would be no need to explain to her his minor indiscretion in taking her on the Scotland road. He would simply press upon her the need for haste in their marriage. He had to believe that she would understand that.

And if she did not . . . He could not even consider the alternative.

Before he could think better of it, his hand moved from his thigh to where hers rested in her lap. He wrapped his fingers around hers, his heart pounding against his rib cage when she responded simply by squeezing his hand. They sat there in the silence of the carriage, neither of them daring to move as their palms touched and their fingers laced together. For a man who had bedded countless women in his life, it was a moment of such profound intimacy that he hardly dared to breathe for fear of ruining it. This sweet creature would be his.

An odd and terrible splintering rent through the evening air, invading their cocoon. Peterson yelled, but it wasn't a warning. It was a high-pitched sound of sheer terror. Christian sat up and pushed the curtains back in time to see the dark green and black of a large oak unnaturally filling the distance between the carriage and the bluff he knew was beyond. A branch shattered the glass, sending it spraying across the carriage. He shifted to shield Violet from the shards as much as he could, but the weight of the giant tree sent the vehicle sliding sideways. The road was so waterlogged from recent rains that it had become a mud slick, which had caused them to slide a few times already. This, however, sent them into a full-fledged skate across the road.

"Hold on!" He shifted, grabbing onto the leather strap above the broken window so that Violet could take his place, safely away from the jagged glass protruding from the sill.

Her cry of fear rang in his ears as she grabbed for her own strap, holding on to it so tightly that her fingers were striped with white. "What has happened?" she yelled.

"A tree fell, perhaps uprooted by the rains." A solid thump as the carriage slammed into a bank of trees knocked the breath out of him. Horses cried out in fear, but damned if he could tell what was happening or where they would end up when this was over. He reached out and wrapped an arm around her waist to keep her from being tossed around the carriage as it whirled. She still held tight to the leather strap, her eyes closed.

Without warning, the carriage tilted, nearly careening onto its side before righting itself again. They were near a river, having crossed a bridge about a mile back. God willing, they were well away from it and it hadn't curled back around. But the carriage tilted again, this time downward, and he knew they were about to fall down an incline.

"Violet, grab onto me!" he yelled, a split second before the carriage gave an unholy screech as metal and glass snapped and twisted. The vehicle fell in a terrible roll that pitched them around inside like marbles in a child's toy. He braced himself against the corner to keep his weight from knocking into Violet. God, he would crush her.

A pain, bright and acute, had him seeing a flash of light as it tore through him on the carriage's second rotation. He fell onto his back, his breath forced out of him in a huff so harsh that his lungs seized. For a moment, he lay there, struggling to draw air as his vision became gray and mottled with flecks of black. When the gray cleared, the sky was filled with the dusky orange light of sundown.

Somehow he had been thrown free of the wildly careening carriage. Despite the pain that lanced through him, he rolled over onto his belly. Behind him the sky was bruised, angry, and black with storm clouds rolling in. Dimly, he became aware of the sound of a terrible grinding, and then all went silent.

Deathly silent.

"Violet." Still struggling to catch his breath, he pushed to his knees, his gaze scanning the ground to find her. There were only the angry marks, deep gouges in the earth, that the carriage had left behind as it rolled down the hill. "Violet!" Coming to his feet, he ignored the terrible pain in his leg and looked for her frantically. If he had been thrown free, then she must have been thrown as well.

Please, God, let her be alive.

She wasn't here. He turned in a desperate circle, hoping

to see the blue of her traveling costume against the mud and brush of the hillside, but she simply was not there. "Violet!"

There was no reply. In a panic, he stared down at the path the carriage had left. She could not still be inside. He would not accept that as a possibility, yet he started running down the hill. His boots slid over the mud so that he half ran, half tumbled down the incline. By the time he reached the bottom, the carriage lay on its side in a river that had swollen to likely two or three times its normal depth. The vehicle bobbed, not entirely swallowed by the brackish depths, but the rushing water pushed it with a force that was frightening. The strong currents in the middle of the river were about twenty meters beyond the carriage's current location, and it was moving toward rushing water. If the carriage reached the depths of the open river, it would be swept away in the power of the runoff that swelled the river.

"No! Violet!" Shrugging out of his coat, he ran through the water as fast as he could, heedless of the pain shooting through his ankle. When the water reached his thighs, he dove in and swam. Moments later he pulled himself up onto the side of carriage, fighting with the door to get it open. The windows were all broken, so the water had rushed in to fill up the carriage. He hoped that she was conscious and able to keep her head above the water, but that hope was dashed as soon as he pulled the door open. She lay still and silent, facedown in the water.

"Violet!" He didn't recognize the cry that tore from his lips. Gripping her with both hands, he pulled her up and turned her to face him. She moved like a rag doll, and her face was slack and tranquil. "Wake up!" Her eyelashes did not so much as flicker. Blood from a deep gash at her temple mingled with the water trailing down her face.

She should have been thrown free. Not him. If anyone deserved death, it was him.

Tilting her head back, he gathered her against him and

covered her mouth with his own, attempting to breathe air into her. She didn't move. It did not seem to be working. A glance confirmed that the vehicle was being pushed ever closer to the river. He had to get them to the bank. If they were carried into the middle of the river, they were both dead.

Please, God, please.

Positioning her carefully across the side of the carriage, he slid down into the frigid water and gently brought her down into his arms. It was tricky, but he managed to keep her head above the water as he swam the few strokes needed to reach solid footing. Once he could touch bottom, he gathered her into his arms and continued his attempts at breathing air into her. He had no idea if it would work, because he had no clue as to what he was doing. His only guide was a newspaper article he vaguely remembered about the topic.

Settling her onto the bank, he struggled to make out her features in the rapidly fading light. "Violet . . . please." His voice broke as he turned her onto her side and struck her back with his palm.

A horrible gurgling sound came from deep within her chest just before water came pouring out of her. Her body twitched almost violently as it sought more air. He held her until the trembling eased and she seemed to breath normally. She had yet to open her eyes, however, and he feared that had more to do with the gash on her head than the water.

Thank God she was breathing. He took a moment to press a kiss to the back of her head. Thank God.

He gently lowered her onto her back, only to realize that she lay there awkwardly. Her right shoulder was raised rather than lying flat. A soft moan fell from her lips when he put his hand beneath her shoulder blade. As he suspected, her shoulder had been dislocated. Working quickly, he tore her dress open down the front, wrenching it down and off her shoulders as gently as he was able. He could work slower now that he was assured she lived, but he was still racing the light, which faded by the second.

Reaching a hand into her chemise, his fingers encountered the smooth skin of her back and roved downward until he reached where her shoulder blade should be. The tendons were pulled tight, and the bone was not resting in the joint as it should. Her shoulder had indeed pulled loose. He did a quick check of the rest of her body. His hands moved down her ribs, her arms, and then underneath her skirt to rove up and down her legs. No bones seemed broken, but he could not be certain. Moving back up her body, he slipped his hand down the back of her chemise again and pressed his palm to her shoulder blade. Then he pulled her arm out and rotated it.

Nothing. Bloody hell! He would have to use more force. Because of his years fighting, he had been responsible for dislocating more than one shoulder, but he had never set one himself. He had seen it done numerous times and had assisted when needed, but always on men, and never on someone as delicate as her. Everything in him rose up in revolt at the force he knew he would have to use.

Gritting his teeth at the pain he knew he was about to cause her, he rotated her arm again, this time with considerable force until he heard a sickening pop and crunch as the tendons gave way. Another moan tore from her lips, and he offered a silent apology.

Gently laying her down, he shrugged out of his waistcoat and tore off his shirtsleeves. He wrapped the shirt around her and tied it to help keep her shoulder stabilized. Then he made a poorly fashioned sling of his waistcoat to keep her arm supported. By the time he tied it off, the sun had completely disappeared and freezing drops of rain pelted his back. He had never seen so much rain in his life as they'd had the past few weeks.

Finally able to raise his head, he searched for some sign of the horses and the driver, but all was silent, save for the steady hum of rain. Had they passed through a town when they had crossed that bridge a mile back? He could not say for certain. His thoughts had been too focused on the girl lying near death before him.

There was no way to deny it. Because of him, she had almost lost her life. A sob born of fury, frustration, and self-loathing tore out of him. Had he instructed Peterson to take them on toward Windermere, they would be safe now. But no. His culpability went further back than that. Had he simply taken her to King's Cross, she would have reached that damned boardinghouse days ago. She would be there now, snug and dry before a fire writing on her manuscript. His own selfishness had intervened to keep her from her fate. His own selfishness had made him put his own desires before hers.

He prayed again. "Let me get her to safety, and I will make things right. I will take her to Windermere and never see her again. Please, if you only help me save her."

Rising with her in his arms, he moved gingerly up the hillside, afraid that one wrong move would jar her and force her shoulder to pop again. No matter how deliberately he trod, he couldn't control the mud and rain that had him sliding down for every few steps he took. He landed on his knees, gasping at the pain that shot through his ankle. His bloody walking stick had been lost in the wreckage. He could not have held it anyway while he carried her. There was no question of leaving her behind to go for help. He refused to leave her alone. At the top of the incline, he adjusted her in his arms and started the walk back toward where he hoped a village would be.

Chapter 13

*Rose had become completely fascinated by
the aura of the man such that he did not have
to lay a finger on her to make his seduction
of her complete. Though it helped that he did.*
V. LENNOX, *AN AMERICAN AND THE
LONDON SEASON*

Violet heard him before she even opened her eyes. His
voice was soft but deep as he spoke in a soothing
rhythm, almost as if he were chanting. Whatever he was
doing, she found it very comforting. She floated in the
space between waking and sleeping, listening to him, surrounded by warmth and comfort.

Christian. She had never allowed herself to call him by
his name. It had seemed too intimate, and indeed, it was.
She could not call him by that name with anyone around,
but perhaps she would try it today in the carriage. A flicker
of anticipation sparked in her belly. He would be surprised,
but then his lips would quirk and that dimple she was coming to love would appear. He was always so careful to keep
his thoughts and feelings hidden, but she had managed to
crack him lately. He liked her. She held no illusions that he
cared for her . . . not yet. But soon.

That pleasant spark slowly expanded, becoming a mildly
uncomfortable burning. What could she say to him before

they parted to hint at her interest? She shifted in her bed, trying to recapture the comfort that was quickly slipping away. She could kiss him. A soft, tender kiss like the one at the ball. Yes, she had done it once, and he had admitted he liked it. She could do it again. The pain had moved up to her ribs, only to center in her right shoulder as if there was an open flame inside her trying to burn through her flesh.

The clarity of the pain rampaging through her body brought forth another realization. This one as startling as the pain. Christian was not talking at all. He was reading aloud.

"I explained to her that I had no parents. She inquired how long they had been dead; then how old I was, what was my name, whether I could read, write, and sew a little; then she touched my cheek gently with her forefinger, and saying 'She hoped I should be a good child,' dismissed me along with Miss Miller."

He was reading *Jane Eyre* to her!

She tried her best to open her eyes. It wasn't easy. It felt as if a feather-stuffed cushion had been placed over her eyes, and she had to move out from under it to open them. Her eyelids flickered, and a seam of light penetrated. It hurt so badly that she closed them tight again. The next time she tried, she saw the hazy outline of his form sitting beside the bed. Her pain receded, and the darkness promised it wouldn't return, enticing her to settle beneath its promised warmth and the comfort of his voice. But she wanted to see him. To talk to him. To ask him why he was reading to her, although she half feared it would make him stop.

"Christian." She spoke his name in part to keep herself awake, in part to gain his attention, but he was unmoved. He kept reading. Perhaps she hadn't spoken very loudly, if at all.

Forcing her eyelids to cooperate, she opened them. He sat at her bedside facing her, but nearly in profile as he held the book open near a lamp. The cover of the book was a dark blue fabric that appeared worn at the corners. It was not her copy of *Jane Eyre*, which was deep red and leather bound. Interesting.

A growth of beard darkened the lower half of his face. His valet would not be pleased if he saw him, but Violet was beyond pleased at the sight. She had never seen a man thus. They were either clean-shaven, or had fully developed beards. There must be some in-between phase, but she had never seen it. In the evenings on their trip, he would sometimes have a light growth that he must have shaved off by himself, because he appeared clean-shaven in the mornings. But this was probably a couple of days' worth. Her fingertips itched to rake over it and feel if it would scrape her skin or be soft to the touch. It made him appear rugged in a way that she found extremely appealing, as if the proper English gentleman had been undone to give way to this man who was far more carnal and raw. He only wore his shirtsleeves and trousers. She had never seen a man so scarcely clothed.

She moved her hand to reach for him, but like everything else, it didn't immediately obey her command. In fact, it didn't feel as if it moved at all, and a pain so white-hot in its intensity that it drew a gasp from her moved through her. It felt as if a poker, hot and glowing from the coals of a fire, had stabbed her.

He looked up immediately and set the book aside. "Violet?" She must have closed her eyes, because when next she was aware, he was suddenly over her, his face swimming in the haze brought on by her pain. "You are awake." This he breathed on a heavy sigh, as if speaking to himself.

He pushed the hair back from her forehead, causing her to wince as she became aware of an extreme soreness there. For that matter, his own face was mottled with bruising along one side—the side that had been facing away from her—and his perfect lower lip had a cut near the corner. "Apologies," he whispered, removing his hand but keeping it nearby.

"What has happened?" Her voice was a mere croak, not

the sort of thing one went for when addressing the man one hoped to impress. An attempt at clearing her throat resulted in more pain somehow, so she gave up.

"Do you recall the accident?"

"Accident?" It would certainly explain the pain she was in right now. "What do you mean?" She tried to go over the last few days, but the attempt only gave her a headache. Their time riding in the carriage seemed endless. Little odd scraps of the days passed through her mind like images in a zoetrope.

His face blanched, turning the palest white she had ever seen it. "Do you remember anything? Do you know who I am?" Stunned by the ferocity of his questions, she could only watch him. "Violet?"

"Who's Violet?" She was a very wicked woman. This was not the time to tease him, yet she had become so accustomed to tugging that elusive smile from his lips over the last few days that the words were out before she could think better of them.

"Oh, dear God!" He fell back down into his chair. "What have I done?" he asked God, presumably, as his face dropped into his hands.

"I'm teasing you." Instinctively, she reached out for him only to have the pain shoot through her arm again. This time she realized that it truly was immobile, because it was somehow tied to her body beneath the layers of blankets. When he didn't look up, she said, "Lord Leigh?" Then louder, "Christian."

He slowly dropped his hands and looked up. It was only then that she noticed that his eyes were rimmed with red and there were dark circles underneath. He was tired and had likely been at her bedside for . . . How long had she been here?

"That was terrible of me. I'm sorry." She reached for him with her left hand, and he reached out and took it, moving forward to bring her palm to his lips.

"You remember?" he asked, his mouth against her skin. "You know who you are?" He kept her palm pressed to his cheek as he looked at her. The hair there was both soft and rough. She longed to rake her fingers across his beard, but she dared not break the moment. His eyes were glassy.

"Violet Roberta Crenshaw," she whispered, because she had lost the ability to do more.

A grin tugged at the corner of his mouth. "Roberta?"

"Never call me that."

"I like it."

He seemed sincere, but she had never cared for the name given her to honor a grandfather she had never met. "We were traveling to Windermere. I remember that much. I remember the days in the carriage . . . the suppers at the inns . . . but I don't know where we are now. What happened? Is this another inn?"

Relief allowed color to flood back into his face. "You are a brat, Violet Crenshaw." He kissed her palm again, taking the sting out his words. He drew a deep breath before looking at her again. "We were in an accident last evening. The rain appears to have uprooted a tree, which fell and hit the carriage. It knocked us off the roadway and into a ravine that was unfortunately overflowing with water. Somehow, I was flung free as the vehicle tumbled down the hill, but you were trapped inside. I was able to rescue you, but not until after you had sustained considerable injuries." If his expression was any indication as it roamed over her face, she imagined her patchwork of bruising to be even worse than his. "You swallowed a great amount of water. You weren't breathing. I was so afraid . . ." But he seemed unable to complete the thought.

He had saved her. The awe that accompanied that thought kept her silent. After a moment, she said, "My shoulder hurts, but I don't seem to be very badly injured."

He reached forward and pulled the blanket and sheet back far enough for her to see that she was not clothed.

Strips of white linen had been wrapped around her shoulder and upper arm, but near the top her skin was shades of indigo and maroon. The bruising likely extended farther down her arm if the pain was any indication. However, she could only think that she was naked while he was fully clothed.

Or rather close to clothed. He wore shirtsleeves and trousers, but both seemed too rough to belong to him. They had to be borrowed. Yes, she was certain of it, because the shirt pulled a bit too tight across his shoulders. She would wager he did not own anything that had not been tailor-made to fit him perfectly.

"Your shoulder was dislocated. I managed to move it back into place, but we must keep it wrapped up to allow the muscle time to heal."

"You put it back into place?"

He nodded. "I have some knowledge of how it is done, thanks to the club."

Her mind swirled with that information. He had saved her and administered aid to her. Had he also disrobed her?

"The physician wrapped it for you."

"Physician?"

He nodded again. "I carried you to the small village we had passed about a mile before the accident. Had I not been so irresponsible, so afraid that your parents were on our heels, we would have stopped there for the night and none of this would have happened."

She could not focus on his self-loathing, because she was too fixated on what he had revealed. Not only had he saved her from the carriage, which must have been flooded with water from the rains, but he had also carried her over a mile to the village and found a physician to attend to her. "Christian." He glanced up at her whisper. "You saved me."

"From a wreckage you would not have been a part of if not for me."

She curled her fingers against his beard, noting how his

eyelashes fluttered in what she could only assume to be pleasure and approval. She was touching him, and he was enjoying it. Her heart soared with the knowledge, even as the aches in her body were making themselves known with every throbbing beat of her heart.

"Perhaps not, but I accepted what fate had in store for me when I took you up on your offer back in London."

He stared at her, perhaps locked in the same odd reality she found herself in, floating somewhere between pain and pleasure.

"What happened to Peterson? Is he well?"

"He lives. He jumped free and only suffered a fracture in his arm. You, however, may have a broken rib. Dr. Mitchell could not be sure. The one certainty is that they are bruised and you are concussed." He leaned forward and gently pulled back the hair across her forehead. "You have an injury here, near your temple, that he had to sew closed."

"Here?" She reached up only to feel a bandage wrapped around her head. "Did he . . . Did he shave me?" It was a ridiculous fear considering how terrible the accident sounded and how close she was starting to realize that she might have come to death, but it was there regardless. Apparently, her vanity would make a strong showing all the way to the end, especially knowing that he was gazing upon her.

Strangely, the question made his lips quirk in that elusive smile she had been searching for. "Only a little. You shall be able to cover it with your hair until it grows back."

Relief made her feel tired. "And you?" Her hand went back to his face, unable to pass up the opportunity to touch him. He leaned into her hand like a cat might. "How badly are you injured?"

"Not very much. I was thrown free early on. I cannot be certain, but I believe the door must have flung open. I merely sustained some bruising and scratches."

"I'm glad." And she was. Now that she knew how terrible things had been, she was so thankful that his life had been spared.

"Here. Drink some water." He moved to grab a glass waiting on the nightstand that held the lamp. His hand gently went behind her neck to cup the back of her head, and he raised her an inch or two, enough that she could drink without choking. She found she was parched. As the cool liquid touched her throat, she wanted more. Finally, he gently set her back and held another cup to her lips. "Laudanum," he said. "It will help you rest. You need rest to heal."

Now she understood why her whole body felt so strange and heavy. It also explained why she felt as if she were floating in this odd interval with him. "I don't want you to leave me."

"I won't." This time he smiled without reservation. "I had to tell the physician we were married, so he would allow me to stay here with you. Now I have nowhere else to go."

She smiled, and he pressed the medicine to her lips.

After swallowing, she asked, "Where is my own copy of *Jane Eyre*? Aunt Hortense gave it to me, and I'd be devastated to lose it."

"Waterlogged, I'm afraid, as were your manuscripts, but I retrieved them and have them drying. They shall be serviceable if not pristine."

At least it was safe, if not a bit worse for wear. And her manuscripts. She was near dizzy with relief that they were salvaged.

"Sleep," he whispered, leaning forward to press a kiss to her forehead. "I promise I shall be here when you wake up."

"Is it nighttime?" she asked, already feeling the weight of sleep pulling at her. She had yet to look past his face to see the room, and now it didn't seem important.

"Yes."

"Where will you sleep?"

"Here." He indicated the chair. "Same as last night."

"No, sleep here with me." The bed was smaller than her bed at home but bigger than the ones at the inns. They could both fit, but it would be snug. She smiled at the thought of being so close to him. Miss Hamilton would benefit from this research. Violet was certain of it.

"I could injure you." He started to pull back, but she held on to his hand.

"Please. Sleep here with me."

He sighed, seemed to reconsider, and then nodded. "For a little while," he said and lay on top of the blanket. The mattress depressed so that she slid a bit toward him. The solid heat of him immediately warmed her side. She sighed as her entire body relaxed into him and drifted off into a medicine-induced sleep.

Chapter 14

❧

He was certain that his penance would be to burn in the fire of his guilt while living in the bright affection of her stare.

V. LENNOX, *AN AMERICAN AND THE LONDON SEASON*

Christian had lied yet again. Although, to be fair, he could not have anticipated how good it felt to lie next to her all night. He could not have known that her small body cuddled next to his would be the closest thing to bliss he had ever felt, or that he would be lulled to sleep listening to the comforting sound of her breathing. Nothing in his entire life had prepared him for how she made him feel. He couldn't have known that he would stay the night next to her.

Women had been a part of his life since his fifteenth year. Soft and beautiful, eager and plain, wealthy or poor, he had not discriminated. His only requirements where they were concerned had been twofold: the time required between meeting them and bedding them must be short, and they must never become cloying. He much preferred the woman who had many lovers to call upon than the one who wanted only him. Toward the end, he had bedded only those sorts of women exclusively.

He had had no inkling or desire to find a wife. The house of Leigh could fall to distant relations for all he cared, his father's legacy along with it. Instead of finding a wife and begetting an heir, his attention had turned to building Montague Club into the name it was today. That included arranging the high-stakes fighting matches that had become so well-known even outside of London. Men and women alike came from all over Europe to watch their matches. However, his own reputation had darkened as Montague's had brightened. Not that he cared for the stain. It kept the wrong sort of company away from him—noblemen who thought their birth elevated them to a superior morality that a few indiscretions could not tarnish.

His reputation had begun to draw women who sought out wicked things. The viscountess who wanted to add him to her list of accomplishments, the disgruntled wife of a foreign dignitary, and once, a princess who wanted to know what it meant to be restrained and dominated. But then something subtle had changed. Those encounters had begun to lose their appeal. They felt hollow and unsatisfying beyond the initial itch they scratched, so he had slowly started to avoid them. His time and energy had been better spent at the club. The more energy he spent there, the more his reputation had grown, until almost every night a woman would arrive on the doorstep in search of him.

Over a year had passed since he had last lain with a woman. Given the fact that his lust was now centered on a girl of nineteen years, he could only believe that his depravity had reached a new low. Self-loathing meant that he should rise and leave her in peace. But he fell asleep instead, the steady in and out of her breath lulling him into the deepest slumber he had experienced in years.

A knock on the door woke him the next morning. He breathed in the scent of lavender mixed with rainwater. Opening his eyes, he saw that her hair was like a cloud before him, and her back was pressed to him, the side with her injured arm propped up against his chest. His erection strained eager and crude against the softness of her right buttock. If his earlier exploits hadn't earned him a place in hell, this would certainly accomplish the task. He closed his eyes, allowing himself to imagine for one selfish moment how it would feel to roll her beneath him and sink into the glorious depths of her body. She would be tight, so damned tight he would—

The knock came again, more insistent this time. Gently placing a hand on her hip still covered by her blanket, he slid out from beneath her, replacing his body with a pillow beneath her injured side. She moaned softly as she roused. He clenched his jaw as it sent a surge of blood straight to his already eager cock. Grabbing the blanket that hung over the back of the chair, he wrapped it around himself and opened the door.

"Good morning, my lord," said Mrs. Mitchell, sweeping into the room with a breakfast tray. Her graying hair was tucked into a tight bun. "I have brought some porridge for the lass. Did she sleep well?"

Christian was immediately seized by a fist of guilt tightening in his chest. He had slept so deeply he did not even know if Violet had awakened. Had she needed him?

She blinked awake, her eyes puffy with sleep. "I slept well." Her voice was raspy.

God, that voice. It sent a frisson of need raking down his spine to settle in his bollocks.

The room was so small that Christian had to step back for Mrs. Mitchell to go around the bed and set the tray on the table near the window. Her doughy arms and figure gave her the appearance of a welcoming grandmother, but she moved with brisk efficiency that would have done any military commander proud.

"Good to hear, my lady," she said as she moved around the room opening drapes and straightening blankets. "Dr. Mitchell will be in shortly for your morning examination.

He is out making his early-morning rounds." When Violet murmured her thanks, the woman turned to him. "Once she is settled, you can come to the table for your own breakfast." Glancing at his beard with disapproval, she added, "I shall find you razor and shaving soap. Dr. Mitchell hardly uses them, but I am certain we can find you something in town, aye?"

"Do not put yourself to any trouble, Mrs. Mitchell. You have been more than helpful." He owed the woman more than he could ever repay. She had helped him undress Violet and clean the mud away from her wounds. She had seen to their every need.

Waving him off, she turned back to Violet. "Will there be anything I can get for you, lass?"

Violet shook her head and then winced at the pain it caused. "Where are we, Mrs. Mitchell?"

Christian tensed. If Violet knew their precise location, she would know that he had lied to her.

"Welcome to the North, lass. Yorkshire, to be putting it precisely."

"Thank you," Violet said, apparently satisfied with that and not understanding that they were not on the way to Windermere.

Mrs. Mitchell nodded and hurried out to retrieve the steaming jug of water she had left outside the door. Setting it on the washstand, she said, "I shall send the good doctor when he arrives."

"What time is it?" Violet asked him when the woman had left.

Christian reached for his watch out of habit, but his clothing had been taken to be laundered and had not been returned to him yet. Their luggage—what had been able to be retrieved—was somewhere in another part of the Mitchells' house. He had been too concerned with Violet to worry about the state of material possessions, except for her manuscripts. Those he had personally retrieved from her

Gladstone bag and set out to dry in the kitchen with Mrs. Mitchell's assistance and assurance that she would not read them. Christian had tried not to read them. He really had, but he hadn't been able to help himself from reading the odd sentence and paragraph. It was as if he thirsted for any knowledge of her he could find. He would take it and squirrel it away for the bleak days when she was well away from him.

A glance out the window confirmed his suspicions. The room had a view over a charming meadow with hills in the distance. "Early yet. Still a bit of pink on the horizon."

She struggled to push herself up out of her nest of pillows, so he rushed to her side to help her. "Rest," he said. "There is no need to rise."

"There is need, my lord. Great need."

Her tone was so insistent that for a moment he could not fathom what she meant. When she looked up at him with a sort of panic in her eyes, he understood. Glancing toward the narrow armoire in the corner, he vaguely remembered Mrs. Mitchell mentioning she had tucked some clothing away in there. "I shall retrieve a dressing gown."

Several nondescript nightdresses in white cotton were folded neatly in a stack. A single dressing gown hung on a hook. It was faded yellow, but soft and thick. Hurrying back to her with it, he helped her put it around her shoulders and sat beside her. Once the belt was secure, he tugged the blanket away so it pooled at her hips. Trying diligently not to look at her shapely legs, he put his arm gingerly around her waist and helped her to stand. She wavered on her feet. Her left hand held tight to his shoulder.

The white edge of a porcelain chamber pot stuck out from beneath the bed. He pushed it toward them with his bare foot. "Hold on to my arm. I can help you—"

"No!"

Frowning, he said, "I can help you to hover—"

"Hover? Good God, no, I could not live with the humiliation. You must leave!" Her face was red, and she stared at him as if he had suggested she run naked through the village. "I can do this alone."

"Then at least allow me to retrieve Mrs. Mitchell. I am certain—"

"Go." She pushed him with her left hand. "I can do this alone."

He was not at all certain that she could, but when she refused to relent, he left her. Dr. Mitchell came up the stairs a few minutes later and found him hovering at the door.

"You appear as anxious as an expectant father, my lord." Dr. Mitchell laughed. He had a shock of white hair on his head with a full beard to match. His cheeks and nose seemed to be permanently red. Unlike his wife, he was rail thin.

"She had to attend to her needs and forced me out of the room."

Dr. Mitchell chuckled again. "'Tis a good sign, lad."

Christian had to agree, but he did not like the idea of her being alone. "She does appear much improved today."

Before the physician could reply, Violet opened the door. His heart clenched at the vivid bruise that bloomed on the right side of her forehead and cheek. Otherwise, she appeared deathly pale.

"I am very pleased to meet you, lass. We have met before, although I am certain you do not remember. My name is Dr. Mitchell."

Violet glanced at Christian in concern, before stepping back to let them into the room. "Good morning, Dr. Mitchell. Thank you for seeing to my care."

Neither the doctor nor his wife had commented on her American accent. That alone would raise suspicion if it were known that she was missing. His only hope was that the small village was isolated enough to allow them this respite. They exchanged pleasantries as Christian followed the man inside. A quick glance confirmed that the chamber pot had been pushed discreetly under the bed. "How did you fare?" He kept his voice low so as not to further her embarrassment.

She flushed anyway. "Fine, my lord. You needn't concern yourself."

He grinned at the spark of fire within her. The tight weight in his chest began to ease. She had to be improving if her spirit was firmly in place.

"Let me help you back to bed." To his surprise, she nodded and allowed him to put his arm around her. Her ready agreement was a sure sign of how fatigued she was.

Once she was settled, Christian moved away to look out the window. A decent man might have left her alone with the physician to conduct his examination in private, but Christian could not stand to be away from her yet. Not when her condition was his fault. He stood, silently absorbing every moan of pain she uttered and wishing it had been him. It was the very least he deserved.

"Very good, Lady Rochester. Very good. We shall get you fit again in no time."

Christian whirled. Aside from a quick mention that they were married, he had yet to tell her the story he had invented. She merely quirked an eyebrow at the name. "Thank you, Dr. Mitchell. Truly, I think the fuss is too much. I'll be fine after a bit of rest."

The physician poured out a small amount of water and rinsed his hands in the porcelain basin. "Aye, plenty of rest for you."

"How long do you suggest we wait before we can travel?" Christian asked.

"A sennight at the least. A fortnight would be ideal." He turned his attention back to Violet. "You must stay abed as much as possible as long as your head is healing." The older man had unwrapped the bandage for his inspection. "The bandage can stay off now. There is no bleeding or seepage," he explained, picking up the cotton batting to be discarded.

"Your ribs are fine and strong. I do not believe them broken, but your arm concerns me. It should stay immobilized for a few more days. Once I am satisfied healing has begun, we can consider loosening the restraint."

"Two weeks?" She looked positively crushed by the news. Who could blame her? She likely wanted to be far away from him.

"What is that in a lifetime?" Dr. Mitchell teased. "Your wedding trip can proceed in due time."

She glanced at Christian, blushed, and looked away. Dr. Mitchell found this very amusing. "Do not concern yourself with me and Mrs. Mitchell," the older man said. "I have already explained things to Mrs. Mitchell, and she has agreed to leave you both to your privacy when possible."

Violet seemed too embarrassed to respond. Christian stepped forward. "Thank you, Dr. Mitchell."

The man said his goodbyes and hurried out the room leaving them alone. Christian retrieved the tray from the table and settled himself in his chair beside the bed. Placing the tray on the bed beside her, he took the lid off the small bowl of porridge. "You should eat. You did not eat yesterday," he said as he brought a spoonful to her mouth.

She took a few bites, likely stewing over the conversation. Finally, after eating half the bowl, she said, "We are newlyweds."

"I thought it would make more sense given your age. It must be clear that we have not long been married." He swirled the spoon in the thick porridge and readied another bite.

"I've been elevated to a lady again," she teased, taking the bite.

"You are Lady Rochester now. I gave them the name, and they assumed the rest."

"Anyone with any sense would know you are a lord. It's in your bearing."

"That is not a compliment, is it, coming from you?"

She grinned. "I do have a complicated history with no-bles. I don't generally prefer them on principle."

He laughed. How could she be in such good spirits at a time like this? The last thing he should be doing is laughing with her. "And me?"

"Oh, I do prefer you, my lord. I have made a rare ex-ception."

She could not mean that the way he took it. Her flirting was simply girlish amusement. "Violet . . . You must know how sorry I am for this."

"No, my lord, do not fret."

"For Chrissake, call me Christian." There should be no ceremony between them. Now that he started, he could not stop himself until he said all. "I should never have stopped you that day on the street. I should have allowed you to walk by. You would have taken the train and be in Winder-mere even now with a view of the lake outside the window beyond your writing desk. You should be happily finishing your manuscript, not here recovering."

"But you were right," she said, putting her hand over his. "We don't know what would have happened. Perhaps my parents would have found me at King's Cross. Or perhaps a timely wire would have seen me delayed at a station along the tracks until they could arrive."

A pleasant hum traveled over his skin. Even now his body responded to her touch like a deviant. Hadn't he done enough? Gently pulling his hand away, he ignored the hurt that crossed her eyes. "But you would have been safe." The words came out more forcefully than he had intended, wip-ing the smile from her lips.

"And potentially betrothed to Lord Ware by now. Is that what you want? Do you think I should simply accept my fate like a good little heiress? Be happy that I get to live my life in luxury?"

"No!" he said emphatically. "Perhaps I should feel that.

But even now, knowing that I almost killed you, I cannot bear the thought of Ware having you."

She stared at him, but it was impossible to read her thoughts. "Is that because you despise Lord Ware and can't bear to see him get what he wants . . . or because of me?"

"I confess initially to some pleasure in removing the object of his desire from his grasp, but it quickly became about you, Violet. You deserve better than Ware. You deserve good things in life, not the distress he would bring you."

The initial joy in her eyes at his confession faded with his last sentence. He had intentionally sidestepped what he knew she was asking. It was no secret that she found him attractive. Her esteem had only grown stronger every day they were together. He had spent his days subtly fanning the flames of her desire, giving her just enough to make her crave more. But he could not do that anymore. She deserved the chance to marry a man of her own choosing, not someone hoping to seduce her into it.

Not him. He glanced down at the bowl and raked up another spoonful.

"Then will you accept that I came with you of my own will? Do not blame yourself for the accident." She took the bite he offered her.

He nodded, but only because he could see no point in belaboring the conversation. He would never forgive himself for what had happened to her. "Yes."

"Good. Let us speak of it no more. I much prefer to discuss how grateful I am for you saving me."

That was another conversation he could not stomach. Saving her had never been a choice. He did not deserve to be celebrated for it. "I would much prefer that you eat and return to your sleep. We can speak of all of this later."

She frowned, but she didn't argue as he made certain she ate the entire bowl of porridge.

Chapter 15

Temptation had never felt as visceral as it did that evening. That was the night Rose knew that the game had become her entire life, and she was willing to risk all to win.

V. LENNOX, *AN AMERICAN AND THE LONDON SEASON*

Several days had passed since the accident, and Violet was enjoying her first proper bath. Well, it was a hip bath, so *proper* was a stretch, but it was luxurious nonetheless. Mrs. Mitchell worked the lavender soap all the way down to the roots of Violet's hair, the soft and repetitive grazing of the woman's fingertips relaxing her.

"Tip your head back." The command came all too soon, but Violet obeyed, tipping her head back so that the woman could pour warm water over her hair to rinse out the soap. After a few dips of a small pitcher into a large pot hanging near the fire, Mrs. Mitchell said, "Good lass. That is done. Let us remove your bandages now."

Violet took in the kitchen as the woman began the tedious task of unwrapping the length of cotton fabric that swathed her ribs and held her right arm secured to her side. When she had begged for a bath instead of the usual sponge bath, Dr. Mitchell had relented on allowing her a little time out of bed to accomplish the task. Mrs. Mitchell had been

THE DEVIL AND THE HEIRESS 153

gracious enough to offer her assistance, and Christian had carried her down the narrow stairs. She had told him that she could walk, but he had insisted on carrying her, to which she had conceded easily because it meant that he held her in his arms. In bed, he kept himself rigidly away from her. When she did bridge the gap between them, he never touched her with his hands. He certainly never held her.

The kitchen was a humble room with an ancient fireplace and hearth on the long side with the window, a cast-iron range and a table for preparing food along another wall, a water pump in the corner, storage shelves, and a larger table in the middle of the room. The hip bath, a steel contraption that was so small her legs hung over the side, had been set before the fire. Modest though it was, the home was quite charming with its plaster wall and thatched roof. She found herself imagining what it must be like to live here in this tiny village with no expectations beyond raising a family and being friendly with her neighbors. She could raise children in the daytime, write in the evenings, and make love to her husband at night. Christian was the husband in her fantasy. It was a silly daydream, because life was infinitely more complicated than that, but that didn't stop her from imagining it.

Deep laughter drew her eye to the window. Christian sat in the warm afternoon sunshine at a small table across from Dr. Mitchell. They were playing chess, and whatever Christian had said had apparently been hilarious. Dr. Mitchell took off his glasses to wipe his eyes. She wished Christian were that at ease with her now. Their days at the inns laughing over their meals seemed far removed from this small cottage.

"You have a good man there, lass." Mrs. Mitchell had long since moved past formality in their relationship, a happening for which Violet was grateful. The doctor and his wife had been kind and comforting during this time. "You're a very lucky woman."

The older woman was looking at Christian out the window. Mrs. Mitchell glanced down at her and raised a brow, a very knowing smile on her lips. Violet blushed and looked away, uncomfortable with the minor deception they had been forced to play out on the nice couple, especially now when she was losing all hope that Christian might come to return her affection. He had been so polite and distant. "He is a good man."

"What bothers you, lass?"

Violet shook her head, staying silent as the woman took off the final pieces of bandage wrapped around her ribs and injured shoulder. She braced herself for the burning pain in her shoulder to return, but it didn't. A tender ache replaced it, but it was a pain she could handle. She had rejected more laudanum as soon as she had been able to sit upright on her own.

The older woman picked up a washcloth lathered with the soap and gently ran it over her bruised side. "Poor child," she muttered.

Trying not to wince in pain, Violet looked back to the scene beyond the window. A light wind ruffled Christian's hair, sifting through the waves like her own fingers longed to do. His clothing had been laundered and returned to him, so he wore those, giving her a new appreciation for how well they fit him. His coat stretched tight across his shoulders, making her gaze linger on their breadth, only to drop down to his chest. He had taken to leaving off his tie in favor of keeping the top buttons of his shirt unfastened. Her gaze lingered on the triangle of skin that would have been scandalously indecent back in London. She longed to press her fingertips there and feel him. He would be warm; she knew that much from the times she had pressed a hip or an arm to his side in bed as he slept. But what would his skin there feel like? Would his chest be heavily furred, like some of the men she had seen once when she had accompanied Papa to the docks? Or would he be nearly bare, like

Teddy? One hot summer afternoon in Newport, she had pushed her fingers between the buttons of his shirt as they kissed.

"He cherishes you," Mrs. Mitchell said, that same knowing look in her eyes as she handed Violet the washcloth so that she could finish her bath. The woman turned away to attend to a stew bubbling on her stove. "I can tell, because he takes very good care of you."

The latter was true, if not the former. Christian had been at her bedside whenever she had needed him. He still insisted on feeding her since she was right-handed, but it seemed to her an obligation and not as exciting as it was the first day. He tried his best not to look at her as he did it. His gaze went between the food and her mouth, only looking up briefly if she spoke, and then returning to his task.

Could she truly blame him, though? No one enjoyed looking after an invalid, which is why she had resolved to get better as quickly as possible.

It was true that he made certain she wanted for nothing. Nothing but his affection; no, his passion. He treated her like a favored younger sister. Not a woman in whom he had interest beyond friendship. "He is a very kind person, though he would likely not admit it."

"Why is that, do you suppose?"

"He has not spoken very much of it, but it seems that his early life was not filled with very much affection and understanding. I don't believe kindness was encouraged."

"Ah, then you must hold a very special place in his heart."

Unable to encourage the pretense of the lie that they were a happily married couple, Violet said, "It is merely the kindness he tries to keep hidden."

Mrs. Mitchell scoffed, adding salt to the pot of stew. "Is that what you believe? He takes care of you because of his kindness?"

Violet paused in her ablutions and glanced back at Christian. Though he faced her window, he had not once attempted to look inside. Perhaps the light was such that he could not see her in the bath, but as foolish as it sounded, she wanted him to at least want to see her nude. Oh! She looked away, disgusted at her own thoughts when he was simply being honorable.

"Yes, I fear he doesn't . . ." How could she explain to this woman that her own supposed husband didn't want her? What a predicament. They were not truly married. He was behaving the way any gentleman should. "I fear that my convalescence has dampened his attraction."

The woman glanced at her again and then out the window. "You don't see how he gazes upon you, lass, when you're not looking. I think he keeps his hands away because he fears hurting you."

This time Violet blushed with pleasure. Her right side was covered in blue and purple bruises, and he did carry guilt even though she had told him the accident and her injuries were not his fault. Could it be true? "Perhaps."

"Here, let's stand up and give you a rinse." She came over and helped Violet rise, pouring warm water down her body. Then she handed her a length of toweling before bringing over a fresh bolt of white cotton fabric for more bandages.

"Might we leave them off tonight? They're uncomfortable for sleeping, and I really am feeling much better."

"All right. Perhaps I can convince Dr. Mitchell that the sling will be enough for the evening. We can wrap you back up in the morning if he insists." She placed the fabric on the table and retrieved a cotton nightgown, helping it over Violet's head. It was clearly borrowed from the older woman, as it hung loose with the wide neck falling off her shoulders. It would be fine for bed, however, because Violet could arrange it around herself.

"It is not my place to say . . ." began Mrs. Mitchell as they walked back toward the stairs together with the woman's strong arm around Violet's hips to support her. Everyone seemed to think that her legs were broken.

Instinct told her this would be about Christian. "Please feel that you can speak freely, Mrs. Mitchell. I so appreciate all that you have done for us."

The woman brought them to a pause at the bottom of the stairs. "I have something that might help. Please do not mention it to Dr. Mitchell. He's a bit more traditional in his thinking than I."

Intrigued beyond measure, Violet nodded. "Of course. It will be our secret."

The woman gave a brisk nod and walked through the swinging door that led from the kitchen to the front of the house. Leaving the door propped open, her purposeful steps took her to the room at the very front, which Violet had been told was Dr. Mitchell's office where he occasionally saw patients. The woman disappeared inside. Shaking her head at the odd exchange, Violet helped herself up the stairs. She would not be an invalid any longer. She was convinced that one reason Christian had pulled back from her was that he found the waiting on her tedious. She couldn't blame him.

"You should not have attempted the stairs by yourself," Mrs. Mitchell scolded a few minutes later when she found Violet upstairs running a brush through her hair. She used her right arm, testing its ability after being confined for several days.

"I am much better. I made it up with no problems." On that note, it was time to start exerting her independence again. "I think I shall come down for supper tonight and eat with everyone else."

"If you insist, and Dr. Mitchell approves." Pursing her lips in mock disapproval, Mrs. Mitchell walked over and held out her hand. Violet could just make out the edge of a small tin.

"What is this?"

"Shh . . ." Mrs. Mitchell glanced toward the door as if she expected them to be discovered in their scheme—whatever it was—at any moment. "It strikes me that your new husband might be concerned about . . . you know . . ." She glanced meaningfully at Violet's midsection and offered her hand again.

"No, I am afraid I don't follow." Violet took the tin from her. It was small and rectangular with a hinged blue lid and the words *Prophylactic, 1 treatment*, written in black ink.

"Getting you with child," she whispered. "He might prefer you not in that condition until you are more recovered. I must say it would be a kind opinion, and I agree. You have plenty of time to begin a family when you are fully healed."

Violet had felt her face heating with every word spoken. "This is . . . this is for me? To prevent a child?"

The woman smiled kindly but shook her head. "For him, lass. I know you are but newly married. Has he not lain with you yet?"

Violet shook her head, her mouth too dry to speak for a moment. Swallowing, she said, "No . . . we were waiting. The truth is that we haven't known each other very long."

Mrs. Mitchell sighed in approval. "He is an indulgent man. Take your time, then. But when you are ready, give the sheath to him. I suspect he will know its purpose." She patted Violet's hand and left her alone.

Violet stared at the little tin, still quite uncertain what it was that she held. She only knew that it was naughty. It had to be if it was meant to prevent conception and she was forbidden to speak of it to Dr. Mitchell. Placing the brush down on the table, she brought the tin closer, as if it were a treasure she had found that warranted further investigation. Her breath caught as she worked the lid open. The unmistakable scent of vulcanized rubber met her nose, though it was faded and not very harsh. The item within was impossible to make out. It was rolled and the color of parchment.

If it was a sheath, then perhaps it was meant to go on that male part of him.

That thought set her imagination down a path from which there was no return. Her entire body warmed, and she noticed the way the fabric of her nightgown scraped against her skin, as if her nerve endings had become highly sensitive. She had thought of what it would be like to lie with him many times in the carriage. Perhaps it was possible . . . if he still wanted her. If she could make him look at her as he had those nights at the inn.

A door downstairs closed with a bang, and a male voice filled the kitchen. Her heart fluttered in her chest like a wild thing looking for escape. She could not allow Christian to catch her with this, not yet. Hurrying to the bed, she shoved it under her pillow.

Chapter 16

❦

He was depravity and his name was Lord
Lucifer.

V. LENNOX, *AN AMERICAN AND THE*
LONDON SEASON

Christian paced in the darkened kitchen, unable to convince himself that he could return to the bedroom they shared and everything would be as normal. He could not believe that because there was no truth to it. Everything had changed. He had seen her nude, and the sight of her had held him captive the rest of the day.

The sun had come out today—a rare and welcome sight—so he had suggested a game of chess with the good physician outside while Violet bathed. His disreputable mind had kept imagining the scene of her bath, but outside and away from her it didn't matter. He was not physically close enough to act on his baser impulses. Impulses that were growing stronger every day. It was to the point where he made certain he awoke before her in the morning, simply to avoid the issue of her having to witness the inevitable morning cockstand he could not seem to control.

But today, things had gone further, almost out of his hands. The bright sun had obscured the window, hiding the scene he knew was unfolding inside. However, he had happened to glance up when she rose from the bath. The very moment a cloud had drifted across the sun. For a single moment that would play itself over and over in his mind from now into eternity, she had stood there gloriously nude. Her breasts high on her chest, their nipples tight as rosebuds, the curve of a hip, the dark triangle of hair between her legs, he had seen all of her. It lasted the length of a heartbeat before Mrs. Mitchell covered her with a towel. After, he had been forced to pretend that all was the same as the moment that had preceded it.

But he was changed. The lustful brute inside him, the one that he had been able to keep a rein on, had broken free. It had taken every ounce of self-control he possessed to stay seated and not go find her in the kitchen and carry her to bed. The meal had been a laughable display. Him sitting there, eating and barely tasting his food, while scenting the lavender from her skin all the way across the table. Though she was completely covered by a nightdress that could have wrapped around her two or three times, and a dressing gown that was tied up tight, concealing her from neck to foot, his lustful gaze still lingered, knowing that she was naked beneath her clothes, unencumbered by corset or petticoat or drawers. He had but to slide his hand up her leg to find her hot and damp for him.

He took the final draw on his cigarette, closing his eyes as the smoke burned through his lungs. Usually, the exhale left him more relaxed, putting a soft edge on things. It was why he had immediately walked to town after the chess game to acquire the luxury, his own cigarettes having been destroyed in the ravine. The absence of them hadn't bothered him until now. He typically only enjoyed the occasional smoke after dinner. But now he needed something, anything, to save him from his own impulses.

Tossing the remnant of his cigarette into the cold hearth, he walked toward the stairs like a condemned man approached the gallows. He could not stay down here all night. She would almost certainly be asleep by now anyway. The lamp on the bedside table was turned low, and her chest rose and fell in an even rhythm. He breathed a sigh of relief and quietly began to disrobe down to his drawers. He reached for the nightshirt borrowed from Dr. Mitchell but decided against it. He rarely slept clothed, and the shirt was scratchy and served to keep him awake. Though he had worn it their first few nights here, there was hardly a need since she was asleep and he would be dressed before she awoke in the morning. Abandoning it, he slipped into bed, thankful she faced away from him on her uninjured side. He could not look upon her beauty tonight. It was too much to ask of himself. He laid as close to the edge of the bed as he dared to keep space between them and reached up to turn the lamp down.

"Wait." Her voice was raspy with sleep, and he cursed himself for waking her.

"Do you need something?" he asked, careful to keep his gaze straight ahead on the ceiling.

She shifted, pulling the blanket taut across his hips. Traitorous creature that it was, his cock stirred at the sensation. He closed his eyes and forced out an even breath.

"Do you think you might rub my lower back? I've been abed too long. It aches." She gave him a shy smile over her shoulder.

"Should I retrieve Mrs. Mitchell?" Please say yes. Touching her would be too torturous.

"No."

"All right," he said, his voice noticeably huskier. Clearing his throat, he sat up. "Do you think you can lean forward?"

She complied, sliding onto her belly. He stared at her small body swathed in yards of cotton fabric and wondered how he could find this so arousing. The outline of her hips and the swell of her arse drew his gaze, and he busied himself by settling the blanket in his lap, lest she see how much he already ached for her. Without the bandages, he had no way of knowing by feel where her bruises were, so he said, "Guide my hands. I don't wish to hurt you."

"Lower," she said when he pressed fingertips to the middle of her back. "Lower," she urged, guiding him downward. "There."

He started softly, pressing the pads of his fingers to the muscles he felt. She sighed, a sound that vibrated down his spine, settling with a flickering and tightening heat in his scrotum. He shifted as his blood thickened like honey in his veins. This was too much to ask of him. He was already drunk on arousal and need. It swam through his head like whisky, making his thoughts give way to instinct and consequences appear murky. His hands roamed lower, until his fingers touched the softness of her bottom. Gratification roared through him, but he forced his hands higher back where they belonged. She didn't seem to notice.

"More pressure, if you please," she said.

Certain all the time that he would hurt her, he pressed down, but she only hummed in pleasure. It was a sound he heard with his cock. Christ! He closed his eyes tightly as his blood roared in his ears. Softness met his hands again, his palms this time. He squeezed, and his hips gave a barely there thrust in automatic response as he imagined sinking into her tight, hot grip.

"Christian." Her aching whisper forced him to open his eyes.

He held handfuls of her perfect arse. It took a herculean effort, but he managed to release her. "Violet." He meant to apologize but could only repeat her name. He had never been this undisciplined with a woman, especially one he was meant to leave alone. He would not ruin her—while it might be too late if people ever found out about this jaunt, he would know that he had not corrupted her.

Surprising him, she turned over and took his wrist with her left hand. As if she sensed his need to run, she said, "Don't leave."

He shook his head, unable to speak for the moment as he saw his own desire reflected back at him in her face. "I have to," he finally managed, his voice tortured and deep.

"Stay." Through eyes that had somehow become disconnected from his body, he watched her guide his hand back to her body. She led it to her left breast, the nipple already puckered. Despite his intention to remove his touch, he caressed her instead, testing the weight in his palm and letting his thumb brush over the tip. Her breath came faster in response, and she never took her wide brown eyes from his face.

"This isn't right," he said, even though his thumb continued to disobey him, circling around her nipple before brushing over the extended tip. He longed to see beneath her nightdress. "I have no claim to you."

"Does that matter? I want this. Isn't that enough?"

He dragged his gaze from her breast to her face. "You don't know what you're asking for."

She frowned, her jaw clenching. "I'm not a child, as you can plainly see. I know what I want. And I know what you want. Now, anyway."

"What do you mean?"

"You've been treating me like a sister. I thought perhaps I had misread your earlier interest."

"A sister?" He was incredulous. How could she possibly think he had treated her that way? He gently tugged her nipple, drawing a gasp from her. "I do not think of you as a sister."

"Then why have you been so distant?"

"Because I have been trying to keep my hands off you." Which is what he should be doing now. With a groan, he finally managed to do just that and pull his hand away.

She sat up, and the nightdress slipped off her shoulder.

His gaze lingered on her creamy skin before he managed to look away. He had to leave and find somewhere private where he could momentarily assuage his need for her.

"But I don't want you to keep your hands off me. I want your touch, Christian." Her voice was breathy, and it shook with her want.

He groaned, clenching his teeth in an effort to keep himself in check. He did not deserve to touch her. "You do not know what I've done."

"I don't care—"

He reached up and covered her mouth with his fingers before she could entice him further. "Violet." But he only became caught up in the sight of his thumb pressed against the pink of her lips. He traced over her bottom lip, savoring the silken feel. "You would hate me if you knew all I've done."

She smiled and he watched, helpless to resist as she bit the pad of his thumb then soothed it with her tongue. When she sucked the tip into her mouth, he groaned again, imagining the sucking of her tight body around his cock. His head swimming in arousal, he could no longer resist. He took his hand from her, only to fall over her, his mouth devouring hers as he held his weight above her with his palms on either side.

She made a sound of triumph deep in her throat as she kissed him back. Her kiss was wet, eager, and wildly inexperienced but intoxicating nonetheless, perhaps because of all of those things, coupled with the fact that this was Violet and he had spent endless hours wanting her, longing to touch her, smelling her scent, listening to her voice. He knew each intonation; the ones that told when she was happy or annoyed or teasing. Somehow in their time together he had learned her like he had never bothered to learn anyone else.

The need for breath made him release her lips, only to drag his mouth down the column of her throat, tasting the salt of her skin. She moaned when he bit her earlobe. The

sound fueled something visceral deep within him. Something that only understood need and want and possession.
He dragged the sleeve of her nightdress down, revealing
her breast to his greedy eyes. Her nipple was drawn tight
and pink.

"Please," she whispered.

He vaguely wondered if she knew what she asked him
for, but just as quickly, the thought was overtaken by instinct. He tongued the distended tip before pulling it into
his mouth and sucking until her back arched off the bed. As
he worked, he shifted onto his side so that he would not
hurt her with his weight, giving his hand the freedom to
pull her nightdress up. Her legs were toned and firm, but
softened a bit when he reached her thighs. She did not hesitate to part them for him.

"Christ," he whispered when his fingertips brushed the
soft hair guarding her sex, dipping between her lips to find
her wet and hot. "Violet."

He rose up only to have her grasp his shoulders as if she
thought he was leaving. "Shh, I'm not going anywhere."

She settled, her palms moving to his front, roving over his
chest and down to his stomach. He shifted away when she
would have roamed lower. He wouldn't last if she touched
him, and he had determined that this would be about her. He
would give her pleasure while taking none for himself. It
would be his penance for daring to touch her, a right he did
not have because he had tried to steal her for himself.

Dipping his fingertip in her honeyed heat, he drew it up
to her clitoris, using her own lubricant to glide the pad of
his finger around the swollen flesh in a teasing circle. She
gasped, her eyes closed tight as she arched into his touch.
God she was beautiful. Her cheeks were flushed, and her
lips parted on breathless sighs as he touched her. He massaged his finger over the sensitive nub, savoring her cry as
he found the pressure she liked best. Her fists clenched in
the bedding, as she gave herself over to him.

Unable to wait any longer, he moved the finger downward to press inside her. She was so tight and white-hot that he stifled a groan, his erection demanding that he take her. Slowly thrusting in a move that urged her body to give way to him, he widened her until he could slip a second finger inside. It was as much as she could comfortably take, so he gently moved them in and out, curling them upward, fucking her with a tenderness he hadn't known he was capable of, afraid that anything harder would rob her of her innocence.

Swallowing thickly, he watched as her head thrashed back and forth, eyes still closed tight against the pleasure. Placing a kiss to her breast, he scraped his teeth over her nipple, before moving down her body. If this was his one chance to touch her, he would do it properly. He would leave her knowing her taste. The nightdress had worked its way up around her hips. He used his free hand to help it further along, baring her to his gaze. She was exquisite, pink and swollen, her lips parting around his fingers. A wave of raw tenderness rose up inside him.

"You're beautiful," he said, his voice thick and unrecognizable. He didn't realize he had spoken aloud until she gasped and stiffened. Her eyes were wide in shock that he was gazing upon her, but her pupils were so dilated with passion that her irises appeared black. Grinning at her, he held her gaze as he lowered his head. Despite his reputation, it seemed she hadn't fathomed such wickedness. Dear God, the things he could show her if given the chance. His thumb ceased its easy rhythm around her clitoris to be replaced with his tongue. He groaned at her sea salt taste, lapping at her to get more of it as he continued to fuck her with his fingers. She threw her head back, her cry reaching his ears as her pussy clenched around his fingers, rippling and tightening with her orgasm. He groaned again as he drank of her pleasure, grinding his cock against the mattress to help ease the ache.

This one night would not be enough. A lifetime of nights wouldn't be enough of her. He eased his fingers from her and lapped at her until she fell against the mattress, languid and sated. His own need, however, coursed through his body, urging him to take her and fill her with his seed. Tearing himself away, he sat on the edge of the bed, fisting his hands at his sides as he tried to keep himself from reaching for her.

"Christian." She fumbled for him, her hand grasping for his thigh but touching his erection instead. They both gasped.

Chapter 17

❦

The plot had worked so well that Lord Lucifer should have felt triumph, for Miss Hamilton was his; but for all the joy, the bitter taste of his own betrayal lingered.

V. LENNOX, *AN AMERICAN AND THE LONDON SEASON*

Violet stared at the length of him barely hidden beneath the white linen of his drawers. The actual flesh of him was obscured but clearly defined in outline. He was both larger and harder than she had imagined possible for that part of him. Testing her newfound knowledge, she squeezed him gently. A groan sounded from deep in his chest.

"You do not play fair." His eyes were hooded and dark with animal intensity. She shivered at the hot weight of them.

"I don't mean to play a game. I simply want to give you pleasure as you gave to me."

"Violet." The way he said her name, breathless and with a husk that promised wickedness, sent a frisson of longing pulsing through her. Her intimate flesh began to ache again. "You know this is not right."

"Why is it wrong?" For the life of her she couldn't remember why it was supposed to be. "Would it be right had I stayed and wed Lord Ware? Would it be right to be sharing this night with him?"

He growled. Growled! The rough sound vibrated through her in a way that was as pleasurable as his touch. "Never say his name to me."

Moving up fully onto her knees, she closed the distance between them until she was at his side, so close his body heat warmed her. The movement pulled at the nightgown, which already revealed one breast, to reveal her other. His gaze caught on the newly exposed peak. She knew that she should feel embarrassed. Once, Teddy had become over amorous and pulled at the lacing of a medieval gown she had worn to a costume ball, nearly revealing her. She had almost died of embarrassment and hadn't met his gaze for the rest of the evening. But things were different with Christian. She felt a little shy, but never uncomfortable or ashamed.

"You didn't answer the question." Empowered by his desire, she released him only to run her thumb over his bottom lip, which still glistened from how he had licked at her. She had never known such a thing was possible.

He hissed out a breath, baring his teeth before licking at her thumb. Desire slammed into her full force as he suckled her, the hot heat of his mouth closing around her. How was it possible to want this so much when he had only recently left her sated?

"It would always be wrong for him to have you. For anyone to have you."

She cupped his cheek, loving the scrape of stubble against her palm, but not as much as she had adored it rasping over her body as he had kissed her. "I see. Then I am to remain untouched and unhad for the rest of my life?"

He groaned and rose to his feet, pacing away from her and adjusting the front of his drawers. His broad shoulders shone pale gold in the low light of the lamp, his muscles flexing under the silk of his skin. She longed to turn up the light to see him better but feared that would send him running, so she didn't move.

"That is not what I meant," he said. He turned to face her, running his fingers through his hair and sending the waves rioting.

She could only admire the breadth of his chest, each pectoral muscle clearly defined. Her palms itched to explore them, and she wanted to curl her fingers in the sprinkling of dark hair that narrowed over the flat plains of his belly. There was an indentation bisecting them that she ached to trace. The hair grew denser just below his navel, arrowing toward his low-slung drawers, half-opened now. She gasped when she saw it. The tip of him rose up, thick and pink, protruding over the top of the linen. The ache between her thighs increased, as if knowing he was meant to be inside her to assuage it.

He saw her take notice and kept his arms up, fingers laced behind his head, as if basking in her study of him. After a moment, he said, "I won't ruin you."

Blinking herself free of the mesmerizing sight of him, she forced her gaze back to his face. "Ruin me? But surely you know that I am already ruined if anyone finds out about our time together. What we do tonight won't change that."

"You are correct, but I will know. I might have touched you, but I didn't take your innocence. I didn't dirty you with my touch."

Her body recoiled before her brain had time to understand what he meant. She flinched as if stricken, gathering up the voluminous folds of her borrowed nightgown to cover herself. "You think me dirty?"

"God, no." He hurried toward her but stopped short of touching her.

"But you would think so if we lie together?"

"No, not at all. I am sorry. I misspoke."

Only he hadn't misspoke at all. He had said the words. "So then if I told you that I had lain with another man before you, you would think me dirty in that case only?" Hurt bloomed in her chest.

"I would never think that of you. There are others who might."

"I thought you were . . . different. I thought you understood that a woman's worth doesn't depend on the state of her chastity or the number of men she's had. You have had women before. Countless ones, if the gossips can be believed. I never once thought you dirty or unworthy."

"Of course you didn't. You are better than them. But there are others who would never deign to be in the same room with you if they knew you let me touch you. You might even feel yourself dirty if you knew all."

"There are those who would not deign to be in the same room with me even now, because my last name is Crenshaw. I don't care about those people. I only care about you, but I can see I was—"

"Bloody hell!" He turned away from her, frustration holding his body taut. "This is why I am rarely honorable. It never goes well."

She needed to be away from him. Still smarting from the pain of his senseless words, she gathered her nightgown once more and got to her feet. She would sleep downstairs, in the kitchen if it meant she could be alone. She brushed past him, her feet bare on the cold wood floor, but he seized her, his fingers tightening on the back of her neck as he dragged her back to him.

"Forgive me?" he whispered into her hair as his arms went around her, cradling her against his chest, all the while conscious of her wounded side. His fingers massaged the back of her scalp as he placed kisses to her unmarred temple. "Please. You are precious to me, and my words were thoughtless."

Precious to him? She hid her face against his chest, uncertain what to make of that. Joy lightened her pain, but the ache still lingered. "Then why would you say it?"

"Because I am a fool who can be careless with his words." He touched her chin, inviting her to look up at him.

After a moment, she relented. She desperately wanted him to be the man she thought he was. His eyes were warm and solemn, filling her with hope. "Please know that there could be a hundred men in your past and I would still admire you and hold you in high regard. I would still want you."

He did still want her. She could feel that his desire had not waned. It throbbed thick and solid against her belly. Her own body responded by clenching in anticipation. "And yet you hesitate to accept what I give you freely?"

He took in a breath, pain crossing his features. "It is because I lied to you. I've been lying to you." His fingertips traced over her face, skating around her stitches and near the edge of the bruise that still lingered at her right temple. "I have no right to accept what you offer."

Reaching up to cup his cheek, she touched his lips with her thumb. He kissed it, and her heart swelled with love for him, even as her belly swirled with anxiety at what he would reveal. *You might even feel yourself dirty if you knew all.* "What was your lie?"

"The truth is that I offered to accompany you north because I hoped to gain your agreement to marry me. I hoped that if we spent time alone together that you would come to see me as a better choice. You would see that I would offer you a certain amount of freedom, freedom you would not find with Ware and men of his ilk."

She shook her head, stunned that the entire time she had been falling in love with him and wondering of his feelings, he had been hoping she would marry him. Falling in love. She had never put such a fine phrase to it, but she understood now that that was what was happening. She loved him. "Why did you never ask me?"

"Because the more time I spent with you, the more I came to admire you. The more I saw you as a woman with your own hopes and dreams. I felt guilt that I had presumed to attempt to force your affection." His voice became self-deprecating and bitter. "I cannot claim that I allowed feelings of conscience to sway me, however. I had planned to ask for your hand on the night of the accident after we stopped for the evening."

"You wanted to marry me?" She could not get over the fact that his thoughts had so aligned with her own.

He nodded, his thumb brushing across her cheekbone. "I am hardly any better than Ware."

"And yet you are."

"No. I caused this." His gaze touched her bruise. "I am worse."

She finally allowed herself to touch him. Her hands drifted over his shoulders and down his chest. She would have sworn his skin rippled in pleasure at the contact. His heart beat a fast rhythm beneath her palm. Biting her bottom lip to shore up her courage, she allowed her other hand to drift downward over the muscles of his belly and to the manhood jutting up against her. A drop of pearly liquid leaked from the tip. She touched it with her thumb, marveling at how silky it felt as she spread it over the head. On impulse, she brought her thumb to her lips and licked the salty taste of him.

"Jesus, Violet." His hands moved down to her hips as he pressed himself against her belly. His entire body trembled with restraint.

"What would you say if I said that I still want to lie with you, even after this confession?" she teased him.

"I would say that it was still unwise. There could be consequences, and I would not have you forced to marry me, despite my initial intentions."

She grinned and swung out of his grasp, privately thrilled with how his hands hesitated in letting her go. Walking slowly but with purpose, she reached beneath her pillow and removed the tin. "What if I said there could be no consequences?"

His brow furrowed as he stared at the tin. As realization dawned, he came around the bed and took it from her.

Pushing the lid open, he asked, "How did you get this?" A good bit of awe tinged his voice.

"Mrs. Mitchell." If she had said the Devil himself, he could not have looked more surprised.

"On the bed. Now."

His voice was growly again, sending sparks of anticipation skittering over her. Laughing, she climbed into bed, half watching as he pushed his drawers down his powerful thighs and put the sheath on himself. So that's how it worked. There was no time to consider further because he reached for the neckline of the nightgown and pulled it down past her hips. When she raised them, he pulled it completely off her, dropping it on the end of the bed. Before she could say anything, he rose over her, blocking out the light as he took her mouth in a desperate kiss. She kissed him back, vaguely aware of how his hips moved into the space between her thighs. She gasped into his mouth when she felt his erection nudging at her belly.

"I shall try to go slow." He ate at her neck, his teeth scraping only to soothe with his tongue. "But I have wanted you for so long." Indeed, his whole body trembled with his need. Then his mouth found her nipples, moving from one to the other to lavish them both with equal attention. As he worked, his fingers found her core, ready and aching. Her body, already fond of his fingers, opened for him readily as he pushed two inside. She closed her eyes, pleasure cascading through her as he moved them in a gentle but firm rhythm that matched his tugs on her nipple. All too soon it wasn't enough. Her body twisted and burned with a need more powerful.

"Christian?" She didn't quite know what she asked, only that the ache he teased demanded more. She needed to be filled.

"Violet." His voice was above her. She opened her eyes to see him staring down at her, a fine edge of pain on his face. "I need to fuck you."

The crude words should have been shocking. She had only ever heard that word in jokes the workmen would shout at one another at Crenshaw Iron. But when Christian said them, they transferred his desperate need to her, so that she shared his fervor. "Yes. Please."

He grinned, revealing the dimple that she so loved. The head of his erection pressed against her womanhood, sliding inside her the smallest bit until he met resistance. But it was only a tease. "I don't want to hurt you. You cannot bear my weight in this position."

No! Had he only meant to torment her?

"Here." He moved off her to stand beside the bed, and she instinctively grasped at him. Gently taking hold of her hips, he guided her to stand before him. Turning her away from him, he ran his hands down her back in a soothing stroke and bent her over the bed. "Let me know if this is uncomfortable."

She didn't know what to say. It wasn't entirely comfortable, but then she didn't know what to expect. His hands moved down her body again, slipping between her breasts and the blanket to pluck at her nipples. Darts of pure need shot directly to her core, making her body clench around emptiness. "Christian."

His soft breath of laughter touched her a second before he kissed the shell of her ear. One of his strong hands moved to grasp her hip, while the other pressed into the bed beside her to hold his weight. "Spread your legs," he whispered.

She obeyed, feeling his hard thighs move between hers. She should feel bare and vulnerable to him, spread as she was and his for the taking, but she loved the feeling of being under his power. He held her hip as he notched himself and gently pushed inside, not stopping when he met resistance. The pressure was incredible. She squeezed her eyes shut and gripped the blanket as he pulled out only to push in another inch. It was a slow back-and-forth, until finally her passage gave way and his groan filled the room as he sank to the hilt inside her.

She felt full of him. Fuller than she had ever thought possible. A burning discomfort accompanied the feeling, but he didn't move, simply stayed still, allowing her to absorb the foreignness of his body within hers. After a moment, his hand reached between her legs, and his fingers played with her clitoris, sliding over it and teasing it as he had done earlier. Little by little, the discomfort gave way to the aching pleasure from before. She canted her hips, caught as she was between the steel of his manhood and the skill of his fingers. The pulsing ache had returned, greedy and demanding more. Except this time he was there, filling her completely, creating a new wave of intoxicating pleasure with her every movement as he nudged against a sensitive place deep inside her.

"Yes, that's it." His voice was serrated with desire. "Fuck me."

A cry tore from her lips, and she tilted her hips again, pushing back. He answered her silent plea by thrusting into her at the same time. A spark of white-hot light shot across her vision. Then he did it again, and again, moving in a controlled rhythm that matched the stroking of his hand. He attacked her with pleasure from both sides. All too soon she was trembling, her breath coming erratically as she cried out into the blankets as wave after wave of gratification broke over her.

Only then did he falter in his pace. He fell over her, holding himself off her with one hand while grabbing a handful of her hair with the other. He pulled her head back and took her mouth in a kiss, his hips losing their rhythm to become erratic and fitful. "Violet." He whispered her name over and over as he pressed his face to her shoulder. Finally, his own cry filled the room, and he found his release with short, quick thrusts of his hips.

I love you. The words tumbled over and over in her head

as she lay there with him, both of them struggling to catch their breath. She wouldn't tell him yet. It was still too soon and he was too skittish. But she would soon.

He pressed a kiss to her shoulder before rising. She could hear him pulling off the sheath as she hurried into bed, shy now that it was done. When she rolled to face him, he was climbing under the covers without having bothered to put his drawers back on. She liked that. Pulling her into his arms, he smiled down at her. "Did I hurt you? Are you injured?"

"No." The truth was that her ribs and shoulder had begun to ache, but she dared not tell him that for fear that he would refuse to touch her again. Shaking her head, she kissed his jaw, his chin, and then his mouth. He kissed her back, and when they parted, the look in his eyes was so warm and soft that she knew he loved her, too, whether he knew it or not. "You were perfect."

I will marry you. She almost said the words out loud but decided to wait, lest she scare him away. He was so intent on being honorable that he might not believe her.

He pulled the blanket up over them and settled his arms around her. "I fear for Mrs. Mitchell's sensibilities if she comes barging into our chamber in the morning."

She smiled as she imagined such a scene. Something told her Mrs. Mitchell would keep her distance come morning.

Chapter 18

He knew that when the reckoning came, it would be harsh and just.

V. Lennox, *An American and the London Season*

THE NEXT DAY
BERKELEY SQUARE

Max took in the white stone facade of the fashionable town house. It stood three windows wide and four floors tall, narrower than most other homes on the street. Despite the fact that every window boasted a window box full of pink and yellow tulips, there appeared to be no one at home. The drapes were pulled closed, and the front stoop had not been swept in days. Leaves, sticks, and other debris clung to the steps, still wet from the recent rains.

He glanced back down at the address on the note that had been delivered to him earlier that morning. "Are you certain this is forty-three?" he asked the hackney driver.

"Forty-three," the man agreed. "Shall I wait for you?" The driver did not seem particularly thrilled by the prospect. His gaze was already scanning the traffic as he readied to pull away from the curb.

"No, not necessary," said Max, stepping up onto the sidewalk, especially when he had no idea what this meeting was about or how long it would take.

He had arrived in London late last night only to find his parents not at home. They had been out at a ball, apparently enjoying themselves while their daughter was God-knew-where. His interrogation of them this morning had led to little information. They had decided to tell everyone that Violet had fallen ill and been sent to Bath to recover. The strong insinuation had been that she had succumbed to a case of nerves. Keeping her disappearance quiet and mini-mizing scandal was, regrettably, their upmost concern. In-stead of reporting her disappearance to the Metropolitan Police, they had chosen—with the help of their friends Lord and Lady Ashcroft—to hire a retired detective. Mr. Spencer was even now combing the countryside, looking for clues. The only information he had reported back to the family was that he had been unable to find Ellen Stapleton, Violet's maid who had disappeared on the same day, and that no one had reported seeing a woman matching her de-scription on any of the trains.

His father had run off to a meeting with Lord Farthing-ton, while his mother prepared for a luncheon, leaving Max to attempt to parse clues from the letter Violet had left. Thankfully, the note had arrived soon after, leading him to this address. Short and succinct and written in a feminine hand, it simply stated: *Come alone. Leave immediately. 43 Berkeley Square.*

Half believing this was someone's idea of a jest, half believing he might find Violet hiding within, he hurried up the steps and rang the bell. After several moments had passed, an ancient man in livery with stooped shoulders and bushy gray eyebrows answered the door.

"Good morning. I am Maxwell Crenshaw. Someone sent me this note." He held up the small scrap of parchment.

"Of course, Mr. Crenshaw." Without further explanation, he stepped back and allowed Max passage.

He vaguely wondered if perhaps he was being led to some nefarious purpose, but curiosity won out. Max stepped inside, declining when the butler offered to take his gloves and hat. The house was stylishly appointed in muted tones of cream, gold, and green. It wasn't overly cluttered in the way his mother preferred to decorate. Everything was orderly and minimal, but in a manner that emphasized the elegance of each item.

"With whom am I to—"

"Follow me, Mr. Crenshaw." The butler turned, leading him down the corridor beyond the stairs. A single light fixture lit their way, leaving the rooms they passed in shadow. Finally, the little man stepped into the room in the back. "Mr. Crenshaw," he announced to whomever waited there.

Max turned the corner to see a woman standing before the cold hearth. She wore a charcoal gray traveling costume embroidered in maroon, complete with hat and gloves. A traveling case sat on the floor near him by the door. He couldn't tell if she had only just arrived, or if he was catching her as she was leaving. She was stunningly pretty in a very untouchable sort of way. Delicate nose, high cheekbones, and pointy chin. Buttery blond hair pinned up in an elaborate roll beneath a hat that perched high on her forehead. Her eyes were a light color, but he could not tell if they were blue, green, or gray from the distance between them. He could only tell that they were expressive, shining with intelligence and censure as they looked him over. Apparently, he had been duly inspected and found lacking.

"Good morning, Miss . . ."

"Lady Helena March." She spoke in the crisp, clipped tones of someone who had already decided something and was growing impatient for everyone to reach the same conclusion. "You are late, Mr. Crenshaw."

The clock on the mantel behind her showed half past ten. He glanced to the butler only to find the little man had abandoned him to face the hoyden alone. "Did we have an engagement I missed?" he asked, walking farther into the room. The drapes were open to reveal a small but neatly kept walled garden that faced the mews beyond. Gray morning light filled the space. "My apologies. Back home we use calling cards and invitations, not cryptic messages left unsigned." He held up the note, and her lashes flickered in acknowledgment of his pique. "I'll have to become accustomed to the way you do things here."

"Thank you for coming. I regret that I could not reveal more in my note, but I could hardly take the chance that someone might see it."

"Someone? Do you mean my parents?"

Her pretty, pink mouth turned down in a frown as she thought over her answer. Finally, she nodded. "Yes, I regret to say."

Interesting. "Lady Helena March, if I recall correctly, you are the one my parents claim accompanied my sister to Bath."

"I think we both know that story is contrived." Her eyes flashed in temper. They were blue. Blue like morning glories. "And Lady Helena is sufficient."

"Do you know where Violet is?"

"No, but I have a good idea. If you please, we should get going." She gestured to her travel bag. "We can talk on the way."

"We're going together?" He glanced to the bag and back to her.

She glared at him as if she wanted to bodily pick him up and tuck him into a carriage herself. "Yes, we have no choice. Huxley has sent for the carriage to be brought round."

"Lady Helena, I don't mean to be rude, but I must insist on you telling me what the hell is going on before I go anywhere with you."

Her lips pursed in irritation, she rang the bell that sat on a small, spindly table next to the delicate-looking settee. Huxley appeared as if he had been hovering outside the room. "Please have a pot of tea brought in."

Huxley nodded and slinked back out again as soundlessly as he had entered. With a sigh, she tugged off her gloves in efficient movements—he noticed her fingers were long and slender—and perched on the edge of the settee as if she intended to go charging off at the slightest provocation. "Please, have a seat," she offered belatedly, indicating the adjacent chair.

Max eyed the piece of delicate furniture warily. At six feet three inches, he wasn't a small man, and he ran solid rather than wiry.

Noting his scrutiny, she said, "A Chippendale original from 1773."

Uncertain what he was meant to do with that information, he simply said, "Impressive."

"I meant that it has held countless men, most of them with conceit considerably larger than your own."

He frowned, uncertain if he was meant to take that as a compliment or if he had been handed the most well-placed insult he had ever received. He mulled it over as he sat, gratified when the chair did not so much as utter a creak of protest.

After he was settled, she asked, "Mr. Crenshaw, could I speak plainly with you?"

"You haven't already?" If this was her being nice, he would truly hate to be the object of her wrath.

She nodded, and he noticed how long and graceful her neck was. "Perhaps I owe you an apology. I am afraid that I have made assumptions that are possibly unfair."

"What sort of assumptions?" He noted she only mentioned the potential existence of an apology without actually issuing one.

She took a moment to answer, looking him over as if

trying to divine his character from his face. Instead of answering his question, she asked one of her own. "Do you know of your parents' plans for Violet, and if so, what do you make of them?"

"If you are asking me if I support their plan to marry her to this earl or viscount or whatever he is, then no, I do not. I was here in London only weeks ago to save August from a similar fate. Believe me, I have better things to do with my life than spend it continuously crossing the Atlantic Ocean to save my sisters. When I find Violet, I am taking her home with me and to hell with their marriage plans. Does that answer your question?"

Instead of being offending by his plain speaking, she actually smiled, a charming little uptilt of her lips that seemed more mysterious than joyful. "I could not agree more. I was beyond shocked when I heard the rumors that he had made an offer and been accepted. I hoped I was wrong, but then Violet confirmed it to me."

"When did you last see her?" Both his sisters had mentioned Lady Helena to him in their letters home, but he hadn't known how deeply their affections for her ran. If Violet had taken this woman into her confidence about the engagement, then perhaps she had shared something of her plans with her.

"She visited me the day before she left. That's when she told me of Lord Ware's attempt on her."

"His what?" His voice came out harsher than he had intended.

She blinked at him but did not seem overly perturbed by the outburst. Waving a hand, she said, "He came to visit and tried to get her alone so they would be caught together. She was able to thwart him, but in hindsight, I think it was the impetus for her plan."

That fucking bastard. After he found Violet, Max would find Ware and make sure he had a few minutes alone with the man.

"When she came, she brought a Gladstone bag and asked me to keep it until she retrieved it. She said it contained copies of her manuscripts and she needed a safe place to store them."

"You didn't think that odd?" he asked.

"Now, yes. I suppose at the time I thought it strange, but I really didn't think much of it. I was packing and our visit was cut short. You see, I was leaving the next morning for my cottage in Somerset. My housekeeper there had fallen ill. She's elderly and meant a great deal to my husband. I had to see to her care personally."

Huxley returned bearing a tray with tea and cookies. As she filled their cups, Max found himself watching her, mesmerized by the graceful movements she had undoubtedly performed hundreds of times. He shook his head no to her offer of sugar and milk. He didn't know why the idea of her having a husband surprised him. Because of her bearing, she seemed older than August, perhaps closer to his own age. Of course, she would be married. The knowledge caused a strange heaviness in his chest.

"Thank you," he said, accepting the cup and saucer from her. "My condolences on your housekeeper."

Her brows drew together as she brought her own cup to her lips. "Oh, she's made a full recovery."

But she had used the past tense; he was certain he hadn't misheard her. Did that mean she was a widow? "About the visit?" he prompted.

"Yes. According to Huxley, Violet retrieved the bag the day she left."

"You mentioned you might know where she had gone." He took a sip of his tea, the hot liquid coating his tongue.

"Yes, but I'm afraid I must have your word that you will allow me to accompany you before I tell you."

He grinned at that, imagining being confined in a carriage with her and her sharp tongue as they tracked Violet down. "And why would I do that?"

"Because you are a man of honor, I hope, and also because you hold great affection for your sister. Anyone can see that."

His grin broadened. "And why would you insist on coming along? Don't you have . . ." He glanced around, uncertain exactly what it was she did with herself every day. "Ladyish things to do?"

She narrowed her eyes at him. "I have plenty to do, but I am setting it all aside because I care deeply for Violet. There is no telling in what situation we might discover her, and she will be in need of a soft shoulder, not your, frankly"—she glanced at his shoulders—"brutish ones."

He was a brute now, was he? She was the one issuing edicts and commands. Gritting his teeth, he said, "Fine. We will go together. Now tell me what you know."

She nodded, accepting his word. "I believe she may have left in the company of the Earl of Leigh. He was a friend of my husband's."

The name had a ring of familiarity about it, but he couldn't place it.

"You might know of him. He is a close friend of Rothschild's. They own Montague Club along with Mr. Jacob Thorne. He seems to have disappeared around the same time as Violet."

Ah, now he remembered. "Why do you suspect a connection?"

She swallowed and glanced down at her tea. "I saw them kiss at a ball."

He tensed. "You don't think he forced her?"

"No." She shook her head, emphatic in her denial. "I think it is more that he seduced her, or perhaps he was even forthright in his offer. He can be . . . charismatic with the fairer sex when he so chooses."

"You think Violet fell under the spell of this scoundrel?"

She shrugged a delicate shoulder. "I know nothing with

certainty, but I believe it possible. There is a rumor that he approached your father for Violet's hand and was rejected."

"Why would someone think that?"

"To be fair, the rumor is that he approached with the intention of courting Violet. He was seen leaving the home, and with no other known business with the Crenshaws, tongues wagged. I am the one who made the leap to marriage because I saw the kiss."

Max dropped his cup back into its saucer and placed both on the table. His parents had not mentioned that once in their morning talk. Had the detective, Mr. Spencer, even considered that connection? Anger drove him to his feet. "Where would he take her?"

"To marry her in Scotland, I assume. Your family is fairly notorious here, and it would be known they do not consent to the marriage. Perhaps Scotland offers a refuge if the marriage is challenged."

"To Gretna Green? Doesn't that only happen in Gothic novels?"

"No, not Gretna Green. There is a residency requirement now for marriage. He owns property there, and I assume coin can ease any other restrictions they may encounter."

Scotland. It would take—"How long will it take them to reach Scotland by carriage?"

"They should be there now."

"Now! Why have you done nothing up till now to stop this?"

She rose and put her hands on her hips. "Your parents were only kind enough to inform me of Violet leaving a few days ago. I wasn't even aware they were using me as her alibi until that time. Had I known earlier, I could have done something. I only returned to London yesterday, and when I called on your mother, she mentioned you would be arriving last night. Forgive me for not trusting her—someone who is highly suspect in her reasoning—with this information. I hoped you would prove vastly more rational."

He stared at her, noting—much to his annoyance—how prettily her anger flushed her cheeks. Holding his hands up in a signal for peace, he said, "Fine. It is done."

Calm again, she said, "Good. Let us leave for King's Cross. I already secured tickets for us to Edinburgh, and the train leaves in an hour."

Chapter 19

He also knew that he had come too far to care about a future without her.

V. LENNOX, *AN AMERICAN AND THE LONDON SEASON*

THE NEXT DAY

It had taken days to get the mule team over from York, but they had finally come around midday. The next several hours had been spent with beasts and men working to drag the mangled carriage from the ravine. After speaking with the foreman as the men finished, Christian could only stare at the extent of the carnage. The ceiling had been bashed in on one side, likely from one of the tree's branches. He couldn't tell which one because the day after the accident a crew of woodsmen had cut it back off the road. The windows were all broken, and one of the doors missing, as was one of the wheels. Part of the interior was twisted in on itself. Violet had been confined within that violence. Her tender, delicate body had been batted around like a child's toy at the whims of gravity and physics. It hurt his heart to imagine it.

"I never realized it was so terrible." Her voice was filled

with awe as she came up beside him, tucking herself into his side.

Despite the fact that he was perspiring from assisting the crew all afternoon, he put his arm around her, thankful that she was alive and well for him to hold. She didn't seem to mind as she burrowed into him. "I will never forgive myself for allowing that to happen to you." He pressed his lips to her forehead, but he could not look away from the spectacle.

Placing her hand on his cheek, she forced him to look down at her. "Stop that nonsense. You could no more control the rain and the state of the road than you can me. Despite what you'd have yourself believe." The sunshine in her smile seeped into him, warming him as it had for days. She wore a simple cotton dress borrowed from a girl in the village for the trip to the accident site. It was white with bits of lace at the cuffs and neckline, making her seem young, innocent, and full of life. And he had nearly robbed her of that life.

Turning to pull her fully into his arms, he pressed his forehead against hers and closed his eyes, heedless of the men who walked around them. "You might have—"

Surprising him, she leaned up on her toes and pressed a kiss to his chin. "But I didn't. Enough of that. Let's go home." Taking him in hand, she started walking toward the Mitchells' house nearly a mile away.

The bruises at the side of her face had begun to fade from blue to green. She had taken to wearing a strip of blue fabric around her head, tied up like a kerchief to cover her stitches. "I feel I'm being abducted by a pirate," he teased.

The men had begun dispersing, having done all they could for the day. A few would stay behind to take apart what could be salvaged for spare parts and scrap metal. Unfortunately, a report had to be made with the local authorities. Christian had given the name Rochester but had been met with looks that bordered on suspicion. It was likely only a matter of time before someone found out about their jaunt north, especially if they were searching for her as thoroughly as Christian would search for her if she were his.

She laughed. "You are, only you come along so willingly like a good lad, you make it too easy for me."

He joined in her laughter as they walked, him leaning heavily on his borrowed wooden cane. At the physician's insistence, she still wore a sling to support her right arm, so she lightly touched his forearm with her left hand, her fingers stroking over the bare skin revealed by his rolled-up cuffs. The afternoon's work had forced him to abandon all pretense of being a gentleman, but she didn't seem to mind.

"Your limp seems more pronounced since the accident. Are you certain you haven't injured yourself?" she asked.

It was the mad scramble to rescue her and the mile sprint to get her help that had done it, but he would never tell her that. Dr. Mitchell had said he had likely pulled a ligament and wrapped it up for him. "Merely overextended it. It will heal with time."

"You should have stayed in bed resting these past days," she said.

"I couldn't."

"Why not?" She looked up at him with her brow creased.

"Because temptation lay there." He grinned.

She colored prettily. He had yet to touch her again after taking her virginity two nights past. Last night he had merely held her, both thankful and bemoaning the fact that there were no more rubber sheaths. Their absence was the only thing that saved him from her lure. He still hadn't forgiven himself for not holding stronger against her charms. She was a woman, entitled to her own needs and wants. She had proven that point, but he was merely a man, and he would not be able to give her up if he sampled much more of her. Even now it would be like giving up his right arm to see her go. Yet, not having her would serve as his penance for daring to take her at all.

Squeezing his arm, she said in a low voice, "It need not be only temptation. You know I am yours."

He didn't know what to say to that. He would not bind her to him unfairly any more than he already had, but the longer they stayed together, the more he was tempted beyond reason.

"Christian!"

He looked up to see a familiar form on the road ahead. Jacob smiled easily and raised his hand as he walked toward them. "Jacob?"

"Your brother?" she asked.

He smiled in genuine joy. "Yes, I sent word to him after the accident." Jacob looked every bit the gentleman in a coat, hat, and gloves as they hurried to meet him.

"I come bearing gifts. A carriage and clothing for you and the miss. The physician's wife told me I would find you here, but I had no idea you had become a laborer," Jacob teased, and pulled him into a quick embrace, slapping his shoulder. When they parted, Jacob's gaze took in the scrapes and bruising on them both.

"Indeed, much has changed since I last saw you, brother," said Christian. The words were true in many ways, and Jacob's dark brown eyes widened in understanding. "I had no idea you would come yourself."

"I wanted to see for myself that you were still alive." Jacob smiled and took Violet's hand. "Miss Crenshaw, I presume?" He pressed a kiss to her knuckles.

"Mr. Thorne." She smiled. "I am so very pleased to meet you. It's wonderful to meet someone from Christian's family."

Jacob kept her hand and tucked it into the crook of his arm as he joined them on the walk back to the village. "He's told you about me, then?" His eyebrows shot up in surprise, and he gave Christian a knowing look.

"Only the disreputable bits," Christian replied, falling into line beside them.

"Ah, then allow me to take the rest of the evening to correct your likely misconception," Jacob said to Violet. "He's the disreputable one. I am the one forced to keep him in line."

"Oh dear, have I chosen the wrong brother?" she asked in mock fright.

Jacob glanced over his shoulder at that word. *Chosen.* Christian looked away, that knowing glance stirring the guilt already threatening to burn him alive and making him feel like a bastard. She had every right to believe their fucking had meant more than that, because it had felt like more than that. Christ, it had meant more than that to him. Being with her had stolen a piece of his soul that he'd never get back from her. He'd yet to figure out a way to let her know that while leaving her.

"Now that you're here, Mr. Thorne, perhaps you can shed some light on the mystery of Christian. He tells me he was terrible to you when you first met."

Jacob threw back his head and laughed. "Now that I am happy to share."

They walked back to the village in amicable conversation, with Jacob answering Violet's questions with charm. The evening was mild, so Mrs. Mitchell set up a table beneath the branches of the line of oak trees that bordered their property. After Christian had a quick wash off, the five of them enjoyed their supper there. Along with carriage and clothing, Jacob had also brought wine, which flowed freely, turning the evening into a celebration of sorts.

When it was time for Jacob to leave for York and the train station, Christian left Violet to the care of the Mitchells and rode along with his brother. They had not been in the carriage five minutes, before Jacob said, "That girl is in love with you. I hope you realize that." His voice was steady in warning.

Christian's guilt, never far from his thoughts, fanned to life. "She's infatuated, yes, but infatuation is not love."

"I have known infatuation before, brother, and that is not it. She worships you with her eyes—"

"A sure sign of infatuation," Christian interrupted him.

"She knows your faults and still holds you in high esteem."

"She has a gentle nature."

Jacob scoffed. "She worries about your injuries."

"She is a kind person." His voice took on a note of frustration, and he knew it was only his guilt, not a reaction to Jacob's assertion.

"Why do you refuse to see what is in front of you?"

"Because it's not real. Love is not real. Infatuation is real, but we all know that fades."

"All right, then. Perhaps I should put it this way. You are in love with her."

Christian shook his head, staring out at the rising twilight. Christ, it was true. He could not lie to his brother, but neither could he acknowledge it. To put words to the ache in his chest would be to open himself up to further anguish. He knew that he had never felt this way about anyone in his life. He would give his next breath to her if she needed it. He had suspected the emotion several nights in on their trip. He had known it with certainty the night he thought her dying. The night he had promised to let her go if she could but live. He had manipulated her, and almost killed her; he didn't know how they could overcome that.

"It doesn't matter how I feel," he finally said. "Her happiness comes first."

Jacob was silent for a moment across the carriage from him as Christian's words settled between them. "What does that mean?"

"It means that I am not good for her. I lied to her, manipulated her. She deserves a man with honor."

"You don't intend to go through with your plans for marriage, then?"

Christian shook his head. "No. We'll leave in a few days,

and I'll take her to where she had planned to go, and then I'll leave her alone."

"And you expect her to agree to that?"

"Of course. We'll correspond a bit, and then the time between letters will become longer, and eventually she'll find someone else to occupy her time and her thoughts."

"Do you really believe her so faithless as all that?" Jacob sounded offended for her.

"It is not that she's faithless; it is that she's infatuated. The emotion will eventually run its course." It had happened before. Despite his intention to only seek out women who did not value exclusivity, it had occasionally happened that the women he bedded wanted more than he could offer them. He had become an expert in removing himself from their unwanted attentions while leaving them feeling as if they were the ones who had grown bored. He also couldn't forget the annoying presence of Lord Lucifer in her manuscript. He was likely insignificant in the grand scheme of things, but he was there. Someone else who could swoop in and occupy her thoughts. The very idea of it grated.

"You know you love her, Christian."

Christian was silent, watching the moon rise to the tops of the trees.

After a moment, Jacob asked, "How is love not real if you yourself feel it for her?"

Another question he could not answer. "Perhaps I misspoke. I meant to say that it is not possible for anyone to love me." No one ever had. Not really.

"Is that how you're assuaging your guilt?"

Christian glared at his brother as the barb hit exactly where it had been planned.

Jacob glared back, not allowing him to look away. "You know what you're planning to do will hurt her. You hope that if you convince yourself there is no love between you then you can leave her."

"I am trying to do what is best for her, what is right." He spoke between gritted teeth.

"When you leave her, it will destroy her. How is that right?" Jacob asked, quite reasonably.

Christian didn't know anymore. Before, it had all seemed very sensible and honorable. He would help her go back to her life as she had intended it, and he would continue on a little broken for it. But Jacob was correct. That was not right, not if it hurt her. Christian really didn't know how to be honorable, did he?

"Do you truly believe that it is love she feels?" he whispered.

"From what I have observed, yes, but you could always talk to her. She seems to know her own mind."

Emotion coursed through him. He didn't quite know what it was, only that it left him bordering on elated and devastated all at the same time. Could she love him? Could she truly be happy with him, and his existence on the fringes of acceptability, and not come to resent him? His own mother had chosen to flee rather than face such a fate.

The house was quiet when he returned. He took his shoes off just inside the front door and made his way to the kitchen and then the stairs. The light was turned down, and she was sleeping. Her chestnut hair was unbound, a mass of waves around her shoulders, and her lips were parted with her breaths. The scarf had been discarded so the stitches shone, a dark, angry slash against her pale skin. He watched her while he undressed down to his drawers, placing his coat, shirt, and trousers over the back of the single chair. He couldn't look away as he slid into bed beside her. This remarkable woman could be his wife of her own choosing. He felt much the same humble awe as he had the first time he'd had this thought in the carriage back in London.

His arm went around her, conscious of her bruising. She slept without the sling, so her right hand covered his easily where it rested on her belly.

"Welcome home," she whispered, eyes still closed.

Home. He understood at that moment he had never had a proper home. The club held a suite of rooms where he rested between work. The house in Belgravia was a cold temple of his father's treasures that Christian had summarily dismantled. Amberley Park had been a prison. Blythkirk had come closest, giving him refuge between terms at school, but it had been a lonely place. Even Thea's welcome had only made him feel that her family had made room for him—and he had been glad of it—but it had never been his home.

With that awareness came insight. Never in his life had he had anyone or anything to care for. Nothing and no one had ever belonged to him. The title meant he had inherited things, buildings, emptiness that he had immediately sold away or neglected. He hadn't cared enough—and indeed hadn't the finances at any rate—to do more than keep them functional. They had all belonged to his father first, which meant they were tainted and not Christian's at all.

Violet was his, or she could be. He had bathed her, cared for her, comforted her as he never had anyone before. She had come to rely on him, and he liked that. No, that was too tame a word. He cherished it, savored having her eyes look to him to fulfill her needs. But could she belong to him as a wife belonged to her husband? Would it be fair to her?

He placed a kiss to her shoulder, the small indentation where her neck met her chest, her soft lips. She smiled at him when he pulled back. This was his home. Her. Violet. The realization was enough to steal his breath.

"I'm glad I was able to meet your brother. He's very charming."

"Not too charming, I hope," he teased her to cover the emotion coursing through him.

"He cares for you deeply. It's plain to see."

"I don't want to talk about my brother," he said, slipping his arm beneath her to gently guide her to lie on top of him, her legs falling to either side of him. Her weight felt good and right. He couldn't stop touching her, letting his palms roam down her back to her hips and up again, careful of her bruising.

"What do you wish to talk about?" she asked, stretching like a cat beneath his touch.

"Something he said to me in the carriage. I haven't been able to stop thinking about it."

Her face sobered a bit in her curiosity. "What did he say?"

His heartbeat sped until he could hear it in his head. He believed Jacob wasn't wrong. Whether her affection was mere infatuation was yet to be determined, but she believed herself in love. It was a truth he had been running from. Marrying her to suit his own needs was one thing, but marrying her knowing that his heart was in the balance was another. What would happen when her infatuation waned? But what would happen if it didn't? If it did prove to be love? His soul trembled at the simple imagining of it.

The words had to be forced out of him. "What do you envision for the future? For us?"

Her smile was back, along with a slight blush. "I hoped we might . . ." She looked away, equally reluctant to put voice to her wants.

"I love you, Violet." The phrase was foreign to him, so hearing the words and feeling them on his tongue felt odd, as if someone else was saying them. His heartbeat belonged to another, and his breath stilled. He had never felt this vulnerable before, knowing that her reaction could completely crush him.

But her gaze met his, and her smile lost its hesitance, a fine sheen coming into her eyes. "I love you, too, Christian. It feels as though I always have."

The words were like a balm to the ragged edges of his

soul. Life came back into him in a rush, filling him up with her. Jacob was right. Sending her away would only hurt her, likely worse than keeping her with him. While he had manipulated her in the beginning like the others, he was the only one who actually cared about her feelings. He had done it to help her, even if it had helped himself.

He cupped her face between his hands and leaned forward to kiss her. She opened to him, touching his tongue with hers and taking control of the kiss in a way that both surprised and stirred him. His cock, already rigid at her nearness, swelled and thickened between them. Finally, he pulled back, unable to kiss her knowing that he couldn't have more. He had neglected searching the village for a chemist and more rubber sheaths in the hopes their lack would help keep him honorable.

"Violet," he groaned, holding her hips when she ground herself against him in an unconscious movement.

"I want you inside me again." Her eyes were heavy with her need.

His hips bucked, and he used his grip on her hips to hold her as he pressed himself against her damp heat, his body once again at odds with his mind. It would be so easy to push his drawers and her nightdress aside.

"We can't." He kissed her chin to soften his words, and he couldn't stop, his lips trailing across her jaw to the perfect shell of her ear. "We don't have sheaths. But I can still give you pleasure." He would give her endless nights of pleasure.

She reached between them, taking him in hand. "Then I suppose you'll have to marry me."

He froze. One look at her face and he knew she was serious. Her eyes were hopeful and slightly wary, as if she harbored a fear that he would reject her.

"Is that what you want?" he whispered, hardly able to believe it even though his disbelief made no sense.

"More than I've ever wanted anything."

He let out a sound he didn't recognize. Part joy, part relief. He held her against his chest as tight as he dared. She held him back, and in that moment he knew that whatever the future held, he would face it with her at his side. His hands roamed down her back to her arse, squeezing the globes until she moaned and leaned up, pulling at her nightdress in handfuls to get it off over her head. Her perfect breasts sat high on her chest, their nipples rigid. He sat up to get to her, holding her on his lap as he took one into his mouth, sucking deeply and drawing a gasp from her as she held his head to her breast.

Reaching between them, his fingers found her wet and sensitive to his touch. As he teased her clitoris between his thumb and forefinger, she bucked and moaned, her fingernails digging into the back of his neck. "Please, Christian, now."

Setting her back slightly, he unfastened his drawers. Greedy in her need, she reached for him, squeezing him in a clasp that mimicked how her body would receive him. He groaned at the soul-shattering pleasure. He could never remember being this eager, this needful with anyone before.

"Guide me," he said in a voice so heavy with desire he didn't recognize it. Lifting her by her hips, he waited for her to notch him at her opening, then he slowly worked her onto him. Up and down, inch by inch, in a slow rhythm until her eager body accepted him and he slid into her fully. She was beautiful, her eyes squeezed tight in pleasure, gasps tumbling from her lips, flush stealing over her.

Pleasure radiated through him at the tight clasp of her body. This was Violet, the woman he loved. Somehow the knowledge put a finer edge on the sheer bliss of being flesh to flesh with a woman for the first time with no sheath between them. The sensation was nearly too raw and vivid to be borne. He knew he wouldn't last. When all he wanted was to pound into her, he held himself still and teased her clitoris, working the swollen bit of flesh as she cried out, bouncing on him in her need.

"Show me how to please you." Her voice was husky in her desperation.

She didn't know that she did just that without even trying. "You're perfect," he whispered, her untutored movements driving him mad with pleasure. But still he waited to join her, teeth gritted in determination as he played with her until her hands tugged at his hair and her breath came in short pants, her orgasm nearly upon her. Only then did he grasp her by the hips and start fucking her the way he wanted.

"Violet," he growled as the unbelievable pleasure took him over, prickling down his spine to where she clasped him so sweetly. She learned quickly, her hips working to meet his rhythm with each thrust into her.

She gasped in his ear, a soft hitch of pleasure that told him she was close. "Come for me," he whispered, burying his nose in her hair so her scent surrounded him. Her fingernails pressed into his shoulders as she tensed, her passage clenching at him in spasms as she found her release. He let go of his control, holding her hips to receive him as he pumped into her over and over again until he exploded. Body and mind finally one, he cried out, certain that she had taken yet another part of his soul.

"I love you." He held her against his heart as he struggled to catch his breath.

She pressed a kiss to his neck, tightening her hold. Even though he was spent, he was reluctant to leave her, and indeed was still lodged inside her, half-rigid in his insatiable need for her. He couldn't stop pressing kisses to her face, the shell of her ear, her brow. This beautiful woman, with all her kindness and goodness, was his.

"When can we marry?" she whispered, pulling back just enough to smile up at him. He loved her smile. "I don't want to wait another day."

"As soon as you can travel we'll go to Blythkirk. We can go by train if you want to hurry." He grinned when she nodded at that. "We can be married when we arrive."

Instead of appearing relieved, she frowned, a line of worry forming between her brows. "What if my father refuses to provide a settlement?"

"Do you think I care about that now?" He took her face between his hands and kissed her. "You're enough for me, Violet." He had been a fool to ever want more than her. "As long as you're in my arms, I have all I need in the world." Words he had never thought to utter in his entire life. Words that were truer than any he had ever spoken.

Chapter 20

❧

*The truth will set you free, but partial truth
can burn you alive.*

V. LENNOX, AN AMERICAN AND THE
LONDON SEASON

The last two days had passed in a haze of sex and tenderness. Even the puffy white clouds that floated overhead reminded Violet of the hours spent with Christian in their tiny bedroom. One in particular appeared very phallic, while another could have been a single bosom tipped with a nipple. The very naughtiness of her thoughts made Violet blush as a smile broke across her face. She lay on a blanket outside with Christian after an alfresco meal of cheese and apples meant to celebrate her birthday. Mrs. Mitchell was baking a cake for the occasion, which they would enjoy that night, a final celebration before leaving for Scotland tomorrow. Christian had surprised her with a silver locket from the village that morning. He had said that he would get her something more suitable later, but that he hadn't wanted her birthday to pass unmarked. She loved the locket and had pressed a tiny wildflower from the hillside within so that she could always remember this day.

"Your thoughts are debauched again, I see," said Christian, dragging a finger down her neck to tease a circle on her skin around the locket.

She wore one of the gowns Jacob had brought her. Though not made for her, it fit well with her corset with only a few modifications. She had decided that today she should get dressed properly, if only to assure Christian that she was well enough to travel tomorrow. He seemed inclined to wait even longer before leaving, and as much as she loved lingering here in this village where the world was at bay and they were simply Christian and Violet, she knew that it was not possible. Very soon someone would find them. She wouldn't be surprised if Max and August had returned, an eventuality that had caused her some grief in the last several days. She should let them know she was fine.

"I would blame you entirely, but you should see what I've already written about Lord Lucifer." She sat up and looked down at him.

He grinned. "I've been meaning to talk to you about your fascination with the chap."

"Are you jealous?"

"Yes, I would have your lustful thoughts reserved for my own purposes."

She laughed. "Am I not to be allowed to even admire another man? Is this what marriage is to you?"

His fingers twirled in an errant strand of hair the wind picked up and blew over her shoulder. She had left it down and tied back with a simple ribbon. "I suppose you can admire whom you like," he said, grudgingly. "But I would have your lust to myself."

Deciding to put him out of his misery, she said, "Then you will be happy to know that Lord Lucifer is none other than you. You and your devilish looks inspired him."

The simple joy on his face sent her into a fit of laughter as she fell over him. Kissing him, she said, "You aren't nearly as fearsome as you'd have others believe, you know."

"Shh . . . don't tell anyone." But he pinched her bottom

and would have tumbled her to her back had she not pulled free.

She had other things in mind right now. They had spent the hour before eating wading around the little brook that sloped through the hills beyond the Mitchells' property. The rise meant they were just out of view from the house, but it would only take them a few minutes' walk to return. His trouser leg had ridden up a bit to reveal his ankle. Pushing on his shoulder to keep him in place, she sat on her knees beside it.

"The swelling has reduced," he said, watching her examine him with her eyes.

"Yes, I noticed your limp has improved with our recent bed rest." She glanced up at him, a flutter of anticipation moving through her at the hooded wickedness in his eyes. She'd had him only that morning. Would this wanting him ever relent? She hoped not.

Gently and with reverence, she traced her fingertips over the scar that ran in a jagged pink line down his ankle. It started at the top of his foot and ran to just under his trousers. Tiny white dots of scar tissue framed it, likely left behind by the thick stitching needed to keep the wound closed. An ache welled within her as she imagined the pain it must have caused him.

"Will you tell me how it happened?"

His initial instinct was to refuse. The pulse of a muscle in his jaw and the shuttering of his gaze said as much. "It is not a pretty story."

Covering the scar with her hand, she said, "I don't need pretty stories."

He stared at where she touched him and then nodded. "My father was active in Newmarket. He had several horses that he raced, and some that he bred to sell. One of his best studs was Bucephalus, so named because he was black with a white star on his brow and near impossible to tame, like Alexander the Great's fabled animal. I still harbored illusions that I could win my father's affection, so when he taunted me into riding him, I accepted the challenge. It was a challenge I lost."

Imagining the sickening scene made her stomach churn with nausea. "What a ghastly thing to do. Dear God, how old were you?"

"Ten years. I was thrown and trampled against the fence. He told a groom to bind my ankle and went inside. A week later infection had set in and a physician was sent for. My father claimed it was because I was too weak, and I believed that for a while."

"I'm sorry you had such a terrible father." She wanted to hold the boy he had been and protect him from the monster. "You didn't deserve that." Leaning down, she kissed his scar and secretly wiped the tear from her lashes. He wouldn't appreciate her pity, but her heart hurt for him.

"Violet." He sat up and reached for her, drawing her into his arms. "It doesn't matter. I believed him for a time, but I know he was wrong. It's in the past."

"You're right. Now we can focus on our own family."

He gave her a look of wonder, as if he hadn't thought that far ahead yet, but he didn't retreat as she thought he might. Instead, his eyes softened with affection and he kissed her. She climbed onto his lap and savored his mouth on hers. Her breath hitched as desire coiled in her belly, but there was no rush. They had days—no, years—of this ahead. When his mouth touched her neck, a shiver of longing teased along her skin.

"Violet!"

They both looked up. A man crested the hill, standing at the top to look down at them. She squinted and brought her hand up to shade her eyes. "Max," she whispered, unable to believe he was here. Scrambling off Christian's lap, she waved and hurried up the hill. "Max!"

Christian came to his feet slower and with considerably less enthusiasm. Max's long-legged stride made him faster, so he met her near the bottom, pulling her into his arms in a hug as he swung her around.

"Ouch!" She twisted until he loosened his grip, easing the pressure on her ribs, but nothing could wipe the smile from her face at seeing him again. "What are you doing here?" She still couldn't believe she wasn't imagining him.

"Are you all right?" His brow furrowed as he took in the stitching and bruising on her head and face. His hand roved down her corset-clad ribs as if assessing her for injuries.

"Yes, I'm much better. There was a carriage accident, but as you can see, only a few scrapes."

"I know about the accident." His gaze, full of accusation and a fury she had missed in her earlier pleasure, swung to Christian.

It wasn't until that moment that Violet realized how the whole thing must look to Max. He must think she had run off with Christian. Well, it actually wasn't far from the truth, was it? She almost laughed at that, but Max was still serious and becoming angrier by the second.

"Did you meet the Mitchells? Aren't they lovely? They've taken excellent care of us." When he still hadn't looked away from Christian, she moved between them to bring his attention back to her. "How did you find us?"

It effectively transferred the full force of his anger to her, which gave her pause. "We had no idea where you were, Violet. Lady Helena is the one who realized Leigh had disappeared at the same time you did." Only then did she understand that it wasn't anger he directed at her. It was fear. His eyes were bright with it. "We went to his estate in Scotland, and with no sign of you there, we had to backtrack through northern England. Thank God, we came across a newspaper. It said that a man suspected to be the Earl of Leigh had crashed his carriage, and a mysterious American had been in his company. We came directly here."

Oh dear. It wasn't good that there was already talk of

them. "I know I should have made contact, but I couldn't because I . . ."

"Because you were injured. Because of him." His anger directed back at Christian, he walked around her, but she wouldn't have it and moved with him. "You take her and then you allow this to happen to her!" he yelled at Christian.

Putting her hand on her brother's chest, she said, "It wasn't his fault, Max. Please calm down so we can discuss this."

"Not his fault? Violet, he nearly got you killed."

"It was an accident, and I am fine. Christian is the one who saved me." She glanced behind her to see Christian standing silently, his hands in fists at his sides. He was so still that a warning rose within her. Something was wrong. She knew he still felt guilty and hated the way Max's words must be landing like barbs in that guilt. "He was escorting me to Windermere. There had been days of rain, and a tree uprooted and hit the carriage. It was an accident."

"Windermere?"

She nodded. "I was going there to a boardinghouse, to stay until I figured out what to do about Mother and Papa and Lord Ware. Christian saw me leave and was kind enough to offer me an escort."

"Saw you leave? You didn't plan to run off with him?"

"No." She smiled, hoping to calm him down, hoping that if he understood there had been no elaborate scheme then he might relax. "He saw me outside the British Museum and stopped to offer his assistance."

Max ran a hand through the hair at his temple, shaking his head as if he'd come to some great realization. Gesturing toward Christian, he said to Violet, "You misunderstand the motivation for his offer of assistance." Max spoke through clenched teeth, and his gaze swung back to Christian. "He wanted to marry you. He never intended you to reach Windermere."

"I know all that." She patted his chest. "He confessed

that his original intention was to escort me in the hopes he could convince me to marry him."

"Did he convince you?"

"Before the accident? No, but in the last several days I have decided that I will marry him." It wasn't nearly how she was hoping to deliver the happy news, but with Lord Ware and her parents on his side, there likely wasn't a happy way for all.

Incredulous, Max looked at her. "Oh, really? Then why are you on the road to Scotland now? I believe Windermere is southwest of here."

She frowned, not entirely certain what he meant. A glance at Christian confirmed the guilt that slashed across his face. He spoke for the first time. "The turn off for Windermere was the morning of our accident. I had planned to ask you that night." His voice had the solemn, resigned tones of a condemned man, which was not at all reassuring.

Turning back to her brother, she said, "A miscommunication. I would have said yes that night." It was true, but the knowledge that he had anticipated her and reacted without her consent itched its way under her skin. She would confront him later about it in private, when Max wasn't breathing his fiery anger on them.

"Do you think it was a happy accident that he found you in London that day when you left?" Max's voice was heavy with insinuation, which caused her to take a few steps backward. Christian stood at her back, but he made no attempt to touch her, which was disconcerting.

"It was a coincidence," she said, knowing that she was being led somewhere she didn't want to go.

"Coincidence," Max repeated, his hands clenching and unclenching at his sides. "Just as it was a coincidence that your maid disappeared on the same day you did?"

"Ellen? What are you talking about?" What did she have to do with this? "Have you found her? Is she injured?"

"Lady Helena hasn't been able to find her, but she has

found that the girl was last seen going to Montague Club on the day you ran away." To Christian, he said, "Perhaps you can shed some light on her disappearance."

Without hesitation, Christian said, "She has been sent to Amberley Park, where I have guaranteed her a position."

Violet whirled, stunned that Christian would know the maid. "I don't understand."

His eyes reflected pain and resignation when they met hers. "I hired her to give me information about you." Taking a breath, he added, "I also had men outside your home so they could tell me when you were leaving."

"You knew I would be running away at the British Museum?"

"No, but I suspected. I knew you had left the bag at Lady Helena's. I knew you were planning to leave."

Betrayal tasted bitter as it clawed its way up the back of her throat. "You planned this, then? The whole trip?"

He nodded, still not bothering to reach for her. Why didn't he hold her? Why didn't he tell her that he loved her and everything would be fine? Every fiber of her body cried out for him.

"He was bitter that our father rejected him as a suitor. When Papa turned him down, Leigh decided to take you another way," said Max.

"No. He didn't ask Papa for my hand." Christian would have told her if he had when he had confessed his plan to convince her to marry him.

"Tell her I'm wrong, Leigh." The assurance in Max's voice sent a chill down her spine.

Christian stood silent, and her stomach clenched in nausea. Her body felt achy and numb all at the same time. "Christian?" she whispered.

"I asked your father that day we spoke outside your music room. He declined in favor of Ware."

Struggling to speak past the ache in her throat, she said, "Then you knew about my father accepting Ware when we spoke at the ball. You knew and were already plotting? You plotted to gain me. No, you didn't want me at all; you wanted my settlement. But why?" He wasn't destitute like Rothschild had been, but then the answer struck her before he even said it. Of course, she had been reduced to the sum of her ability to increase his holdings, just like with Ware.

"Blythkirk. I needed money for Blythkirk, but Violet, I wanted you." He took a step forward, but Max intervened, walking to her side.

"Do you actually think our father would allow a conniving bastard like you a settlement? What would you have done when he cut Violet off?"

Violet already knew the answer. Her voice quivering in pain, she couldn't look away from the guilt on Christian's face. "The house in Manhattan? The stocks?"

Max's head swiveled to look down at her. "He knew about those?"

She nodded, feeling like an absolute fool. "I told him everything." What a complete and utter fool she had been. "He baited me, and I played right into his hands." Part of her didn't want to believe it, but the truth was written on Christian's face.

"It all would have been yours upon your marriage to her," Max said to Christian. "You planned to sell it all, didn't you? You son of a bitch. You planned to gut Violet's holdings for your own selfish gains."

"That was my plan, yes."

"I love that house." Aunt Hortense had left it to her because she had stayed there the most. They had built the greenhouse in the back together, planted the rose garden, spent hours arranging the books in the library. Her voice was thick with unshed tears, forcing her to swallow past them. "How could you?"

"I didn't know, Violet," Christian said. "I meant it when I said that you are all I need. I wouldn't have sold it, not now, not without your consent."

"Easy to say, but how can I ever believe that now? You lied to me. You treated me exactly like every other man, used me as a commodity to meet your ends."

Before either of them could react, Max swung. She shrieked as his fist hit Christian's cheek, nearly knocking him over. "No!"

Christian's entire body reeled with the blow, and he whirled and crouched as if bracing himself for another one. "You get one, Crenshaw. Do not attempt another."

Max moved as if he indeed would, but Violet was not going to allow them to fight over this, especially when she still needed answers. Putting herself between them, she faced Christian. "When did you plan to tell me the whole truth?"

"I told you the truth."

"Not the entire truth. Not how you schemed. Not the depths you were willing to go to get what you wanted," she said.

"He seduced you to get what he wanted. He doesn't deserve any part of you," said Max.

The painful truth of that statement hit her right in the chest. Christian had seduced her. He had used his pretty words to make her fall in love with him. What if none of this was real? He hadn't told her the truth, not when he had held so much of it back. What if he still held himself back and she had merely fallen in love with this facade of him?

She had fallen in love with a facade. If most of it wasn't true, then how could any of it be real? "I don't even know who you are."

"Violet." The pain in his voice nearly ripped her heart in two. When he would have stepped toward her, she held up her hand.

"No, I don't want to talk to you anymore. I have to go." She turned, her body chilled with the aftermath, but she stopped as something he had said came back to her. "Do you remember the day you came to my home with Rothschild looking for August?" At his nod, she continued, "That day when you tried to convince me he had been faithful to her, I asked why I should believe you. You said that I should not ever believe you." She took in a shuddering breath. "You warned me, but I was too infatuated to heed it."

She felt like she had just lived a hundred years at once. Her body hurt with the pain of his betrayal. "Take me home, Max. Please."

He wanted to stay. She could feel his body vibrating with anger, but he put his arm around her instead. "This isn't over, Leigh. We will discuss this later. I expect to see you in London to settle this. Don't make me come find you in Scotland."

Christian didn't follow, and she didn't know what to make of that. She wanted him to tell her she was wrong, to plead with her; yet she knew she wouldn't believe him. Not now. Not when her heart had been torn open and left bleeding. How could she ever trust anything again? Memories of their nights on the road swept through her head as she trudged up the hill. He had held himself away from her, only opening pieces of himself bit by bit like tiny little treasures he would give over to her keeping. She had thought it a sign of his growing affection, but what if it had all been carefully planned, calculated to have her take his lure? Along with the memories came the snatches of gossip she had heard about him. Reprobate, womanizer, blackguard . . . This was precisely how a man like that would play her affections. What had made her think she was any different?

Lady Helena was waiting for her at the Mitchells' front stoop. Violet had almost forgotten that Max had mentioned her. Worry creased her brow, and she hurried down the steps to meet her. "Oh, Violet," she said, pulling her into a warm embrace.

Tears gathered in Violet's eyes, but she refused to allow them to fall as she hugged the woman back. When she would have thought she'd prefer to bear this pain alone, she found herself grateful for Lady Helena's comfort.

"Let us gather your things, dear," she said in her typically efficient way. "We can be on a train for London this very afternoon."

Violet nodded, unable to speak past the pain clogging her throat. Inside, she found that Mrs. Mitchell seemed very concerned, clucking like a mother hen as she hurried from one room to another, helping Violet gather her scarce belongings into her bag. Thankfully, the woman did not ask questions.

At the stoop, Violet said, "Thank you for your kindness, Mrs. Mitchell. Please convey my gratitude to Dr. Mitchell. I'm sorry I won't see him to say goodbye." The man had left early in the morning to attend the birth of a gentry woman in the next village and had not returned.

"Of course, I will. Please do write and let us know how you get on, lass."

Violet agreed and allowed Max to help her into the carriage. She had no idea what Mrs. Mitchell had been told, and she dared not ask at the moment. The weight of her complete humiliation and devastation was all she could bear right now. The silence in the carriage was deafening. Tiny houses and shops and people going about their day passed by her window as they drove through the charming village she had temporarily called home. The entire time, she could feel the weight of Max's gaze on her. He was disappointed, and he had every right to be. "I am very sorry for the trouble I put you through, both of you."

Beside her, Lady Helena took her hand, holding it with both of hers and giving her fingers a squeeze of compassion. "We are simply glad to have you back safely."

"Violet," Max began, "I will make that bastard pay—"

"Mr. Crenshaw." Lady Helena's voice was sharp as a whip lashing through the carriage. "Perhaps we should wait to discuss particulars in London. Now is not the time."

Violet hadn't noticed the tension between the two of them before, but it was plain to see. Max's eyes darkened with a storm she had rarely seen in her brother, and never directed at someone as kind and gentle as Lady Helena. Yet, there it was. For that matter, Lady Helena's own gaze flashed with fire, but she banked it quickly. Max looked away first. Something had definitely happened between these two.

Lady Helena seemed to remember herself and gave Violet a reassuring smile. "We shall get you home to your own bed tonight, though it might be quite late."

Dread twisted her belly into knots. "I'd prefer not to go home. I don't want to face Mother and Papa just yet." She didn't know how she could ever forgive them completely for Lord Ware.

Max frowned but said, "We can go to a hotel."

"Or she could stay with me." To Violet, she said, "I am happy to have you for as long as you like. Whichever you prefer, dear."

"Yes, thank you." Violet squeezed her hand in gratitude.

"My thanks," said Max, his gaze lingering on the woman.

Violet turned her gaze back to the window, where it stayed for the rest of the trip. She had made a foolish mistake by following her heart, and she very much feared that she would spend the rest of her life paying for it. No matter how angry she felt, a small part of her wondered: What if it had all been real? How was she supposed to know?

Chapter 21

❖

*Some would believe that his marriage to the
fair Miss Hamilton even after his deed was
uncovered was a sign of how deep his devilish proclivities ran; some, however, knew
that it was his last attempt at salvation.*

V. LENNOX, *AN AMERICAN AND THE
LONDON SEASON*

There was no question of them not marrying.

Violet had known deep in her bones that would be
the case. Although she had spent a great deal of her time on
the train pretending that she would be fine, pretending that
she could become a hermit and live her life out in a boardinghouse writing her novels, she knew that simply wasn't true.
She would not live her life as a pariah. The minor scandal
that would have followed her only a short time ago when
she was running away to a boardinghouse would have
barely made ripples back in New York. Certainly, none that
a Crenshaw fortune couldn't calm.

God. It always came back to that, didn't it? She was always to be reduced to the worth of her father's bank account. Damn Christian. He hadn't made it so, but he had
given her a glimpse of how it would feel to be valued for
something more. But it had only been a lie.

However, this scandal was much more serious than running away to a boardinghouse. While her parents had cre-

ated that ridiculous story about Bath that had kept the gossipmongers at bay for a while, Christian's absence had been noted. Max's arrival in London and subsequent disappearance had only fanned the flames. Then everyone had discovered the news about the carriage accident. This scandal would not die away without leaving a stain. She would have to face it. There would be no running away.

Max opened the gate leading from the mews to the back garden of Lady Helena's Berkeley Square home. He used the back entrance, because Lady Helena had decided it would be best to not be home for the time being. Speculation was ripe about where Violet was hiding—Huxley brought in the paper every morning—but she was content to keep them guessing until the inevitable wedding.

"Max is here," Violet said to Helena, who sat working at an elegant desk in the corner. Heart firmly in her stomach, Violet opened the door for him. He had come directly from a meeting with Papa and Christian at Montague Club. Their first meeting beyond an exchange of angry correspondence. She had noted that Christian had not once attempted to send her a letter or contact her in any way.

"Good afternoon." He put an arm around her and kissed the top of her head as he had done since she was a child. "How are you feeling?"

She forced herself to smile and say, "Better." Though it had been half a week since she had left Christian, she still vacillated between love and hate. It couldn't have all been a lie, could it? Not those moments when he stared at her with such joy. One couldn't fake that, could one? Or those times he had touched her so intimately. How could one convey so much tenderness in a touch and not feel it? But he was a practiced libertine and had perfected his craft, she would remind herself, and it was that very thinking that had gotten her in trouble.

"Good afternoon, Mr. Crenshaw."

Max stared at the woman, his gaze roving downward as

she stood to greet him. Violet bit her lip to hide a genuine smile. Having been born with an invisible marriage bull's-eye on his back, Max generally kept his distance from women in Society. Violet's own friends back in New York tended to fall all over themselves in their attempts to meet him or compliment him. It was simply too bad that he would be returning to New York soon and would not be able to further his acquaintance with Helena.

"Lady Helena." He inclined his head, but instead of taking a seat, he walked to the fireplace.

Violet noticed the set of his jaw and the rigid way he held his shoulders and sank down onto the settee.

"I shall leave you to discuss things," said Helena.

"No, stay, please." Her calming presence had been a comfort to Violet. After Helena sat next to her, Violet asked, "What happened at the meeting?"

Storm clouds darkened his gaze, and he glanced away as if he didn't want to say. "There is no need for you to concern yourself with these petty negotiations, Violet. Let Papa and me handle them for you. You'll see the final contract before it's signed."

"No. It concerns me, and I must know. I am not a child anymore, though I have perhaps behaved impulsively. I will go into things with my eyes open from now on."

The muscle in his jaw shifted. "Leigh has refused to marry you unless Papa increases the money he offered to settle on you."

You're enough for me, Violet. As long as you're in my arms, I have all I need in the world.

Lies. The tiny flame of hope that had been clinging to life in the depths of her heart was snuffed out. The pain tore through her more vicious than any she had ever felt before. It would have crumpled her had she not already resolved to prove—to herself and everyone else—that she was a perfectly responsible adult who made perfectly reasonable decisions. As it was, she had to swallow several times before she could speak. An ache pressed against the back of her eyes, but she refused to allow tears to fall. "What was Papa's initial offer?"

Silence was her answer.

"Max, please."

Scraping a hand along his close-cropped beard, he said, "Fifty thousand dollars."

August and Rothschild had been given one million plus an annuity. She knew that the small figure was meant to show Papa's displeasure with Christian, and yet she could not help but feel it quantified her own worth to him.

"Papa came up to one hundred thousand," Max continued. "But Leigh maintained that he would not agree to a penny less than five hundred. That is where we left things."

Rising, she walked to the window, her arms tucked against her stomach as if she could hold herself together so the pain wouldn't rip her apart. "How much did Papa plan to settle on me in the agreement with Lord Ware?"

Again, her question was met with silence. Finally, he said, "Same as August. Remember, there were mineral rights in the exchange."

Of course. Mineral rights. Male conceit. None of this really had anything to do with her. She was simply the body being transferred along with the cash. Her stomach churned with nausea. "What will happen if Leigh proves true to his word?" A rarity, that. "If he refuses to marry me?"

"Papa already has an attorney looking into charges that can be filed. Kidnapping, endangerment, breach of promise, to name only a few."

She squeezed her eyes shut as she imagined the circus and endless fodder that would cause. She would never be able to show her face in public again. How had she been such a fool? To run away from Lord Ware only to fall into the same trap, but in an infinitely more painful way, was too humiliating to bear.

"Don't worry, Violet." Coming up behind her, Max ran

his hands over her shoulders in a soothing massage. "It will not come to that. I promise I won't let it."

"How will you stop it?" She turned and looked up at him to ascertain his confidence. He seemed resolute and unworried.

"Papa is angry now, as he has every right to be, but he is above all a shrewd man of industry. Dragging this out will only damage all of us, and Crenshaw Iron will suffer."

Crenshaw Iron would suffer. Her own suffering counted for much less when contracts might be held up in Parliament if the men took offense to Papa attacking one of their own. She had never wanted another life as much as she did in that moment. A life where she could be who she wanted to be. The Mitchells' cottage came to mind, but she forced it out as she did every moment of every day when thoughts of that happy time threatened to surface. "Will Papa be convinced of that?"

"Yes. I have full confidence that he will relent. Five hundred thousand is a reasonable offer, and he'll come to see that. Once we have reached an agreement, we'll obtain the special license and you can be married immediately. I believe a ceremony by a civil registrar will be most expedient."

"I agree." Helena spoke for the first time. "We need to minimize the scandal so it can begin to fade away. You can marry at the General Register Office, with a church ceremony to follow in a few weeks, if you prefer."

"No." Violet shook her head. "The civil ceremony will suffice." She couldn't imagine acting out an elaborate wedding in a church where everyone pretended they were happy and this marriage was a blessing.

"I'm sorry, but I have to go. Papa has another meeting scheduled with the attorney soon, and I would be there to stop him doing something rash." Pulling her into his arms, he said, "Please try not to worry. This will be sorted out very soon." When he pulled back he bent a bit to look her in the eyes. "Unless you want to leave. You don't have to go through with any of this. We can go home."

"No, I won't live my life as a recluse. But have you been able to transfer the deed to Aunt Hortense's home?" They had decided it best to have the property moved to a trust controlled by Max. Violet owned the property, and if they were in New York, it would still be hers upon her marriage, but under British law it would transfer to her husband. Indeed, even she would be British afterward. There was no telling the legal ramifications if Christian chose to sell it.

"I am working on it, yes, but I cannot promise it can't be undone."

She nodded. That would have to be enough. "And you've made it clear that I do not expect to reside with him?" It wasn't a concession that could be enforced, but she felt better knowing the expectation was established from the beginning. She would not pretend this marriage was a real one, not with the stain of his betrayal marring it.

"Yes, he did not push back on that point."

"Good." She didn't mean it, though, no matter how much she wanted to. The man she had loved would fight for her. She wanted that man. Not this one who would likely prefer his freedom.

"I'll send word the moment the settlement has been finalized." Max kissed her forehead and left the way he had come in.

Violet joined Helena on the settee.

"All will be settled soon," said Helena.

"Yes, I know. I simply cannot help wondering how I could have allowed myself to be deceived so."

"Perhaps you weren't as deceived as you'd have yourself believe."

"How so?"

"Your feelings were real. You spent days with him, and I'm convinced that at least some of that revealed his true character."

He had saved her. That was the part Violet was struggling with. If he were completely mercenary, would he have chased the carriage toward the river and pulled her out? Would he have carried her on his injured ankle?

"He did sit by my bedside while I was unconscious and read *Jane Eyre* aloud to me."

"Then perhaps at least some of the affection he returned to you was real, as well."

"Perhaps." She had to believe it was true or else she might go mad. She couldn't go through her entire life questioning her every instinct. "But that doesn't change the facts of the matter. He lied to me and used me for his own gain."

"No, it doesn't," Helena agreed. "I do not mean to urge you to forgive him. I only hope to reassure you that your feelings, that you, are not at fault here. The blame is entirely with him."

"Thank you, Helena. I appreciate that." Violet didn't entirely agree, but to know that her friend believed it was a comfort. "If only it would take the sting out of his not agreeing to marry me unless Papa gives in to his demands. Whatever affection he feels for me apparently isn't deep enough to overcome his financial concerns."

"He is a fool."

And she along with him.

The wedding took place a few days later, on a Sunday by special dispensation to avoid the public spectacle that might have occurred otherwise. Christian held the power, so Papa had agreed to his settlement demands the morning after they had been made, just as Max had predicted he would. Violet walked up the grand staircase in the North Wing of Somerset House to the first floor as if in a dream. Her parents had been waiting downstairs when she and Max had arrived. There had been a stiff and achingly formal greeting between them before Max took her arm and led her upstairs to the office of the general registrar.

She took a breath to calm her nerves as a servant opened the door. Inside, Christian, Jacob, and the man whom she assumed to be the registrar rose as their group entered. He was an older man who stood behind a rather large desk that had been wiped clean of everything except a ledger that appeared to be some sort of register, a Bible, and another book opened to a page. She dared not look at Christian full on, not if she intended to get through this.

She had seen enough to know that he wore dove gray trousers and a charcoal morning coat with a deep blue tie and waistcoat. It was in sharp contrast to how she had last seen him in shirtsleeves and bare feet. Though handsome, he stood rigid and cold, unapproachable, and yet she had no choice but to go and stand beside him. He would be her husband by the time she left this room, a fact that still didn't seem real.

She wore a gown of thin batiste that buttoned up the front with pretty bits of lace along the chest, at her cuffs, and along the skirt. It had a short, ruffled train. Helena had helped her add a lace veil, though they had pinned it so it didn't cover her face and instead trailed down her back. The gown itself wasn't strictly speaking a wedding gown, having been made for the eventuality of attending a summer party. There had been no time to have a true wedding gown made, as well as no need, since there would be no large church wedding. Violet had chosen this one because it was the prettiest of the few white gowns she owned. Like an idiot, she hoped he liked it, and then despised that the thought had crossed her mind.

Swallowing thickly, she came to stand beside Christian and inclined her head when the registrar greeted her and her family. Her parents took their places next to her, with Christian and Jacob to her left and Max behind her. Christian made no move to grasp her hand, not that she was expecting that. She held no flowers, and August wasn't even here to share the moment with her. It hardly felt like a true wedding at all.

"Let us get this done with," Papa said, his voice harsh with anger.

Done with. Another transaction he wanted finished because it hadn't quite worked out the way he wanted.

"Perhaps you would prefer to wait downstairs." Christian's voice was clipped and precise with his own anger. She grimaced inwardly at the coldness contained within it. He sounded like a stranger to her.

The registrar cleared his throat, apparently deciding it would be best to move things along, and picked up the open book. The air was thick with antagonism. "We are here today to join the Right Honorable Christian, Earl of Leigh, to Miss Violet Crenshaw in matrimony. If there would be any who would voice an objection to why these two shall not be joined, let him speak now." There was only the slightest pause before he continued. "Very well. Let us proceed with the vows." Looking at Christian, he said, "My lord, if you would be so good as to repeat after me."

They faced forward, staring at the registrar instead of each other. Fitting, she supposed, for what amounted to a sham. The inflection in Christian's voice did not change as he repeated his vows. Neither did hers, though it was because she forced herself to speak them in a clear voice past the lump in her throat. There was no ring pushed onto her finger in a moment of tender urgency, there was no kiss to celebrate. There was only the registrar saying, "You are now man and wife."

"There. That is done," said Mother, nodding with a smile as if she had accomplished some task and could put it behind her.

"If you could sign here, my lord." The registrar pushed the ledger over.

Christian picked up a pen and signed his name with a flourish. His fingers were long, graceful, exactly as she remembered them. She blinked away as soon as she noticed her own thoughts.

"Now you, my lady." The man shifted the ledger to her.

Christian offered her the pen, and she accepted without touching him. Her fingers trembled, so she paused, forcing a calm as she began to sign her name. She almost wrote Crenshaw. A dot of ink spread on the paper as she caught herself, turning the little curl at the beginning of the C into the beginning of an L. She was Violet Leigh now.

"Thank you, sir," she said, giving the registrar back his pen. The strength of her voice had been all used up, so it was barely higher than a whisper. And then it was over, and time to reconvene at the Crenshaws' rented townhome for the wedding breakfast. They all left exactly as they had arrived, in three different carriages.

Chapter 22

*Rose, for her part, had no interest in playing
the role of savior. She knew what many did
not, and what some only learned after tribu-
lation. True redemption came from within.*

V. LENNOX, *AN AMERICAN AND THE
LONDON SEASON*

Christian was certain that he would never forget how
beautiful Violet had looked when she walked into the
registrar's office and became his wife. It was a day he
would remember for the rest of his life. He regretted many
things. How he hadn't been honest with her when he should
have, how he had stolen her away to begin with, and even
how she didn't have a proper wedding. But he would never
regret making her his wife, even if meant living with her
disappointment and dealing with that nest of vipers she
considered family.

When he and Jacob walked in, the Crenshaws' townhome was bustling with activity. Servants moved from
room to room, carrying in last-minute flower arrangements
and setting up platters filled with glasses of champagne for
the guests who would be arriving soon for the wedding
breakfast. Having only arrived moments before them, Violet and her family still stood in the entryway discarding
their outerwear.

"Leigh," Maxwell Crenshaw greeted him. "Mr. Thorne."

Her father simply glared at them both. He didn't know if Jacob's presence had been expected, but no one objected.

"Hello, Mr. Thorne." Violet gave his brother a tiny smile, studiously avoiding looking at Christian. His heart twisted from the coldness.

"I would have a moment alone with my wife before the guests arrive," he said, handing his hat and gloves to a footman.

"I'm afraid there is simply no time, my lord." Mrs. Crenshaw indicated the photographer, who had set up a camera and his equipment farther in where the curve of the staircase could serve as a backdrop to their wedding portrait. "We must get your photograph finished before guests arrive."

"Nevertheless," said Christian, "I must insist."

Mrs. Crenshaw frowned, but Violet said, "It will take but a moment, Mother." She led the way into the music room, her shoulders back and head high as if she were going to meet her dark fate.

As he closed the door behind him, secluding them, he could not help but notice how pale she was. Dark shadows under her eyes indicated she hadn't been sleeping well. It appeared as if her stitches had been removed, but the veil and her hair had been artfully arranged to cover the wound. Her bruising had faded a bit, and what was left was disguised by a layer of powder.

"I rather hoped you might wear your pirate scarf." The words were out before he knew he had meant to say them.

"I am sorry to disappoint you." Her voice was all business and impersonal.

He hated that he had done this to her. Could she so easily forget how he had accused her of being a pirate? The way they had laughed? She seemed to look through him rather than to see him. He wanted to pick her up and take her out of here, to spend the night in his bed showing her how he regretted hurting her.

He took in the fine batiste, almost sheer in its delicacy, and the artful way it clung to her curves. "You are beautiful."

She glanced down, but not before he saw the blush that touched her cheeks. "Thank you."

Reaching for the ring in his pocket, he walked over to her. "I have brought you a ring. I wanted to give it to you alone rather than before your family."

"Oh." She hadn't been expecting one. His heart cracked a little at that.

"Here." He took the ring out of its little velvet pouch and waited for her to offer her hand.

"I don't need a ring," she said, staring at his hands as if they meant to do her harm.

"I would very much like for you to have it. It is expected for a woman of your station."

Her brow creased, but she nodded and gave him her hand. He gently grasped her fingers. To touch her again after a week apart was bliss; heat and the faint hum of a current seemed to work its way up his arm to settle in his belly. His body recognized her immediately as need tore swiftly through him, the need to hold her against him and inhale her sweet scent, to feel the beat of her heart. The gold ring held a rose-cut emerald set in the middle of two matching diamonds with a scrollwork band. He pushed it onto her finger, only to have her withdraw her hand the second it was done, as if she couldn't abide his touch.

"Thank you," she said, examining the ring.

"Do you like it?"

"Very much so." His joy at those words was diminished with her next. "I suppose an extra few hundred thousand dollars allows for some extravagance."

"Crenshaw shared the contract negotiations with you." Bloody bastard.

"Of course. Why wouldn't he?" This was almost an accusation; her eyes flashed at him.

"That's why you've been so cold. I understand now."

"No, I don't think you do. Your lying would have been enough to justify my being cold, but there is really no need to have this discussion now."

He stared at her, trying to see some hint of the woman who had smiled up at him so sweetly and held him as if she never wanted to let him go. This woman was aloof, and though her anger was justified, he could not understand how she could so easily put her feelings for him aside. Perhaps he had been taken in by her and he had been right all along. It had been mere infatuation and it was already fading. Admittedly, he had helped it along, so he didn't blame her.

"I negotiated the settlement for you."

"It is always good to understand the figure the men in your life put on your worth." Bitterness filled her voice, and she turned away from him, facing the window that looked out over the street. "But you cannot pretend it was for my benefit. I know you refused to marry me if you didn't get what you wanted."

"A negotiation tactic. Christ, Violet, I wanted you so badly, I ran away with you. It wasn't the money."

"Really?" Fire lit her eyes as she fixed him with her stare, stopping him when he would have closed the distance between them. "Then you would have run away with me had I been penniless? Had I not possessed a stock portfolio, or property in Manhattan? Had you no hope of collecting any funds?"

"Had I known you as I knew you in Yorkshire, yes."

"Which is a fancy way of saying no." The fire in her eyes gave way to sadness that was unbearable. He stepped toward her, but she moved away. "How convenient for your better financial sense to make a reappearance now that we are back in London."

"Your father's initial offer was insulting. You deserve far more than fifty thousand dollars."

"Lucky for you we are one and the same under the law, and you were able to negotiate more money for yourself in the bargaining."

"Violet—"

She held up a hand to stop him. "No, I understand now that this is always how it was meant to be for me."

"You don't understand." He walked to her but stopped short of touching her. "You are meant to live with fine things. I would not have you give them up because of me, because I was selfish to want you for myself. What I did was wrong, and I know that now."

She moved away from him, giving him her back as she put space between them. He hated that he had made her despise him so much. "Is this all you wanted?" she asked without facing him. "Guests will be here soon."

He suspected she was blinking back tears, because her voice had thickened. He tightened his hands into fists to keep from reaching for her. "I have placed the funds in an account under your name. You can access it at any time. The documents have been left at the Belgravia home for you."

"And you are on the account as well?"

"Well, yes." He'd had to open the account and add her name to it.

"Then you can access the funds as well."

"Yes, but the funds are yours."

"Then they are yours, too."

"I cannot control the laws, Violet. I only know that I want to give it to you, and you can use it as you see fit."

"All right. I believe we should return now." She appeared resigned, but not nearly as aloof when she turned toward him. Her face fell in dejected acceptance.

"Violet." He sighed, reluctant to leave things like this and wanting to take her into his arms. "Let us talk. Do you not remember—"

"Christian, no." For the first time he saw the struggle on her face. Her fight to keep her pain from showing to the world. Her eyes glistened before she was able to blink back her tears and calm her expression. This was the Violet he knew. "We cannot talk. I'm sorry, but it's not possible. You lied to me, and you manipulated me. I don't know how to think of that, and the truth is that I cannot be near you right now. If we talk, then I will be lost.

"I don't know what is wrong with me that I cannot think clearly when you are close by. I am not very sophisticated, perhaps. But when you touch me, I am not able to think as I should. I lost myself to you once, and it hurt me terribly. I cannot allow it to happen again."

She could have stabbed him with a knife and it wouldn't have hurt as badly. He would welcome that pain over this. "Then we are to simply exist, near each other but never with each other?"

She nodded. "It's all I can offer you now."

"Violet . . ." He could hardly believe what he was hearing. "Once we are away from your parents, and have some time to—"

"Please understand. I have lived my entire life under the thumb of my parents. I ran away only to run straight to you. I need to be on my own for a while. I need to know my own mind and make my own decisions. I cannot have anything to do with you. Not if I want to stay true to myself. If you have any bit of affection left for me, you will honor me in this."

If? His love for her had not faded since the day her brother found them near that brook. In fact, it possessed him, like a wildfire, willful and uncontrollable in its passion. "Of course I do."

She flinched, and he didn't know what to make of that except that his affection hurt her.

"Then please keep your distance."

He took in a breath, nearly gasping at how it raked over the jagged edges of his heart. "As you wish," he said when he could finally speak past the pain.

She nodded her thanks and walked out of the room. When he had finally recovered enough to follow at a much slower pace, he found her in the entrance hall, her mother fussing over her veil and hair to arrange them for the portrait. He stood there watching as the photographer took her photograph in two different poses. His heart hardly dared to beat.

"My lord." Mrs. Crenshaw smiled, seemingly the only Crenshaw content with her new son-in-law, and beckoned him over. "Now let us have one of you both together."

He glanced at Violet. She gave him an almost imperceptible nod. Walking over to join her, he allowed the man to place him just beyond her shoulder, so that she stood mere inches away, her body heat warming his front. Her scent teased him. It was the French perfume he remembered from the ball, but underneath was her own sweetness that he recognized so well. He had breathed it off her naked skin, licked it from her, and fallen asleep floating in a cloud of it.

"My lord, over here if you will." Christian had been staring at her neck. The photographer lifted his arm, finger raised to show them where to look.

Before he knew what he meant to do, Christian put his hand on her waist. Her breathing changed, but she didn't step away. He promised himself it was the last time he would touch her uninvited. When he would have dropped his hand, she covered it with her own, a soft, gentle touch that nearly brought him to his knees with his need to have her in his arms.

The photographs were over much too soon. She drifted out of his arms, and the guests began arriving. They set up in the drawing room beside each other on the far side of the room, but never touching, to greet the well-wishers. Most of them had come to gawk and ascertain for themselves how much of the gossip was real. She smiled at the appropriate times and laughed when she was meant to, but she wouldn't look at him. It was the same throughout the meal. Near but so far away she was unreachable. Less than two hours after he had given her the ring, it was time for them to leave.

They left together for appearances. Following her into the carriage, he sat across from her, reminded of their trip north not so very long ago.

She waited until the carriage was in motion before she said, "Helena believes that after a week we should begin to be seen in public together to help minimize scandal."

"What do you think?"

"I suppose she's right. If it takes a few times for people to see us together at a ball or the theater to stop the gossip, then we can certainly endure it."

Endure. There was no better word, save for *torture*, perhaps, to describe how it felt to be in her presence and know she wasn't his, that his own actions had pushed her away.

"All right. If that's what you want."

She nodded and returned her gaze to the window. He tried to be civil, to do the same, to be polite and honorable, but he was none of those things, and he could not change himself to become that man. Instead, he couldn't keep his eyes from her as he tried to get a handle on the brute within him that wanted to take her in his lap and kiss her, show her that they were meant to be together and this being apart was unnatural and not good for either of them. He managed to keep to himself, but only because he knew how very badly she needed him to.

All too soon they arrived before the house on Upper Belgrave Street. The white stucco and stone-clad exterior blended with those around it. He had never liked the place and would have sold it if his pride could have borne it. It had felt much better to take it apart piece by piece, undoing the years of work his father had bestowed upon it to make it grand. Now he was condemning Violet to live here with its barren walls and empty corridors. She deserved a real home, something he was coming to realize he wasn't capable of providing her.

Her trunks had been brought over as soon as the contract had been signed to allow the servants time to have things settled for her arrival, but this would be her first visit. When a groom opened the carriage door, he started to move, but she was faster.

"Goodbye for now," she said. "I'll send you a note once I decide on our first outing together."

She didn't want him to see her inside.

"I shall await your word." He nodded and sat back in the seat, a lump settling in his stomach as he watched her hurry up the steps and disappear inside. For the first time in his life, he longed to be welcomed within those walls. He watched the door until the carriage turned the corner, taking him to the club.

Chapter 23

Lord Lucifer realized that his life would unfold in one of two ways: with her beside him, or apart from him. There was no question in his mind which version he meant to live.

V. LENNOX, *AN AMERICAN AND THE LONDON SEASON*

The door to her new home opened, and Violet stepped inside to be greeted by a skeleton crew of servants. "Welcome home, Lady Leigh. My name is Winston, your butler." The man was tall, portly, gray haired, and very polished. His manner seemed reserved, if proficient, and she didn't detect any of the skeptical deference she sometimes felt from the servants in other London homes. Perhaps this would go very well.

"Good afternoon," Violet said, taking in the expansive marble floors in the entry hall. They gleamed white and gray from a fresh cleaning. White columns spanned the two-story foyer to a ceiling inlaid with gorgeous moldings. Two crystal chandeliers would light the space at night. It was an impressive entry that was only marred by the golden wallpaper that had faded to a brownish-yellow, the discolored rectangles left behind where paintings had once hung, and two pedestals obviously missing their busts.

"Will you be expecting Lord Leigh?" Winston asked. He

had the grace to look her in the face instead of peer behind her at the carriage she knew must be retreating by now.

It was a fair question, but it still caused a pang of longing to sting her chest. "No. Not today." Nor any other day. She swallowed past the unexpected lump that welled in her throat.

His polite expression didn't change. "Very good. Please allow me to introduce you to the staff."

The servants were made up of Winston, a footman, the cook, and a scullery maid. They all seemed very polite if a bit wary to meet her. She couldn't blame them. Not many brides arrived on their wedding day without a husband to a home that had likely been shut up for years.

"I am very happy to meet you all," she said after the introductions. "I am certain that we can get along very well together." The maid and the footman curtsied and bowed before disappearing to the back of the house. To the cook and Winston, she said, "I hope to meet with you both over the next day or two to sort out any needs you might have."

"What time would you prefer your dinner tonight, milady?" Cook asked.

She paused, never having had the question posed to her before. In all her life, her schedule had always been influenced by someone else's needs. Dinner had been at the leisure of others. When Mother returned from visiting, when Papa finished his meeting, when Max could work stopping by into his schedule, when August could put her reports aside. The power of this decision was heady. "Please have a tray sent up at eight. I won't dine in the dining room tonight." Though maybe she would now that she thought about it. She had her own dining room.

The woman did not blink at the order and gave a curtsy before she scurried off to the kitchen.

Turning to Winston, she said, "I'll have a tour of the house now before going up to rest."

"Very good, milady."

The tour took about a half hour. It was obvious that the main floor had been divested of all its treasures. Although the furniture was mostly intact, it was all very old-fashioned, leading her to believe that the house had not been refurbished except for minor comforts since it had been built some thirty-odd years ago. Much of it was in need of new upholstery. The walls and carpets were uniformly faded, and the wood floors were dull with discolorations in the varnish where more valuable possessions had once stood.

This is what Christian had meant when he had told her that he sold off everything of value. He was so smartly put together in his suits and walking sticks that she had hardly dared to believe that his poor finances had all been true. Max had assured her that his income was enough to support a stylish lifestyle, and the basic upkeep of this grand house, but it fell far short of bearing the strain of Amberley Park and the complete refurbishment needed here. She tried to imagine the boy he had been, dealing with the overwhelming burden of a failing earldom, and her heart hurt.

The only portraits remaining seemed to be family members. She found one that she was certain was his mother. The beautiful woman was very stylishly dressed and appeared to be no more than Violet's own age at the time. She had light brown hair and the gray eyes that she had bestowed upon her son. Her expression was happy, but she somehow seemed lost.

Later she found two that she was certain were of Christian. One was a small painting of him as a boy of around eight years lounging with a hound by a stream. His face was open and confident, not yet closed off as she had seen him so often before Yorkshire. The other was a more formal portrait, likely done after he had inherited. His shoulders were already wide, but his frame was still wiry, and his expression was glacial and haughty. She imagined this was the boy who had come to Thea seeking vengeance. Thank goodness the woman had shown him a better way.

The final portrait hung near the upstairs landing that led to the bedrooms. A life-size man stood glaring out at her. His hair was the same rich shade as Christian's, but it was cut much shorter, and his eyes were darker. However, they held the same gleam of wickedness that she had seen in both Christian and Jacob's eyes, except there was a coldness about them absent from those of his sons. His lips were thinned in a line of haughty disappointment. She imagined it was the look he had given Christian when he'd fallen from that horse. Despite the similarities to her husband, she despised him on sight.

"The late earl," said Winston respectfully.

"Have it removed to the attic."

He didn't reply, and she couldn't tear her eyes away from the earl to ascertain if his silence indicated displeasure.

"Immediately," she added. She would not allow the man to sit as a portent over the house any longer.

"Yes, milady, Thomas and I will see to it."

She nodded, and he led her to her bedroom. He stopped at the door, politely not stepping over the threshold, so she peeked inside. It was of a good size with perfectly serviceable furniture, but like the rest of the home seemed a bit tired and faded. She was happy to see that the windows overlooked the garden.

"This room adjoins the late earl's chamber. It is also the only bedchamber fully furnished. Lord Leigh uses it when he sleeps here, but that hasn't been for some years." Likely not since Montague Club and the suite of rooms he kept there, she imagined.

Slowly, she took a step into Christian's room. She could find no sign of him from the dulled damask bedspread to the armoires already filled with her clothing. He was long gone from this place. Before melancholy could set in, she said, "This will do quite well. Thank you, Winston."

"Will your lady's maid be arriving soon?" he asked from the doorway.

"No, I'm afraid I'll need to hire a new one." Ellen was at Amberley Park now, and Violet didn't think she could trust her even if she were brought back. That betrayal still stung. She had borrowed Helena's up until now. "It appears we'll have to hire several new members of the staff."

"I expected as much, milady. I shall see it all arranged tomorrow."

"Thank you, but I would have candidates sent over from Lady Helena March's charity, the London Home for Young Women."

His brow creased with disapproval. "The fallen women, milady?" He whispered the word *fallen* as if it were a curse he couldn't speak of but had no choice.

"They are merely women fallen on difficult circumstances. She assures me there are several that have been well trained for the task. They simply are in need of someone to hire them. We could also hire a couple for the rest of the positions."

"Of course," he relented, inclining his head. "Certainly, you will wish to retain more footmen as well."

"You mean besides Thomas?" Wasn't the one footman enough?

"Well, yes." His expression indicated that it was only expected. "You will need footmen to serve at the table when you entertain and to assist your guests."

She took in a breath, certain that Winston might very well be moved to resign on the spot once she explained. "I am well aware of the custom, but I have decided not to honor the tradition. Maids can serve my guests just as well as footmen."

"But . . . you . . . milady." His mouth closed as the battle raged within him. His need for continued employment won, so he bowed. "Of course."

Her voice gentled. "You will find me to be a very generous and caring employer once we discover our way together."

"I expected nothing less, milady."

Nodding, she added, "I would also like the names of several firms with experience in renovations. I would like to see this home restored as soon as possible. Perhaps even new livery. In this I will be appreciative of your expertise and judgment."

That seemed to meet with his approval as his shoulders relaxed. "Of course, milady."

"That will be all for now."

He bowed and left her.

For the first time that day, a genuine smile touched her lips as she inspected the room. This would be her home, and if Christian's words were true, she would have the funds to make it her own. There would be no one to second-guess her choices, no one to tell her no. Now she understood why Helena had chosen not to remarry. She could get used to this freedom.

But could she get accustomed to the loneliness? The bed was freshly made, the bedspread likely a sunny yellow damask that had faded to brown, nearly matching the wallpaper downstairs. Was this the bedding Christian had used when he slept here? Would she feel the imprint his body left in the mattress? Would he ever hold her again? No, she couldn't allow her thoughts to take her down that dark path.

Her exploration revealed a package wrapped in the finest paper she had ever seen set on the table near the window. A large red ribbon held it all together. Picking up the note set on top of it, she read:

My dearest Violet,

A belated birthday gift along with my regrets for not celebrating as we should have.

All my love,
C

Tears filled her eyes as she touched her chest where the locket rested beneath her clothing. She wore it still because she couldn't forget the morning he had given it to her, nor how she had felt, dumbstruck and silly with her love for him. A terrible but true way to describe the sheer bliss that had surrounded them. Blinking away the tears, she unwrapped the package revealing four books: *Jane Eyre*, *Wuthering Heights*, *Agnes Grey*, and *The Tenant of Wildfell Hall*. A quick examination revealed them to be all first editions.

Dropping into the chair, she read his note again two more times. Her finger traced the *C*. As much as she despised what he had done, she couldn't stop herself from missing him.

T he next several weeks saw Violet writing madly on her story about the American heiress in London. She had thought the anguish would distract her or make her too melancholy to write, but in fact, the exact opposite happened. She wrote whole chapters over a matter of days, when before it would have taken her weeks. It was as if every bit of sadness she felt was infused in her pen and served as the fuel to push it across the paper. Much to her surprise, she found herself focusing on the budding romance between Lord Lucifer and Rose Hamilton instead of the larger social commentary she had originally planned. She wrote every part of them on the page, holding nothing back, not even the parts she knew she would have to edit out or be forced to wear the modern equivalent of a red *A* on her chest. On the pages, she could control their story as she could not control her own.

Her own story was not turning out quite so well. She and Christian attended several balls and theater events together. They always arrived separately because Violet had insisted upon it. She still didn't trust herself to be near him, and the request wasn't that out of the ordinary. Most fashionable couples spent the evenings out, following their own pursuits, coming together at one function or another for appearances. It wasn't lost on her that her own marriage, despite her best intentions, had become like theirs. Living a life separate from her husband was not how she had ever envisioned her future, and in fact was why she had so rebelled against her parents' plans for her.

Except Christian was not Lord Ware or Hereford. He had not imposed himself upon her. He had not issued any restrictive edicts that would see her life curtailed to suit his whims. According to Max, he had not attempted to touch Aunt Hortense's home. Her situation could be exponentially worse, which is why she didn't allow herself to linger on those thoughts. In the evenings she wrote, and in the daytime she turned her attention toward renovations, choosing wallpaper, varnish, and furniture to make the Belgravia house a home.

Only in the past several days had she begun to suspect that adding a nursery would need to be prioritized very soon. Her courses had not appeared since before she had left for Windermere, she felt tired more than usual, and her breasts ached in a way they never had before. The prospect of having a child—Christian's child—filled her with as much happiness as it did uncertainty. They had never talked about children except for that day when he had told her about his injury. Would he welcome the news? Would he see it as another burden? How could she even tell him now with this terrible rift between them?

None of this was ever how she had imagined her life to be.

The suspicion weighed heavy on her mind as she sat trying to pay attention to the opera *Lohengrin* with Christian beside her. Her parents sat in the row in front of them with Lord and Lady Ashcroft, who had been gracious in inviting them all to share their box. Helena and her brother, Lord Rivendale, sat on her other side. Despite appearances, she had not spoken to her parents at any length, nor did she plan to in the near future, and Max was due to leave soon for New York. She exchanged letters with August often, but it wasn't the same as having her sister here. She was very alone in this. Besides, sharing her suspicion with them could not compare to the joy she wished to share with Christian.

He sat beside her, stiff and formal. His thigh was only inches from her, reminding her of how they had sat in the carriage and how he had invited her next to him. She had luxuriated in his touch that day. Even now there was a part of her that screamed out for him. That was the part that frightened her. She would tell him when she was certain, but she was afraid that her irrepressible feelings for him would overpower her. If she told him before knowing her own mind, surely she would be lost to him again. It was best to wait.

She glanced to her right only to find him not watching the opera at all. His gaze was on her instead. It was not the first time she had noticed. When the music lowered, she leaned over and whispered, "The performance is on the stage." She tried not to take in his scent, but it was too late. Even as her mind rebelled, her instincts sought the remembered comfort of him.

"I prefer this view," he said without taking his eyes from her.

She stared at him fully, noting the intensity of his eyes and how they pulled her in. It was like that between them every single time she saw him. Him drawing her to him without even trying, and her attempting to keep her sanity. Even when she looked away she could feel the heat he emanated, could remember the way his touch felt, and her hand would ache to find his. Would such a small comfort compromise her so deeply?

Yes! Every fiber of her being knew that if she allowed herself one small comfort, her affection-starved heart would revel in it, glutton itself in the luxury and demand more bit by bit until she was as lost as she had been before. Giving him everything while demanding nothing in return. Even knowing the danger he posed to her heart, she had to make a fist to ensure she wouldn't reach for him. Her body craved the flood of solace and contentment that being held in his arms would bring it.

"Excuse me," she said, rising from her seat to brush past him as the anger that always accompanied such thoughts made an appearance. Pushing the curtain aside, she stepped out into the corridor that would lead her to the stairs and the cool evening air.

"Violet?" he whispered as he came out behind her, catching up to her when the stairs were in sight.

Since the opera still raged on, the corridor was empty with gaslights flickering at intervals, but they were turned very low so that his face appeared in shadow. She could still see his concern, and it tugged at her treacherous heart.

"Are you ill?" he asked, coming to a stop only inches before her.

"No, I'm angry, Christian." She kept her voice low, and hopefully the music drowned out anything said between them from reaching ears only too eager to hear. Speculation about their living separately had been raging for weeks.

He nodded. "My apologies. I'll keep my gaze to the stage."

Shaking her head, she said, "It's not only that."

"Tell me." He searched her face and seemed to come to some resolution. "Tell me what I can do to win you back and make you end this punishment."

"You think I'm punishing you?"

"Yes, that is very much how it feels. I know that I deserve it, so I haven't pushed, but you don't deserve it, and I can see that this estrangement is hurting you, too. Let me—" He reached for her, and she moved back out of instinct and self-preservation.

"Christian, please don't."

He paused and ran a hand over his jaw, clearly frustrated.

"I'm sorry I can't move forward yet, but you hurt me deeply. Not only did you wound me, but you made it so that I cannot even trust myself. I don't trust my instincts. I don't trust that I know anything about anything, certainly nothing about the things that I thought I knew."

She wasn't making any sense, but pain furrowed his brow, and he made no move to speak.

Taking a deep breath, she started again. "You see, I gave you everything, my hopes, my dreams, my future . . . my heart, you had all of it. I held nothing back from you. And you manipulated those feelings. You lied to me. The entire time I gave everything, you held back. I was too stupid to know that I was supposed to do the same. I don't know how to move forward with that. I don't know that if we do move forward that you'll be honest. I don't know that you even know how to be honest.

"Please understand that while I am angry, none of this is to punish you, Christian. I do it to save myself."

His eyes glistened suspiciously, and that tore at her heart even more. She despised hurting him. When she would have turned away, he grasped her waist, making her pulse leap in excitement as her body remembered the pleasures his touch could bring.

He didn't attempt to kiss her as she thought he might. Instead, he whispered, "Perhaps it would be best to take some time apart, then. No more performances for the gossips."

She took in a serrated breath. "Yes, that seems wise." It was certainly too painful for them both to continue as they were. Two broken people stumbling around each other, trying and failing to heal.

"Know this, Violet. I love you." His eyes were so fierce and earnest, she believed he spoke the truth. "I will love you until I draw my last breath. When you are ready, you will find me waiting."

Her own eyes filled with tears as pain and tenderness warred for space in her heart. Leaning up on her toes, she kissed him, an achingly sweet kiss of loss and heartache. When she pulled back, he let her go, dragging in a ragged breath. She turned before she could talk herself out of it and hurried outside to summon her carriage. The only way through this was forward, but she didn't know if she had the strength to make it.

Montague Club was busy by the time Christian returned that night. Usually, the jovial atmosphere allowed him to push whatever worried him to the back of his mind. He could forget it all for a time in drink, gambling, or fighting. That had not been true ever since he had returned to London without Violet. For the first time in his life, he felt that a part of himself was missing. That she had taken it with her, and he would never be whole again. Worse, he didn't know that he wanted to be whole without her. The idea of finding joy in a life without her in it filled him with disgust.

Ignoring the patrons he passed, he walked through the entry hall and up the stairs to seek the sanctity of his suite, already loosening his tie. He would send his valet away and spend the rest of the night racing to the bottom of a bottle of scotch. It wouldn't solve anything, but it would dull the ache in his chest enough that he could make it through another night with the guilt doing its best to eat him alive.

He was pushing open his door when Jacob called to him from down the corridor. Christian ignored him and continued into his room but left the door open so that his brother could enter if he wanted. Of course, he wanted. Jacob could never leave well enough alone. Dismissing his valet, Christian shrugged out of his coat and poured himself a drink as Jacob entered.

Dressed in full evening wear, Jacob closed the door behind him and leaned against the doorjamb. "I take it the evening did not go well."

"She despises me." Christian took a sip, letting the scotch warm a path to his belly where it joined the guilt gnawing at him. "I do not blame her, and yet . . ." He took another drink. He could barely restrain himself from going to the Belgravia house and forcing her to talk to him. Shaking his head, he said, "We've agreed to not see each other for a while." It had seemed the only sane choice when he saw how very much his presence upset her.

"I doubt she despises you."

"I hurt her deeply. I don't know how to convince her to forgive me for that."

Jacob walked farther into the room, his face a study of serious thought as he sat on the sofa. "I don't think you can convince someone of that. She either will or she won't be able to."

Christian took the sofa opposite his brother. "Very helpful."

"No, I mean that perhaps you're coming at this from the wrong angle. You've compromised her trust in you. Once trust is lost, you can't see its return by simply willing it to be so."

He was right, but it sounded very much as if he meant Christian was to give her up. "Then what do you suggest?" he asked, holding his breath to await the answer.

Jacob sat forward, forearms on his knees, to look him in the eye. "Deeds, brother. When words no longer hold meaning, deeds speak louder. Prove to her that she can trust you."

Deeds. The guilt and scotch swirled together in his belly, but Jacob's words burned through them, an incendiary flame that scorched everything but his resolve. Deeds were the only way to have Violet in his arms again. They were the only way to prove to her that she could trust his words. The only way to have her.

He knew exactly what he would have to do.

Chapter 24

❦

The task before him was to convince the woman he loved that he was worth the hand she had given him. He set himself to this task with his whole heart.

V. LENNOX, *AN AMERICAN AND THE LONDON SEASON*

SEPTEMBER 1875

I have wonderful news to announce." Helena raised her voice slightly to be heard over the din of conversation in her drawing room. The board of directors of the orphanage was concluding its monthly meeting. After the usual fiscal report followed by progress made the previous month, the members were discussing the need for a capital campaign to finance the task of procuring a new home and school to house the working mothers and their children.

The London Home for Young Women had begun as a way to fulfill a need Helena had identified from working with the orphanage. Working mothers, usually unmarried women, sometimes wanted to keep their children instead of giving them up but were unable to with the orphanage's current resources. She had converted a floor in the orphanage for this purpose, but it had grown so much in the past year that it needed its own space separate from the orphanage along with its own board of directors. Violet was in attendance because Helena's passion for the cause had influenced her to help.

"Well, what is it?" Violet asked, setting her cup and saucer down. "You can't hold us in suspense any longer." She hadn't seen Helena look this excited in the short while she had known her.

Helena's smile widened. "I received notice from our solicitor that a substantial donation has been made to help take the London Home for Young Women forward. We can begin looking for a building immediately. The donor, however, wishes to remain anonymous."

"How wonderful," said one of the women.

Another asked, "But how is this possible, Lady Helena? We haven't yet begun to solicit donations beyond our families." The five women all looked to one another as if hoping someone knew the identity of the mysterious donor.

Helena looked at Violet, a very knowing and very appreciative glint in her eye. Thankfully, she glanced away before anyone else could catch her. Violet had no idea what the look meant.

"It was a surprise to me as well. However, it means that we must make finding a space a priority," Helena continued. "I believe it would be appropriate to form a committee for the purpose. Lady Leigh, would you like to chair this committee?"

Caught completely unaware, Violet opened and closed her mouth several times like a fish out of water. Another woman seconded the motion, and before she knew it, she had been voted chair of the committee to find a new location for the London Home for Young Women. She didn't mind, not really. The charity had become close to her heart in the months she had been volunteering under Helena's guidance, but the entire exchange was odd.

The meeting went on for several more minutes after the excitement, but finally the ladies adjourned and made their way out. Violet stayed behind to speak to Helena alone. As soon as the door closed on the last board member, Helena turned to her. "How are you feeling?"

Violet automatically touched her belly. Her pregnancy wasn't known yet, but she had shared the information with August, Max, and Helena. All those close to her except Christian. She would have to tell him soon, however, because she didn't want anyone else beating her to it. Her body had already begun to change in many ways. She wore her corset loosened, her face had grown fuller, as had other parts of her, and she was hungry nearly constantly. It was only days before someone noticed. He would be hurt if he didn't hear it from her.

She had even begun to feel that fluttering sensation that told her the baby moved and grew inside her. It had happened a few days ago, and her first thought had been to tell Christian, to share it with him, but they hadn't talked in months now, and she was no longer sure of her reception if she approached him, even though she missed him more and more each day. Their time apart had given her the space she needed to feel comfortable making her own decisions and learn how to trust herself again. It had also made her wonder if his infatuation had faded. He had said that he would always love her, but she still didn't know how she could trust that when so much of their history was based on lies.

Pushing those thoughts aside, she said, "Much better lately, thank you. My fatigue and nausea seem to have passed."

"That's so good to hear." Helena led the way back to the drawing room. "I hope you don't mind me recruiting you as I did for the committee. It only seemed right that you take the lead since this was such a very generous contribution. It would have taken us months and months to raise this sort of funding. Why, we're nearly a year ahead of where I dared hope to be. But if you feel that you may not be up for it, I completely understand."

"No, of course I don't mind, Helena. I am happy to help in any way that I can, and I believe we can find something within the next couple months. Certainly, well before the baby is to be born in February. It's only that I'm afraid I don't understand. You see, I already donated my portion, and I had Mr. Clark set up an annuity." Christian's solicitor had paid her a visit shortly after she had taken up residence at the Belgravia house. They had been in regular contact since to establish how her fortune should be managed. Along with a lump sum donation, she had set up an investment that would see the charity given a fixed amount every year.

"I know that, but my solicitor believes that you arranged it." Helena frowned.

"Interesting. Why would he think that?" It would not be from her parents, whom she had not spoken to at any length beyond social functions. She intended to speak to them, but it would be much later, once she had finished establishing herself. "Perhaps it was Max?"

Helena colored prettily, and her face softened somehow. "It's not from him. He already made a pledge. Besides"—she glanced toward the door even though everyone had left them and her aged servants were in the kitchen—"the solicitor mentioned Lord Leigh, though his name shall never appear on any documents. We both assumed that you had appealed to your husband."

Shock prickled her skin. "No, I haven't spoken to him yet about it."

No one but August, and the gossips who continued to speculate about the state of their relationship, knew that she hadn't spoken to him in months. No one but her immediate family knew that he would not be able to summon such a large donation from his own personal wealth. Had he used her funds? The funds that he had sworn were hers alone? She didn't think he would, but she hadn't actually required Mr. Clark to show her the monthly transactions.

"Is everything all right?" Helena asked.

Violet nodded, but she didn't know.

"I don't have to tell you how much this means to us. We can help to improve so many lives. Many more children will be able to be raised by their mothers instead of given away. We can train and educate even more women to improve the jobs available to them."

"Yes, it's wonderful. I shall tell Christian myself how his gift has been received." It was wonderful. The unease swirling in her belly was due to the fact that he hadn't told her any of this.

Helena smiled. "You must be very proud of him."

"Well, yes . . ." There was something more in Helena's eyes, something lurking behind that statement. "Why do you say that?"

Helena rose and walked over to the desk where newspapers had been left to pile up in various stages of being read. Rifling through them, she retrieved the one she was looking for. "He had an essay published on the need to reform married women's rights. It's caused quite a stir among the stodgy set."

Violet accepted the newspaper from her. She had stopped reading the papers when the gossips had decided her relationship with her husband was too much to ignore. When they had begun to write of the rift between them, she had told Winston to keep all the papers for himself.

The article's headline read, "Marriage Turns Devilish Earl into a Saint for Women." The reporter began by outlining the argument Christian laid out in his essay: that married women should possess their own legal identities and be allowed to control their own assets. The reporter referred to the essay as "a love letter to his wife." She couldn't help but smile at that. Was that why Christian had written it? Was he wanting to win her back, or did he really believe those things? Or were both possible?

The piece went on to discuss speeches Christian had

given earlier in the summer regarding protections for women and children who worked in factories. She hadn't known about those. While some supported his stand, the newspaper maintained that many were offended by his insinuation that those needs exist. The article even commented on the fact that the Belgravia house was staffed by only women, as if it were further proof of Christian's taking the side of the women. The assertion wasn't quite true, given that Winston and Thomas still held their positions, but close enough to the truth to print, apparently.

"Leigh's essay is on the next page if you want to read it," said Helena.

Violet turned the page and skimmed his words, hearing them spoken in his voice in her head. He admitted with humility that he had not deigned to notice the abysmal state of the law in regards to women until his own wife had been forced to hand over complete control of her finances to him. He had been unable to find a legal way for her to even receive an allowance from her family without it passing through him. He had looked! A tender ache swelled in her chest. If he was so troubled by the law, then certainly he had been telling the truth about not wanting her settlement. Love unfurled in her heart after months of shielding itself.

"He has changed so much since your marriage, Violet. You've influenced him for the better."

She saw his face as it had been that night in their tiny bedchamber above the Mitchells' kitchen when she had mentioned marriage. A shy and tender sort of hope had passed over his features as he had offered his heart to her. These actions she would believe from that man. Perhaps that man was who he really was. Perhaps the man before, the man who had schemed to marry her for his own will, the man who had lied to her, was not who he was at all, not underneath where it mattered.

"I don't believe that people truly change," she said.

It was true of her parents. This mercenary side of them had always been present. Violet had realized that over time as she had examined their actions here in London and compared them to their actions back home. They were the same people, but circumstances had changed. Perhaps the same could be said of Christian. Perhaps he had been warm until circumstances he had faced as a child had made him cold to protect himself. It didn't mean that the warmth was gone, only that it had been hidden deep. She had gotten too many glimpses of his warmth to think it had never existed.

"This side of him has always been present." No matter what else had happened, that much was true. She was certain of it.

"Well, you certainly brought more of it out of him, my dear."

She had. Being together had brought out the best in both of them. If she was right about that, then she had wasted so much time.

"Helena, I'm sorry, but I must be going." It was late afternoon, and she still had to drive home to retrieve her ledger before going to Mr. Clark's office before he left for the day. She would get to the bottom of this right now. Knowing where he had acquired the funds for the donation would answer a few of her questions.

"Of course." The woman rose with her. "Is everything all right?"

"Yes, I think so."

She called out a quick goodbye and hurried to her carriage, giving her direction to her driver. On the entire drive, she wondered if perhaps she had been as right as she had been wrong. Infatuation would have passed, so what she still felt for him was love. It wasn't a spell or a trick. It was her own heart. But how could she trust him if he had done what logic said that he must have? If he had used her funds for the donation?

Traffic was slow, and with the stop at home it was an

hour later when she stepped into Mr. Clark's office. She had only been here once before, because he usually came to her home. She wasn't surprised that his clerk failed to recognize her.

"Good afternoon, madam." The young man stood and gave her a respectful once-over, though the creases in his forehead wondered what she was doing here.

"Good afternoon. I do not have an appointment, and I apologize for bursting in like this, but I must speak to Mr. Clark at once." She glanced toward the closed office door beyond, hoping to catch a glimpse of the man through the glass.

"My apologies, madam, but he is extremely busy. If you would like, I can make an appointment for you." He was already pulling an appointment diary from underneath the papers littering his desk.

"No, I must speak with him now. Tell him Lady Leigh is here."

The man dropped the book, his eyes wide in shock. "I shall try, my lady." With that he knocked on the door once before disappearing inside. When he returned a moment later, it was to nearly run into her standing at the door awaiting him. "Yes, he will see you now."

She walked through the open door to see Mr. Clark hurrying into the coat he had arranged on the back of his chair. Several ledgers were open on his desk as if she had caught him in the midst of working on something important. "My apologies, Mr. Clark. Thank you for agreeing to see me, and I hope to not take up too much of your time."

"Of course, my lady." Pushing his spectacles into place on his nose, he indicated she should seat herself across from him. As she accepted, he hurried to close the ledgers and stack them in an orderly fashion on his desk.

When she had first met him, she had noted he was younger than she had expected for a solicitor, probably Christian's age. The solicitors she knew from Papa were all well into middle age with portly builds from all the hours spent at their desks. From their earlier conversations, she had gleaned that Mr. Clark seemed very capable, plus he had worked for Christian and Montague Club for several years now. Rothschild and August also recommended him. She was certain that she would get the truth from him.

"What may I do for you today, my lady?" he asked, taking his seat behind his desk.

"I have come because I would like to see the ledgers you keep for my accounts."

"Of course you have that right, my lady, but might I ask if there is something specific you are looking for?" His gaze went to the ledger she held in her lap.

Unable to meet his gaze, since she was questioning his very earnestness, she said, "I have brought my own ledger from home where I have kept track of the renovation outlays and my own personal expenses over the last months. I would compare them with your own records."

To her relief, he didn't seem offended, but merely curious. "Is there a problem with your allowance? As you know, your renovations have come out of a different account."

"Yes, I know. I have kept the accounts separate here as well." She tapped to indicate the heavy ledger in her lap. "If I may but look at your ledgers and compare."

He gave her a nod and rose to pull open a drawer in a cabinet farther behind his desk, his movements slow but precise as if he still questioned her intent. Retrieving a file held closed with string, he unwound it and presented her with a piece of parchment from within. "Perhaps it would be best to start from the end and work our way back if need be. This is your statement of account from July for your allowance, and here is the one for your general funds. I am content to send my clerk to your bank should you need a statement from them to verify the amounts match. If you find they are not as you expected, we can certainly delve into the ledgers to determine why."

She studied the papers; each of them held columns of figures labeled debits or credits along with the category the funds or expenditures had been sorted into. Max and August had spent time explaining the concept to her back when she had originally begun investing her own money with her brother's assistance. They were not foreign concepts, and her own ledger was arranged in a similar fashion. The problem was that both totals were very near to what she had been expecting.

"This seems to be as it should," she said.

When Mr. Clark was quiet, she risked looking up at him. "Forgive me, but you seem startled by that. Have I given you cause to doubt my stewardship, my lady?" Twin lines of concern formed between his brows.

"No, Mr. Clark, you have been very kind and capable. It isn't you that I question. It is only that I received news today, and I am uncertain what it means."

She knew the moment he understood what she was talking about. His brows rose and his eyes cleared of uncertainty. Taking the papers back, he stuffed them into the file and placed it upon the desk as he retook his seat.

"I am certain you understand that I must commit myself to the confidence of my clients," he said.

"Yes, I understand. But I would have it confirmed that Lord Leigh directed you to donate a significant amount to a charity organized by Lady Helena March."

He swallowed. "I cannot betray his confidence in the matter, as much as I might wish to, my lady."

"Fine, but you could tell me if he used my money to do such a thing. I am correct in thinking that he could use my money if he so chose?"

"Yes, if he chose to utilize your funds in that way, then there would be nothing stopping him, but having been acquainted with both your wishes and the wishes of Lord Leigh, I feel confident in assuring you that he is a man of character in that regard."

She breathed out a sigh of relief, and the fist of dread that had made itself known since her chat with Helena completely loosened its grip on her heart. "Then where did he obtain the funds for such an endeavor?"

Lips pursed, he appeared pained by the question. "I cannot say, my lady."

The first gust of anger roused within her. "You cannot say. Could you say if the positions were reversed? If I were the one spending large sums and he came in demanding to know where they had been obtained, could you say then?"

His mouth opened, but then he closed it again and could not meet her eyes. "I can no more control the law than I can control where Lord Leigh chooses to spend his money."

"Of course you can't. I merely wish to know a simple thing. Where did my husband get the money for the donation?"

"Lady Leigh, certainly you can understand the position you put me in. If Lord Leigh wishes to keep the sale of his private property to himself, then I cannot go against his will in this. As much as I wish it were otherwise, I cannot tell you."

She gasped at that. His private property. As far as she was aware, the only property owned by him was the house in Belgravia, Amberley Park, and Blythkirk. Perhaps also the club, but Jacob and Rothschild owned part of it as well. Since her home was safe, Amberley Park was entailed and picked clean as far as she could ascertain, that left Blythkirk, or his portion of the club. "He would never sell his portion of Montague Club. Besides, it's his only reliable income." Aside from the annuity from the investments Mr. Clark had arranged with the bulk of her settlement. "It would be far too early to recognize any of the income from the annuity, yes?"

"Correct, my lady, it would be foolish of him to sell his interest in Montague Club at this time."

"Then Blythkirk. He sold Blythkirk?"

"My lady, as I have mentioned, his will is that all matters are kept private."

She stared at him, unable to believe that Christian had sold the one thing that had meant the most to him, the one thing that had started all of this. Without his love for Blythkirk, and the fire that had nearly destroyed it, he wouldn't have attempted to run away with her. "Blink if he sold Blythkirk."

He blinked.

Chapter 25

✤

*Lord Lucifer might have the Devil in his
eyes, but his heart belonged to Rose, and she
planned to keep it safe for all of her days.*
V. LENNOX, *AN AMERICAN AND THE
LONDON SEASON*

Christian grabbed the bar and pulled himself up until his feet left the floor and his chin rose over it. Pushing out the breath he'd been holding, he allowed himself to drop back down in a slow and controlled movement. He repeated the exercise in three sets of ten repetitions until the muscles in his arms, shoulders, and core screamed for mercy. Even then he did one more set to make certain he was good and exhausted.

Physical exertion was the only way he could get to sleep anymore. It couldn't all be alcohol induced, not when he had full days scheduled and needed a clear head. He had taken to retiring to the gymnasium in the club most nights after the majority of patrons had left for the evening. He would finish his shift on the floor and then come here to relieve his excess energy and frustrations on the equipment. The room had originally been a ballroom. It was large and still boasted the fine wallpaper, moldings, and chandelier that had graced it when Thea had presided over the house.

The ring in the corner was where most of their scheduled fights among the patrons and exhibitions occurred. The rest held equipment for exercise.

Sweat dripped from his hair and ran down his back as he let his feet touch the floor, a twinge of pain darting through his ankle.

"Ready now, milord?" Kostas, the attendant, asked, walking over with linen and batting to wrap his hands. Hitting the sandbag was how Christian preferred to end all of his exercise sessions.

"Yes, thank you." Christian held the batting to his knuckles while Kostas wrapped the linen between his fingers before winding it around the cotton and his hand.

"You simply cannot—my lady, this is not done. We have confidentiality to maintain." A commotion sounded from outside the open double doors. Christian recognized the voice of the club's night butler a moment before he heard a feminine voice say in a distinctly American accent, "I do not care for your confidentiality agreement. Had you fetched my husband like I asked, this wouldn't be necessary."

Violet! Hand wraps not yet tied off, he hurried to the door just as she rushed into the room. She paused and looked faintly appalled when she saw him. The initial burst of joy he felt turned to caution. Shirtless in breeches and boots, his usual costume for bare-knuckle brawling matches that he had taken to wearing while exercising, he understood how he must look to her. Beastly and unrefined. His true nature. Perhaps it was only right that she saw him like this. There should be no pretending between them, not anymore.

"Is everything all right?" he asked. It was late, and she wasn't dressed for a ball. He couldn't fathom what had brought her here at all, much less at this hour. He didn't dare think that she was here for any sort of reconciliation. He wouldn't be able to deal with the disappointment when he learned he was wrong. Something must have happened to make her barge into the club.

She appeared to have trouble finding her voice, swallowing several times and looking away only to look back at him. The two other men who had been using the equipment had paused to watch them. "I think so. I must speak with you now, though. Privately."

Assured that she was well, he began unwrapping his hands. "We can go to my suite." At her nod of agreement, he handed the wraps off to Kostas and accepted the length of toweling in return. He wiped his face of sweat and shrugged into the dressing gown Kostas held for him.

The butler gave a huff but left them. Without a word, Christian accepted his cane from the attendant before leading her through the empty back rooms to the corridor that led to the second floor, which was where they all kept their personal rooms. The entire time he was aware of her, silent and rigid next to him, her censure a near tangible thing. If he had held any hope that her visit was a conciliatory one, he would have been mistaken. Luckily, he had given up that hope long ago as a fool's blind faith.

Holding the door open for her, he followed her inside and closed it behind them. It made a deceptively quiet but ominous click. Suddenly, he was afraid to let her talk. Afraid that she would say the very words he knew to be true but had not been able to face this whole time. She wanted a divorce. He could not bring himself to imagine that she wanted anything else, not after her months of silence. If she asked for a divorce, he would be powerless to do anything except give it to her, but not before he shamed himself by falling to his knees and begging her to stay.

"Could I get you something?" He walked to the sideboard and poured himself a glass of water from the chilled pitcher that was left for him each night.

"No, thank you."

From the corner of his eye he watched her hover, decide to take a seat on the sofa, only to change her mind at the last second and walk to the window. She was as beautiful as he remembered. Her hair shone under the gaslight, and her skin seemed luminous. In profile, he was reminded of how she had looked the day he had asked her father for her hand. The day they had sparred in the entryway outside her music room. Christ, what a fool he had been for her. He had loved her even then.

When she turned back to him and caught him watching, he couldn't look away. She knew he was besotted with her, and he would look his fill until she left him. Her face was rounder, as if the angles had been softened in the time since he had last seen her. He couldn't be certain, because they were covered by her gown, but the effect seemed to extend to her shoulders, and even her breasts appeared fuller than he remembered. God, he knew every inch of her so well, he actually felt saddened that he had missed these changes. That she was somehow different than she had been with him and he had missed out.

That made him look away. He was mad for her. *Madness.* It was the only word for the obsession that coursed through him. He would have thought it would have faded with her absence, but it had come roaring back with her return, greedy for all he had missed.

"Why are you here?" His voice was harsher than he meant for it to be.

She approached him, only stopping an arm's length away. He didn't have the heart to tell her that she had ventured too close. He took another drink of water to give himself something to do besides grab her.

"I read your essay. I thought it was very good."

Her approval soothed him like a balm, seeping into the dark places he kept hidden. It was dangerous to allow himself to react to her so, but he couldn't help it. "Is that why you've come? To tell me you approve of my stance?" A stance that would greatly benefit her. Yet even as he thought it, he didn't care. She approved and that was enough.

"I also read an article about you in the *Times*. It men-

tioned your speech about children workers and the need to
further limit their workday, and also the one about women
in factories. I hadn't known about those, but I very much
appreciate your support. I suppose you might not know this,
but I have been working with Helena and her charity—"

"I know." He knew because he soaked up every bit of
information about her like a bloody desert thirsty for rain.
"I know, Violet."

Her lips parted in surprise as if she might have had
doubts that he was mad when it came to her. "Why did you
make those speeches?"

"Because they are just and good causes." *Because they
are things you support, because I want to be close to you
even if it is by association.* God, how low he had fallen.

"And yet you didn't support them before?" Before them,
she meant.

"I did. Only I was more selfish then."

She was silent for a moment, her too-knowing eyes seeing far too much in his face. He glanced away and walked
to the dressing room to discard his towel. The other room
was his bedchamber, which rounded out the three-room
suite, which meant his bed was close enough to be enticing,
but it might as well have been on the other side of London.
She was still standing by the sideboard when he returned.

Torn between needing her to go to spare himself the
pain of hearing her ask for a divorce, and the tiny flicker of
hope that dared think she might want him again, he simply
watched her, knowing the next few moments could and
likely would alter the course of his life.

"Christian . . ." She began to walk toward him, her pace
slow and deliberate, and his heart pounded against his ribs
as if trying to reach her on its own. Twisting her fingers in
front of her, she said, "Lady Witherston has asked if I might
be inclined to donate to her house for unusual birds. It
seems she believes that the only way to make the public
appreciate their splendid plumage is to breed them and con-

tinue to produce the terrible hats she wears. If I were inclined to favor her charity, would you also make an
impassioned speech about it?"

"If you wish it," he whispered, afraid to move, unable to
lie, unable to breathe. If he allowed her to know the terrible
power she held over him, he didn't know if he would survive its misuse.

She stopped mere inches from him. "Why did you write
the essay about women's property rights?"

"One day I hope to make permanent and lawful the
agreement we made. One day I will make certain you are
given control of your settlement."

For the first time, her expression cracked. She wasn't
cold or rigid but warm and soft. "Is it true that you sold
Blythkirk and donated the proceeds to the London Home
for Young Women?"

He shook his head. Clark had assured him that the donation could be made anonymously. Christian had insisted
upon it. "It doesn't matter."

Her palm touched his bare chest between the lapels of
the dressing gown. He stared at her hand, certain she could
feel the thundering of his heart.

"It matters to me, Christian. That was your home. It was
a place you loved, and I won't have you selling it for me."

"It was not my home. I thought it mattered, but it
doesn't." *You are all that matters.* "It was a shell of a building. I know what real loss feels like now, and that was a
mere echo."

Tears shimmered in her eyes. "Then tell me, is it true
that you still love me?"

His own eyes went blurry, making her face swim before
him. He wanted to protect himself, but he couldn't stop the
words from pouring out, not if they might convince her to
give them another chance. "Surely, you realize that my love
for you has not been ended by your absence. You must
know that I have loved you from our very first meeting, and

I will continue to love you long after I cease to draw breath. If you but ask it, I will make any speech, give any donation, sell the clothing from my back to see you satisfied."

"Christian." She breathed the word, and it filled his soul as she fell against his chest.

Slowly, as if his own imaginings had conjured her and she might disappear with his touch, he brought his arms around her. She was real, flesh and blood and heat. He tightened his grip, a part of him still afraid that she might vanish.

"This can't be healthy for us," she whispered against his chest. "This all-consuming love that we feel."

As if confirming her words, his heart seemed to stutter in his chest. "Love?" he repeated.

Lifting her head, she stared up at him. "Yes, I love you still. I tried to convince myself it was mere infatuation, but it wasn't. It isn't. I love you now as much as I did in Yorkshire. Perhaps more, deeper. Reading your words and knowing that you are willing to face criticism from your peers to see our agreement made legal . . . I know now that you really meant it when you said you didn't care about the settlement anymore.

"And seeing you now . . ." She ran her palms over his shoulders and up so that her fingers could clench the hair at the back of his head. His scalp prickled at the pleasant tug. "It's as if no time at all has passed, but also as if a lifetime has passed us by. I don't want to go another day without you. I don't want to wake up without you. I don't want to wonder in every gnawing moment that I have alone what you are doing or if you miss me."

"Yes," he whispered, taking her mouth. She opened for him so sweetly. "I miss you constantly." He kissed her again. "I love you constantly." Another kiss. "Can you ever trust me again?"

"Yes, yes, of course." Her hands slid inside his dressing gown to explore his naked chest as if she couldn't stop touching him. "You are a good man, and I knew that all along."

"I'm sorry for ever making you doubt me. I'm sorry for not being more open. It's hard for me, but that's no excuse."

Her dark eyes softened, shimmering gold in the gaslight as she took his face between her palms. "No, it's not, but we can start anew. If you still want me—"

He pulled her against him again. "Jesus, Violet, of course I still want you. I never stopped. I want us and what we discovered in Yorkshire." His kissed her jaw, craving her taste and the salt of her skin. She wore the perfume she favored, but underneath he could smell her.

"I'm perspiring." He had only just now realized that he was likely ruining her gown. "I was training." He tried to push her away, but she only brought his mouth to hers.

"Yes, I know. I saw. It's why I'm rather in a hurry."

So the look she had given him hadn't been censure after all. She had been fighting her desire for him. It was as plain as day in her eyes. He laughed, and the beast in him slipped the reins, clawing at her clothing as he tried to find her beneath it. She made a sound of anticipation and pushed the dressing gown off his shoulders before helping him with her fastenings. Something ripped, but she didn't seem to mind. As soon as he yanked her gown away, followed by the corset, he saw the locket he had given her lying on her chest, and it stopped him cold.

"You kept it."

"Yes." Her heart was in her eyes. "I wear it every day. Sometimes I take it off for balls, but I put it back on before going to bed."

That would explain why he hadn't seen her wear it in the weeks after their wedding. Her gowns for going out in the evenings all had lower-cut necklines. Groaning as a wave of affection crashed over him, he picked her up and stormed through the suite with her to his bed. There he unwrapped her, ravenous in his need. But so was she. As soon as she was divested of petticoats and chemise, she pulled him on top of her, her greedy hands at the waistband of his breeches.

"I can't wait any longer," she said.

He was inclined to agree. As he sat back to unfasten the breeches, he couldn't take his eyes off her, afraid she might disappear because this was all a dream. She was the most gorgeous thing he had ever seen. A pink flush stained her pale skin as she laid back against the pillows, thighs spread for him. Her sex glistening with her need. This was his home. Her. This woman who had taught him so much about love and forgiveness. Blythkirk and all the rest be damned. None of it meant anything without her.

He crawled over her, his body trembling with need and emotion. She reached between them, guiding him to her where he felt only the slightest resistance before he filled her up. They both cried out at the sensation; for once there was no need to be quiet or discreet in their pleasure. The tight grip of her body was the closest to heaven he would ever come. He tried to savor it, to relish the feel of her, the smell of her, but it had been so long he knew he wouldn't be able to prolong it. Her legs wrapped around his waist, and she arched toward him, tightening herself along his length.

"I won't be able to last." His voice was more of a growl than anything else.

"Good," she said, doing it again, her nails biting into his shoulders.

"Violet," he groaned. "I love you."

"Show me," she sighed, as he moved within her.

He was lost. Winding her hair around his fists, he held her tight and thrust into her like a man who had been denied this pleasure for too long.

But apparently so had she. She rode him as he rode her, and when he came, her body shuddered with his as he lost everything within her.

* * *

Violet didn't want to close her eyes to blink, afraid that she would wake up and this would all be a fantastic dream. Her heartbeat was only now starting to return to normal as she lay beside him. Her husband. Taking his hand, she brought it to her lips, feeling his own kiss at her temple in response.

"I'm sorry I took so long. I think of all the time—"

"Shh . . . it was time you needed, time we both needed. I understand." He touched her cheek, taking her mouth in a kiss that was only just starting to lose the tinge of desperation. Rising up on an elbow, he smiled down at her, his dimple making an appearance. His smile was so loving and accepting that it filled her heart with a warmth it could barely contain. "I love you, and we will never be apart again. That's all that matters."

"You'll come home with me in the morning to Belgravia?" A part of her still expected him to refuse. The house must remind him of his father.

He surprised her by nodding as he rose, unlacing his boots to drop them off the side of his bed, followed by his breeches and drawers. "You've renovated it, I hear," he said as he turned to her, taking first one shoe off and then the other.

"I have. It's almost unrecognizable." It wasn't until that moment that she realized she had been so determined to change it completely for him. She watched as he kissed the arches of her feet, before reaching up to divest her of her stockings. Arrows of pleasure darted through her with each touch. Her body was a greedy thing, already wanting him inside her again. "We don't have to live there, though, if it makes you uncomfortable."

He gave her a wicked glance. "As long as I'm with you, I have everything I need."

He trailed kisses up her legs to her thighs and the curls

hiding her from him. Then he kissed her belly, pausing as he took in the slight swelling he had probably been too busy to observe before. She dared not breathe. He couldn't suspect. It was hardly noticeable to her, but his gaze was filled with awe when he looked up at her.

"You're with child," he said.

"Yes," she whispered.

His face transformed with joy as he looked back down to where their child grew. His hand swept over the slight bump in a tender caress. "That explains these." He grinned wickedly and rose over her, his gaze on her breasts. "They've grown, and your nipples are darker." His tongue licked around one before drawing it into his mouth. She gasped at the pleasure it sent pulsing through her. Releasing her, he lay beside her and gathered her into his arms. "There was a time I thought I would never have children," he said, his lips brushing her cheek as he spoke. "But it seems only natural with you."

"Then you're not disappointed?" A part of her hadn't been certain he would welcome fatherhood.

"No, never. From the moment I knew I wanted you as my wife, I imagined children in that future." He was silent for a moment, then he asked, "Are you disappointed?"

"No. Why would I be?" She looked over at him to see that he seemed pensive.

"Because you must think that I'll be a terrible parent."

"No—"

"I promise that I will be a good father. I know that you must wonder—"

"I don't wonder, Christian." She smiled at him. "You are a good man and nothing like your father." Something she knew with absolute certainty. Relief softened his features.

"Good, because I imagined that we would grow old together with children and grandchildren around us." He admitted that in the same way he had admitted his love for her in Yorkshire, in a way that was almost shy, as if he expected the information might be received with anything less than the overpowering happiness she felt.

"When did you imagine this?" She couldn't resist asking, her hand pressed against his beloved face.

"Truthfully? I imagined it the night I first saw you at the ballet with your family. But I knew it was something I had to make happen the day I asked your father for your hand."

Her smile only grew larger. "Had I but known, I could have saved us a lot of trouble. I was convinced you saw me as little more than a child."

"Never that." He laughed, and the rich sound penetrated her, warming her. God, she had missed this with him.

"I have other news to share, about my writing."

"About that . . . I've been thinking that we should have your manuscript printed. A private printing that we can distribute—"

He stopped talking when she shook her head. "There is no need, my lord. I have a publisher."

"What? Really?" He grabbed her hips and rolled to his back, bringing her astride him, his face alight with joy.

"I received the letter and contract only yesterday. The *Atlantic Monthly* in Boston wants to publish it as a serial this winter." Her initial urge had been to tell him about it. Before August, before Helena, he is the one she wanted to share in her news.

"That's excellent, Violet. I know it will be a success. We should celebrate. And then we'll celebrate again when your second manuscript is finished."

She shook her head again. "Then we should have a double celebration tonight. I already finished it."

"You did?"

"It's all I could think of these past months. Lord Lucifer and his annoying brooding. He wouldn't leave me alone."

She giggled when he tackled her to the bed, rising over her. "I'm glad he tormented you as you tormented me." He began kissing his way down her body.

"I'm afraid you're likely to be disappointed when you read it."

He paused at her belly and raised his head. "You're going to allow me to read it?"

She shrugged, feeling shy despite the fact that she was lying naked in his bed and at his mercy. "If you want."

"You know I want to." If possible, his eyes gathered intensity as he returned his attention to his task.

"As I was saying, it's all terribly droll and melancholy. He finally gets his comeuppance in the end when Miss Hamilton rejects his suit in favor of—Ouch!"

He bit her inner thigh. It hadn't really hurt as much as it had sent a pang of longing directly to her core. After soothing the bite with his tongue, he looked up and said, "She can reject him all she wants, as long as the real Miss Hamilton becomes Lady Lucifer."

"The real Miss Hamilton is already Lady Lucifer, and you didn't let me finish. She rejects him but has a change of heart and they live happily ever after."

"As it should be, Lady Leigh." The Devil was in his eyes as he gave her a wicked grin and went back to his play.

She decided to wait until morning, when they went back to the Belgravia house, to tell him she had instructed Mr. Clark to purchase Blythkirk back from its new owners. A man could only take so much excitement in one day.

Acknowledgments

Thank you to the entire Berkley team for all of the wonderful things you do to make my ideas into actual books. You all are fantastic at what you do, and I'm so thankful I get to work with you. A special thank-you to Sarah Blumenstock. You are an amazing editor and I don't know where I'd be without you. Nicole Resciniti, thank you for going to bat for me a thousand times. Laurie Benson and Tara Wyatt, you both read early versions of my work and talk me off the ledge when I need it. Thank you for always being there. A special thank-you to Jenni Fletcher for catching all of my egregious English errors and Americanisms and setting me straight. To my Unlaced ladies, I appreciate your generous sharing of knowledge and our monthly chats with tea. Nathan and Erin, Saturday mornings wouldn't be the same without you.

Finally, a very big thank-you to my family. I couldn't do this without your support and understanding. Thank you for helping me do what I do. Love you!

Don't miss

THE LADY TEMPTS AN HEIR,

coming in Spring 2022 from Berkley Jove!

Maxwell Crenshaw had left New York for London three times this year. The first time had been to save a sister from a marriage she didn't want. The second time had been to find his other sister who had run away from a marriage she didn't want. This time he was in London to see his father who had been on his deathbed ten days ago when Max had set off from New York. Thank God the message that had been waiting for him in Liverpool indicated there had been substantial improvement in his condition. But it didn't change the resolution he had come to on the ship. He planned to convince his parents that it was time to come home. London had been disastrous for the Crenshaws.

"Max! Thank God you're here." The front door of the Crenshaws' townhome on Grovesnor Square had barely closed behind Max and his secretary before Mother came sailing out of the drawing room, arms outstretched to greet him. Handing off his hat and gloves to a manservant, he met her halfway. She looked as well put together as usual, her gown was the height of fashion and diamonds flashed at her wrists and neck. She was pale, however, a sign of her worry.

He held her for a moment longer than necessary, noting how her shoulders trembled. "I came as soon as I could." Since Papa and August had come to London in the spring, Max had assumed control of the American operations of Crenshaw Iron Works. It was a job he had been born and bred to do, having worked alongside his father since he was twelve years of age, but it was very demanding. Thankfully, having to come to London twice in the spring had forced him to delegate duties, so he had left the office in the capable hands of a manager.

"I know you did. I'm so happy you're here." Pulling back enough to see his face, she patted his cheek as if he were a child. "Mr. Winslow." She greeted his secretary. After their pleasantries were exchanged, she instructed the footman to show him to a bedroom.

Taking Max's hand, she tugged him toward the stairs. "How was your voyage?"

"Fine. What have the doctors said?"

"His heart is weak, but you'll have to ask August for the specifics." She waved him off. "She's up with him now. You know me. I can't keep track of those medical terms. The important thing is that he is improving. They believe that with rest he will recover."

"He's been working too hard." It wasn't a question because they all knew how much the man worked. He was up early every morning and spent the evening at all the social events London had to offer. He wasn't resting like he should. "You both must come home to New York." At least there they maintained a more conventional schedule.

"You'll have to take that up with Papa."

She smiled, but he could sense her reluctance. She didn't want to leave the social acceptance they had found in London. With one daughter married to a duke and another married to an earl, all ballrooms were open to them. Things were different in New York. As new money, the Crenshaws had been excluded from the upper echelons of society. Mrs. Astor kept her list of the best families in New York and his family wasn't on it, or they hadn't been before the marriages into nobility.

While this had never bothered anyone but his parents, the allure of acceptance had proven too much for them to resist. And it looked as if it was proving to be their downfall. First, they had sacrificed their daughters, and now Papa's health.

Clenching his jaw to keep from insisting, he held his breath as she pushed open the door to Papa's bedroom. August rose from her seat beside the bed, but his gaze went past her to the man lying back against the pillows. His breath caught in his chest at how pale and wan his father looked. Papa, who was always so in control of the world around him, appeared to have lost at least twenty pounds, possibly more. His skin seemed to hang on his cheekbones. For the first time, Max understood how close they had come to losing him, and it left him feeling weak.

"Max." His father's eyes lit up in a way that made the tightness in Max's chest ease the tiniest bit.

"I'm so glad you're here." August closed the leather-bound journal she had been holding and hurried over to hug him.

"Good afternoon, Papa. August."

His sister smiled up at him, but she looked exhausted. Blue tinged the pale skin beneath her eyes and lines bracketed her mouth where he hadn't noticed any before. She had worked at Crenshaw Iron since she had been old enough to insist upon it. At first Papa had humored her interest in numbers and analysis, but she had proven herself to be more than capable. She had come to London with their parents to help build the European branch of their business,

and she had excelled in the task. Max had a sinking suspicion, however, that she was as overworked as Papa, a condition that had likely worsened as she had shouldered their
father's workload while he convalesced.

"What are the doctors saying?" Max asked, releasing his
sister and walking over to the bedside to squeeze his father's disturbingly frail shoulder.

Papa gave a low cough. "You know doctors. What do
they ever say? Rest, take in fresh air." He shrugged. "I'll be
better in a few days."

August's brows drew together in concern. "You will improve, Papa, I have no doubt about it, but it will take weeks
to recover from the attacks."

"Attacks? There was more than the one?" Alarm caused
Max to speak louder than he meant to.

Mother gave a soft mew of displeasure and left the
room, as if the conversation was too much for her. August
put a calming hand on his back.

"It was only the one at Farthington's soiree," Papa said.

"We were all at a party hosted by the Earl of Farthing-
ton when the attack happened," August explained. To her
father, she said, "No, the doctors are certain you had another two days later."

Papa waved his hand as if the event wasn't worth mentioning.

Her mouth turned down in displeasure. "We were home,
and he was supposed to be resting. But he was drowning in
reports and correspondence that he had sent over from the
office behind my back. He had another episode."

"It wasn't as severe as the first one," Papa interrupted.

Ignoring him, August went on. "The doctors called it
angina pectoris. Essentially, it's pain of the heart caused
from periodic loss of oxygen and is a sign of heart disease.
They suspect there is an accumulation of fatty tissue com-
pressing the organ."

"I am as healthy as an ox."

"An ox with a heart problem." August shot back but walked over and gave him a kiss on his cheek to soften the words. "I have to go now. Evan sends his regrets for not accompanying me. He had a meeting with his estate manager. We have a dinner to attend, but we'll stop by and check on you on our way home." To Max she said, "We can talk more tonight, but let's have breakfast in the morning to discuss how to proceed."

Max agreed, and she departed, leaving the room feeling eerily still in her wake. The only sounds were the ticking of the clock on the mantel, and the chime of the doorbell downstairs. "Healthy as an ox?" Max said, taking a seat in the vacated chair.

One corner of the older man's mouth turned upward, and his eyes seemed to visibly fade. "She worries too much, so I play along."

Max's own heart seemed to stutter in his chest at his father's admission. "Then you did have more chest pain?"

Papa nodded. "A bit, yes, there was another time as well, but I didn't see a need to mention it. What are the doctors going to do? They've prescribed plenty of rest, bone broth to thin the blood, and a tonic." He gestured toward a brown glass bottle with a cork stopper on the nightstand.

What indeed? The energy that had spurred Max onward since he'd received the telegram about Papa's health drained as if someone had pulled the plug. Running a hand across the back of his neck to ease the tightness there, he said, "I've arranged to stay several weeks, longer if needed. August and I can see to the office here while you rest. After that, once you're stronger, you and Mother will return to New York with me."

"Leave London?" His face closed in mulish disagreement. "No, I can't see that happening until at least the spring. Perhaps longer. I've been working all summer on plans for India. We already have production underway to lay a thousand miles of track. As a matter of fact, I was hoping to take a trip there before returning to New York."

"A trip to India?" A trip like that could kill him. "Are you out of your mind?"

"Not now, obviously. I had hoped for January, but I concede it might not be the best time, so perhaps in March before it gets too terribly hot. I'll need to see the progress we're making with my own eyes. The railroads will have begun by then. No, don't give me that look, you remind me of your sisters. I will be better then."

"Papa, this is absurd. It is far too early to discuss trips abroad. Besides, you know I don't approve of this India expansion."

"I am aware of your feelings on the matter." Sighing, he added, "I suppose you're right. There are more important matters to discuss now."

Max's stomach churned in warning. "No, you need to rest and recover. Everything else can wait."

"I'm afraid this can't." His father's full moustache twitched in a way that it always did when he had to deliver unpleasant news.

Max sighed and sat back in the chair, stretching his long legs out before him and crossing them at the ankles. The upholstery creaked in protest. At six feet and three inches in bare feet with a solid frame, protesting furniture was a common problem. There was no escaping what was coming, so he might as well get comfortable. "I believe I know where this is heading but say it anyway."

"We need to begin thinking about the family legacy." The lines on his face seemed to deepen.

Max had been prepared to suffer through a monologue about the need for him to take the lead in their European venture, which would have effectively taken that role from August. While Papa had been somewhat supportive of her role in the company, he considered it an indulgence and wasn't above taking it away. Max was not prepared for *this*. "The what?"

"The legacy. I would like to have a hand in guiding my grandchildren through the ranks of Crenshaw Iron. I must admit that this . . . spell has given me cause to consider the fact that I may not be immortal as I had once hoped. In fact, I wonder if I will live long enough to see grandchildren through the ranks at all."

Max swallowed against a lump threatening to clog his throat. "Don't speak that way. Violet is with child now and due to deliver in the new year. August could—"

"August has informed me in no uncertain terms that she plans to wait to have children. Besides, her firstborn son will be too busy learning how to be a duke to run Crenshaw Iron. The same goes for Violet's child, and neither of them will be Crenshaws. They won't carry the name, and they'll have responsibilities here."

Max wasn't entirely insensitive to his father's suggestion. All his life he had embraced the Crenshaw legacy, begun by his grandfather, and imagined his own son taking over the reins of the company—though now that August had proven herself so adept, perhaps that mantle could be picked up by a daughter. While he had welcomed the idea, it had always been one that would be realized far into the future. Into his thirties. Not now at the age of twenty-eight when his life was so busy. He had assumed he would have another five years at least before considering the responsibilities of a wife and child.

"Let's talk about this later, Papa. As you said, you will recover."

The older man shook his head, his groomed and oiled hair shining in the lamp light. "We must speak of it now. While I do believe I will recover somewhat, I am not so foolish to believe I will be as good as before. I'm old, Max, but I still know a thing or two about planning for the long run. We must begin laying the foundation now. I want you married by the end of the year."

"Good God, Papa, that's not even two months!"

Papa held up a placating hand. "Yes, I'm aware. I'll settle for an engagement."

Max regarded his father through a narrowed gaze. The man was shrewd when it came to negotiation. He would bargain with the devil himself to get what he wanted, and Max felt no relief in the knowledge that he was his son. One only had to look at how Papa had negotiated August into accepting her marriage to see that. There would be consequences if Max chose not to agree to his terms.

His jaw clenched in anger, he said, "You're trying to manipulate me, to use me like one of my sisters."

The corner of Papa's mouth quirked upward again. "Aren't you and August always harping on me about equality amongst the sexes? Well, I have taken your words to heart. A son should marry just as a daughter should."

"I don't know what you have planned, but I will choose my wife. I won't have some brainless pawn served up to me."

"You would never stand for that. I would have nothing less from you. Despite how you might feel about my machinations in the past, I do appreciate the fact that when I'm gone August and Violet will be left in good hands. I have only wanted what is best for them."

Now Max was genuinely bemused. "I don't understand. If you don't have someone in mind, then why—?"

"Oh, I have several young women in mind. Amelia Van der Meer for one." Max was already shaking his head, but Papa continued. "Her father is a good friend and respectable businessman."

"Is she even Violet's age?"

"You mean the Violet who is now married with a child on the way?"

"I won't marry someone so young." He needed a wife he

could talk to about his day over dinner, not one who would smile mindlessly at him as she fell over herself to see to his needs. The memory of the one time he had been foolish enough to allow Amelia to corner him at a party sent him to his feet in a state of agitation. Rubbing a hand over the back of his neck, he walked to the pitcher on the bureau across the room and poured himself a glass of water. Miss Van der Meer had all but pawed at him in her bid to keep him to herself.

"I understand," said Papa, but Max rather thought he didn't. "That's why I don't want to suggest anyone. It's not so much who the lucky young woman is as long you marry soon." There was a brief pause, then he added, "But there are a few who shouldn't be considered."

Curious despite himself, Max asked, "Who?"

"That woman you've been seeing, for one. She's much too old and everyone knows her true nature. The only reason she's allowed in respectable society is because she's an Astor cousin."

Lydia Sheffield was a widow who was wealthy enough not to need to remarry. She was thirty-three and had no interest in having children or settling down with Max. That's why they got along so well. Their standing engagement on Thursday evenings kept them free to enjoy other pursuits during the week without entanglements. "Lydia wouldn't have me, so you're safe there."

"That's reassuring. Any woman you choose would need to be respectable, of course. Wealth would be a boon, but not necessary. Did you have anyone in mind?"

Unbidden, an image of Helena came to mind. She was looking at him in disapproval, with a slight smile curving her generous lips, after he had just informed her that she had been wrong. Violet had run away with Leigh, and Helena had insisted they go to his Scottish estate to find them. But none of the staff there had heard from the wayward couple. After that, he and Helena had spent several days combing the countryside for his sister before finding her with Leigh in a small village outside of York.

Nothing untoward had happened between Max and Helena on the trip, they had both been too worried for Violet's safety to entertain a flirtation, except something *had* happened. The devil if he knew how to describe exactly what. He had become familiar with her every emotion and how each of them reflected on her lovely face. He admired her intelligence and her quick humor, and in the months since he'd been unable to stop thinking of her.

She wouldn't want to marry him, though. She was settled in London and Somerset, and her family was here. It wasn't as if he knew her well enough to even consider marriage, but he liked what he knew about her. There would be no vapid dinner conversations with her.

No. She was a lady who inhabited a completely different world. He didn't know why his thoughts were even wandering in that direction.

"I do not, because I don't plan to be married anytime soon. This conversation is premature to say the least."

Disappointment crossed Papa's face, but it was gone as easily as it had come. "I thought you might think that."

Taking another drink of water, Max longed for it to be something much stronger. "What are the consequences you've come up with for not finding a woman to marry?"

Papa sighed. "I don't think we need to delve into consequences. I trust you will do what's right."

He despised this part of his father's character. The man was so ruthless in business that he had forgotten how to not be ruthless when it came to his family. He wanted what he wanted when he wanted it, and he had such faith in his vision being the right one that he manipulated anyone and anything to get it.

Clenching his jaw, he said, "But there is one. Tell me."

The air was thick with rising antagonism. There was a moment of silence before the man answered. "August has a new project she's excited about. The Prince Albert Dock. She spent all summer on a proposal and is close to securing a deal."

"And it'll be profitable?"

"Oh yes, it's a tidy sum which will help Crenshaw Iron get a firm foothold here in England."

"But?"

"But I'm prepared to block the project if I need to."

"You would stop a project you know is profitable to force me to marry? She would be crushed." It wasn't really a question. It was simply that Max couldn't quite believe the depths his father would stoop.

"I think you and I both know that there will be no need for that. Think of it as an incentive. If you make the right choice all will be well."

Nausea roiled in his stomach. "Right. An incentive." Setting the glass down on the bureau with a hand shaking in fury, Max went for the door. "I'll let you rest."

He tried not to slam the door behind him but wasn't successful. Outside, he paused and drew in a deep breath followed by another. His collar felt suffocating. In one deft motion, he loosened his tie and stood for a time with his fists clenching and unclenching at his sides. The need to hit something had never been so great.

What he wanted to do was to go back downstairs, walk out the door, and summon a carriage to take him back to the train station. He could be on an ocean liner tomorrow headed back to New York where he would continue to live his life in peace and run the American branch of Crenshaw Iron as he saw fit. He had been put in charge. It would take a vote by the board to remove him, no matter what his own father might prefer. Max had gained their respect, so he was certain his father's vote wouldn't sway them.

Before he even quite knew what he was doing, he was at the top of the stairs and moving down them. Guilt made it feel like he was walking through mud that sucked at the soles of his boots, but he kept progressing like an automaton. It wasn't until he reached the bottom that he made himself stop. His hand gripped the banister so tight the wood bit into the palm of his hand. He could not leave August to whatever fate their father would give her.

Would she be fine without Crenshaw Iron? Yes. Max had seen her with her husband and knew how happy they were together. Evan supported her and would happily take her on in the full-time running of his estates and their investments. Her life would be full and in time she would become accustomed to her new role. But there would always be a part of her spirit that would be crushed by their father's callousness, and she would likely never heal from it. She would always know that he didn't respect her enough to not use her for his own gains. She would always know that she was second in his estimations. And this rift in the family, already begun by their parents trying to marry off their daughters, would be complete, never to be mended again.

"Max!" August's voice rose in pleasant surprise as she stepped out of the drawing room.

Pulled from his thoughts, he still felt as if he were moving through a fog. "I thought you had left," he said. Mother and another woman walked out of the room behind her. It only took a moment for his heart to come to a stuttering halt in his chest as he recognized the woman to be Lady Helena.

"Wonderful," Mother said, her pallor and demeanor much more cheerful than it had been when she'd led him to Papa's room. "You won't miss out on greeting Lady Helena."

He had to make himself release the bannister and act like a civilized human, even as anger and something dangerous coursed through him. He wasn't prepared to see Helena again, not like this. He had expected it to happen one evening at a dinner or a ball. Not in his parents' home when he had just been fed the most damning ultimatum.

"Lady Helena." He paused to clear the gravel from his

throat. "How good to see you again." There was still the slightest hint of venom in his voice. He hoped she wouldn't think it directed at her.

"Mr. Crenshaw." She sank down into a proper curtsy.

God, she was lovely. From the top of her buttery blond hair to the delicate curve of her cheekbones to the tips of her pebbled leather boots, she was polished and proper. The epitome of a lady. When her gaze met his he was struck anew by the color, a pure cornflower blue.

She raised a brow, and he knew she had detected his tone as well as the livid anger likely visible on his face. "My deepest sympathies on your father's health. I am happy to hear that he is improving."

"Yes, it is a relief." His voice was tight. His mouth went dry and he couldn't bring himself to say anything more. On the crossing he had imagined their meeting many times. He would complement her and watch the color rise in her cheeks. He would tell her how he had missed her wit, but in such a way that she wouldn't suspect he had thought about her at night while alone in his bed, or by day as he traveled from one meeting to another.

"I hope you will be staying in London for a time," she was saying.

"Yes, of course he is," his mother said. "We are very much looking forward to the dinner with your parents later this week. Will you be there?"

"Oh yes. It will be lovely to see you all there." Her gaze settled briefly on him before flitting away again when he didn't respond. "I am afraid I have to be going now."

"I'll walk out with you," August said, giving him a strange look. She knew him well enough to suspect something was wrong. He would have to figure out a lie to tell her before she came back later tonight. He refused to wound her with the truth.

Helena looked back at him, and he mumbled a goodbye. Her lips turned down in disappointment, and he realized perhaps it was for the best. He'd be heading back to New York soon.

As the front door closed behind them and Mother hurried past him up the stairs, he had to wonder if she was going to chat with Papa. If they had planned the entire thing, and his anger once more returned to the forefront. No, they wouldn't get away with this.

Papa had known Max's weakness and hadn't hesitated to exploit it. He had anticipated that Max's own affection for August and his loyalty to this family would keep him in line. But he had underestimated one thing. Max, in his own way, could be just as ruthless and cunning as their father when it suited him. He was a Crenshaw, after all.